THE
OLD
ROGUE OF
LIMEHOUSE

ANN GRANGER

HEADLINE

First published in 2023 by
HEADLINE PUBLISHING GROUP

First published in paperback in 2023 by
HEADLINE PUBLISHING GROUP

1

Cataloguing in Publication Data is available from the British Library

ISBN 978 1 4722 9015 1

Typeset in 10.85/15pt Plantin by Jouve (UK), Milton Keynes

Printed and bound in Great Britain by Clays Ltd, Elcograf S.p.A.

Headline's policy is to use papers that are natural, renewable and recyclable
products and made from wood grown in well-managed forests and other
controlled sources. The logging and manufacturing processes are expected
to conform to the environmental regulations of the country of origin.

HEADLINE PUBLISHING GROUP
An Hachette UK Company
Carmelite House
50 Victoria Embankment
London EC4Y 0DZ

www.headline.co.uk
www.hachette.co.uk

Ann Granger has lived in cities all over the world, since for many years she worked for the Foreign Office and received postings to British embassies as far apart as Munich and Lusaka. She is now permanently based in Oxfordshire.

For more information about Ann Granger's previous Victorian mysteries as well as her other crime novels visit www.anngranger.net.

Praise for Ann Granger's previous Victorian mysteries:

'Her usual impeccable plotting is fully in place' *Good Book Guide*

'An intriguing tale, with period detail interwoven in a satisfying way' *Oxford Times*

'Characterisation, as ever with Granger, is sharp and astringent' *The Times*

'Period colour is nicely supplied . . . This engrossing story looks like the start of a highly enjoyable series' *Scotsman*

'The book's main strength is the characterisation and the realistic portrayal of London in the mid-19th century' *Tangled Web*

'Murder most enjoyable' *Bournemouth Daily Echo*

Dedicated to the memory of long-time and dear friends Angela Arney and Isabel Dunjohn. We shared a love of books, of writing, of travel and much else. I wish I could still just pick up the phone . . .

'Will you walk into my parlour?' said the Spider to the Fly,
'Tis the prettiest little parlour that ever you did spy;
The way into my parlour is up a winding stair,
And I have many curious things to shew when you are there.
Poem by Mary Howitt, pub. 1829

Chapter One

Inspector Ben Ross

'NOW, IN France, as I've heard it,' said Mr Jacobus, 'they recognise what they call a crime of passion. Love, Mr Ross, being a powerful motivation. People goes quite mad on account of it. It's a recognised defence there, is pleading a crime of passion.'

He gave a chuckle which rippled through his double chin. Propped on his neckcloth, it resembled nothing so much as a tiered blancmange, and his mirth was followed by a bout of wheezing. Finally, the chin stopped wobbling. He mopped his watering eyes with a spotted handkerchief.

'Well, I've heard that, too,' I told him, when he'd regained his composure. 'But I can't tell you if it's true or not. All I'd say is, if you should find yourself in France, and be unwise enough to murder someone while there, I wouldn't put my trust in pleading a crime of passion. I think you'd need a little more by way of defence.'

'I dare say you are right,' he said. 'You being an officer of the law and knowing about such things. But I'm a sentimental man, Mr Ross, and I like to believe it.'

He heaved a deep sigh. He also liked to believe that an ancestor had arrived in England, in 1688, in the retinue of William of Orange. Or should I say that he liked other people to believe it? It might even have been true; but probably wasn't. Did he actually believe it himself, in his heart of hearts? At any rate, like many a rogue, he had his story rehearsed; and he stuck to it.

He had observed, when I arrived, that he had not seen me for a while. He'd spoken reproachfully, as if I were a relative who had failed in his duty, not a police officer trying to do his. I had replied that I had been otherwise engaged; investigating a case of murder in the countryside. Jacobus expressed himself sorry to hear I'd risked such an adventure. He had a horror of sparsely habited areas and told me he never left London. Somehow this had led on to his observations on crimes of passion. Perhaps he'd hoped I'd entertain him with details of my rural exploits. If so, he was out of luck.

We sat in his stuffy parlour on the first floor of his narrow little house, which was squeezed between an ironmonger's store and a tavern. I imagined these neighbours kept it upright, like a slice of bread in a toast rack. The house was of some antiquity. It had but one room on each floor, accessed from a rickety staircase with an alarming sideways slope to the treads. But it was three storeys high plus an attic. You might think that the exertion of climbing up and down the stairs would have led to its owner losing some of his considerable weight. However, this did not seem to be the case. I guessed that Jacobus, unless forced to emerge from his lair, used the staircase only to leave his bedroom of a morning and return to it at night; seldom descending to the ground floor and instead spending the greater part of the day crouched in this parlour, like the spider in the poem. The building's framework was of wooden beams with crumbling brick between them, and the parlour window jutted out over the street. The window sections were latticed with tiny diamond-shaped panes of uneven glass. They had a greenish hue and were probably already in place when William and Mary ruled, with or without the help of the mythical Jacobus ancestor. Whenever I called upon Jacobus, I would shout up to him from the street and he would fling open this latticed window and throw his key down to me so that I could enter.

I'd never known the window to be opened for any other reason. We were near the river and docks here, in Limehouse, and any air let in would have been fouler than the bad air indoors. It would also have allowed the hubbub of the street below to rise and invade the room. The tightly closed windows at least served to keep this noisy world at bay.

Jacob Jacobus himself was a large man to be living in such cramped quarters. He was in his sixties, quite bald, with a complexion as pink and clear as that of a baby. Twinkling blue eyes peeped out from his chubby cheeks, and his general appearance was as haphazard as that of his house, or the details of his business. He wore a rusty black frock coat and chequered trousers. Beneath the coat was a brocade waistcoat bedecked with a gold chain that led to the half-hunter watch tucked into the little pocket, out of sight now, but I'd seen him consult it in the past. That, too, was gold.

He gave as his profession a dealer in antiquities, comprising paintings, old books and objets d'art. Occasionally he did sell some chipped piece of porcelain, a work of reference now a century out of date and riddled with bookworm, or a murky oil portrait. All this came from his 'stock in trade', as he proudly referred to it.

He had often invited me to view this cornucopia of junk, which was stored on the ground floor beneath our feet. 'Any time you wish, Inspector!' This meant he wanted me to see it because it was his 'cover'. I had duly glanced around it on a couple of my visits, though both of us knew I was wasting my time. All of the dusty collection of works of art, mouldering volumes and knick-knacks that comprised it were, it goes without saying, lawfully acquired and accounted for, even if the items themselves were mainly fakes. I did not, for one moment, suppose Jacobus made a living from them. As far as Scotland Yard was concerned, he was almost certainly a fence, dealing in stolen items of much higher value. Unfortunately, the Yard had never been able to prove it. He always had paperwork of some kind to establish the legitimacy of anything we inquired about. If he didn't, then he denied any knowledge of the items in question; and we couldn't prove it. He was a clever fellow, was Jacob Jacobus.

But he was worth a visit because, from time to time, he passed on a little information regarding stolen items. Although never, of course, about any bit of business of his own. He called this 'doing the police a little favour', and saw it as a kind of insurance.

'He'll slip up one day, and we'll have him!' Superintendent

Dunn liked to say. 'In the meantime, he has his uses, old Jacobus.'

I doubted it, myself. With my wife, I had just returned from the New Forest. I'd been there on police business. She had been there on a holiday with the widow of her god-father, Mrs Julia Parry. She had once been Mrs Parry's companion, and the lady liked Lizzie to address her as 'Aunt Parry'. This use, or misuse, of a lapsed connection was like Mr Jacobus's claim to a tenuous connection with William of Orange. It served the claimant's purpose.

The reason I was here with Jacobus today was that Scotland Yard had been called upon to investigate a number of significant burglaries in wealthy households in the capital. We were in the midst of what is called 'the Season' by those with social aspirations. It has always appeared to me to be nothing so much as a marriage market for the wealthy. That means a round of parties, balls, entertainments and so forth, that requires the opening up of town houses, ostentatious displays of family plate and jewels and a soaring number of reports of house-breaking. Unusually, we had no case of murder on our hands at the moment. This situation couldn't last, but it had led to my visit today.

'Can't have you twiddling your thumbs, Ross!' Superintendent Dunn had declared. 'Before long I dare say we'll hear from Wapping that a body has been fished out of the Thames, or that someone has poisoned his landlady. But, in the meantime, go and see Jacobus. If there is anything in the wind, he might see fit to mention it. Get along well with him, don't you?'

'Another little glass?' inquired Mr Jacobus solicitously now.

We had been sampling a bottle of his homemade apricot schnapps of which the old fellow was very proud. If I drank a second tot, I'd leave the house with the beginnings of a thumping headache. I declined, stood up, and collected my hat from a small antique gate-leg table. Jacobus claimed it had belonged to his mythical ancestor. As with most things owned by Jacobus, we couldn't prove that it hadn't; and didn't believe for a moment that it had.

'You'll let me know if you should hear any whispers of the items of jewellery I mentioned being offered, as it were, on the unofficial market?'

Jacobus chuckled. 'You're a wit, Inspector Ross! And you've got a turn of phrase. Bless me, it's a pleasure talking to you. Call again, my dear sir, I might have something for you. There again, I might not. You'll mind how you go down the stairs, won't you? The cleaning woman I employ has been washing them down, and they can be a tad slippery when she does that. She likes to splash the water about. It makes it look as though she's done a thorough job. She's never done one yet.' He chuckled again.

During the latter part of my visit I'd been aware of sounds outside the parlour door, on the staircase. When I emerged into the stairwell, I saw just below me the cleaner in question, or at least I saw the top of her head and a faded mop of reddish hair untidily pinned up. She pulled aside the bucket to allow me to pass and looked up.

A grin spread across her face. ''Ullo, Mr Ross!' she exclaimed. 'Didn't know it was you calling on the old feller.

Remember me, do you?' She wiped her hands on her grubby apron and settled back on her heels.

'Good grief, it's Daisy Smith!' I replied.

I'd met her at the time when a serial killer called the River Wraith had sought out his victims among the many prostitutes working along the banks of the Thames. Daisy had then been one of that sisterhood, a lively, pretty red-head. She had lost her looks but not her London sparrow chirpiness. She sat down on the step and looked up at me. 'Go on, then,' she ordered. 'Be a gent! Tell me I ain't changed. I'd still catch the eye of one of the young swells about town.'

Sadly, that wasn't true. The few years since we'd last met had not treated her well. Her skin had coarsened and become lined. She had lost one of her two upper front teeth and this caused the sibilants to whistle faintly as she spoke. Her skin was marked with the scars of infection.

'I would've known you at once, Daisy,' I replied courteously.

'No, you never would!' she retorted. 'You'd have gone on past me and out the front door, if I hadn't reminded you.'

I felt myself flush because it was true. 'I've been calling on your employer, Daisy. My thoughts were elsewhere.'

'What d'you want with the old villain, then? You won't tell me, will you? I know that.'

I didn't know quite what to say, so asked, 'How long have you worked for Jacobus?'

'Strictly speaking,' said Daisy, 'I work at the pub next door.' She paused to pin up a stray lock of hair with her reddened hands, then continued, 'I live there, too. Got a

room in the attics. But the old man owns the pub, too, so
you could say I do work for him. Same as Tom behind the
bar, though he calls himself the landlord. I don't just wash
the stairs. I come in first thing and bring Mr Jacobus his
coffee and muffins. Early evening, I bring him in his dinner from the pie shop down the road. Last thing of all, I
come in at night, help him into bed and lock up the house
when I leave.'

'You take care of him, then? And you have a key?' I
remarked. I was wondering just what was included in 'helping him into bed'.

'It's Tom who's got the key, strictly speaking,' Daisy
corrected me. 'I ask him for them, as needed. The old man
don't go out hardly ever. He can't manage the stairs; and
he's got a mortal fear of open spaces.'

I recalled his dismay when I'd told him I'd just returned
from the country. 'I wasn't aware he was a man of property,' I said now. 'Other than this house.'

'And the ironmonger's next door!' said Daisy. 'He owns
that building too.'

Whatever business Jacobus was engaged in, he obviously did well out of it. The 'stock in trade' certainly would
not have paid for it all. I would report all this to Dunn in
due course.

In the meantime I fished in my pocket and found a couple of florins, which I gave her. 'Good to see you again,
Daisy.'

'Ta!' she replied, pocketing the coins. 'Likewise! Mind
how you go.' She grinned at me. I wondered how she'd lost
the front tooth. 'See you again, I dare say!' she said.

Indeed, we would meet again and much sooner than either of us then suspected.

I paused in the street, the throng eddying around me. It is not a quiet area. Its narrow, twisting thoroughfares are always crowded. Almost any nationality you care to name can be found, and a Tower of Babel of languages assaults the ear at any one time. Many of the speakers are sailors off the various ships using the docks, and where there are sea-men, there are plenty of taverns, not to mention brothels, gambling and opium dens and eating houses serving food from around the world. Add to this mix the newly arrived immigrants from all parts of Europe and further afield, all seeking a better life, although I feared many didn't find it here. But many were determined to thrive and set up all manner of businesses in cellars and rooms that doubled as the family living quarters.

Thanks to Daisy, I now knew that the tavern also belonged to Jacobus. It, too, appeared of considerable antiquity. A creaking sign on the façade announced it to be the Crossed Keys. I knew that name was linked to St Peter. This, together with its medieval timbering, made me won-der if it had been a church property before the monasteries had been abolished by Henry VIII. Perhaps it had been a hostelry for pilgrims. But on the other hand, this might only be its latest name. A clock was displayed on the front-age as required by law, since the advent of the railway and the standardisation of time throughout the land. It now uttered a discordant jangle and began to sound out the hour. I checked my own pocket watch against it. It was twelve noon. The place was doing brisk business. Labourers, costermongers, cabmen and flashily dressed fellows whose occupation was dubious passed in and out of its doors on their way to take a restorative pint or two. I also glanced at the ironmonger's shop on the other side of Jacobus's house. It looked from the outside like a respectable enough business.

I wondered if the old fellow owned other properties elsewhere; and in just how many pies he had his stubby fingers.

As I had been studying others, so they had noticed me and marked me down as a police officer. No matter I was not in uniform. They knew me for what I was; and someone I'd seen enter the tavern had informed the landlord. He came out and stood in the doorway staring at me. This, I supposed, was Tom, of whom Daisy had spoken. He was a tall, strongly built fellow with straw-coloured hair; and a nose so knocked out of any true shape that I could only conclude it had been broken several times. I guessed he might once have graced the prize ring. We assessed one another as opponents at the beginning of a boxing match might do. I held his stare and eventually he turned and went back inside.

I was also being observed during this time by a group of ragged grimy urchins. They had the glittering eyes and sharp stares of sparrowhawks. Many of them would already have tried their hands at petty crime; and as they grew older would graduate to serious law-breaking. Their portraits would one day grace the Yard's rogues' gallery.

The ragamuffins also recognised my calling; of course they had. To confirm this, one of them shouted, 'Rozzer!' They sent up a derisive cheer before they scurried away in all directions like a disturbed ants' nest. The clock reminded me that I should already be back at the Yard and I set out at a brisk pace.

Chapter Two

IT WAS a good thing I hadn't stayed any longer with Jacobus. On my return to Scotland Yard I was intercepted by Sergeant Morris before I had managed to reach my desk. He loomed up and blocked my path, looking flustered and out of temper. This was not unusual, and on spotting me he appeared to cheer up. If he was pleased at my arrival, I was put on my guard. Now what had happened?

'Good job you've come, sir!' he growled in what he imagined to be a whisper. 'The superintendent's been asking for you for the last half an hour. He's got a lady with him.'

'Old or young?'

'She's of a certain age,' said Morris in an attempt to sound genteel. It didn't work. He abandoned it. 'And she's got a bit of money by the looks of her. You're to go straight in, sir.'

'Any idea what it's all about, Sergeant?'

'All *I* know,' said Morris, 'is that it concerns emeralds.'

Not yet another theft from a wealthy house! 'Single stones or jewellery?' I asked resignedly. Every officer we had was already engaged in trying to apprehend a jewel thief or find his takings. Silently I cursed 'the Season' and all the extra work it brought us.

'Family heirloom!' declared Morris. 'Or so the lady reckons. They all say it's family heirlooms that have gone missing. You're nobody if you don't have a family heirloom or two knocking around the place. Mrs Morris has a teapot that came into her family in the days of the second King George, she reckons. She sets great store by it, though it's nothing I see as particular. But that's heirlooms for you. You don't have to like 'em; you just have own 'em. Or if you're really rich, you just have to be robbed of 'em. If no one tries to rob you, that means you don't have anything worth taking; and the rich don't want that thought of them. On the other hand, they all want the stuff found and returned, double-quick. Don't hang about, sir, I beg of you. The superintendent has worked himself up into a fair old state. I can't tell you any more, on account as I don't know any more about it than that! The lady,' he concluded in a martyred voice, 'did not see fit to confide in me.'

So, like Jacobus, he'd been left in the dark.

I entered Dunn's office to find not one but two females present. There was clearly some difference in status between them. The room was dominated by a formidable lady in late middle-age (at my estimate). I am not a judge of ladies' fashions. I rely on information from my wife for that. All I can say is that I'm glad the crinoline has lost its popularity. This visitor's skirts, which earlier would have been supported by the frame, were now drawn back into a waterfall of material projecting to the rear below the waist. She wore a velvet jacket with braid trim, and a hat with a narrow brim and a quantity of tulle swathed round the crown like a turban. Beneath the hat, a pair of very sharp eyes assessed me. Then, as if we realised each of us was studying the other, she abruptly turned her gaze back to Superintendent Dunn.

I briefly assessed her companion. I used the word advisedly because 'paid companion' she clearly was. I judged her about fifty years of age, perhaps a year or two less, a plain woman, but with strong features and intelligent eyes. Her dress, too, was plain to the point of severity. She had clearly been brought along for convention's sake. I suspected from her general demeanour that she had been in the complainant's employ for some time. It was not an occupation I'd wish on any woman.

Constable Biddle was also there, seated discreetly in a corner with an open notebook on his knee. I am well acquainted with Biddle. Not only he is part of the force here at the Yard but he has also been walking out with our housemaid for a couple of years, despite the vigorous objections of his possessive mother.

'Ah, Ross!' exclaimed Dunn. 'There you are at last.'

He was looking somewhat harassed himself. He turned to the visitor and said, 'May I introduce Inspector Ross, ma'am? He is one of our most experienced officers.'

The hawkish gaze beneath the tulle turban was again turned on me. 'Indeed,' she said. 'Does he know why I am here?'

I took it upon myself to answer. I don't like being addressed indirectly. 'Not in any detail, ma'am. I was told by the sergeant that it is a case of missing gems. But that is all.'

It wasn't intended, but I had managed to annoy the caller.

'This is not a simple theft!' she said sharply. 'We are speaking of an exceptional necklace of emeralds, with smaller diamonds, set in gold, and made in South America for my late husband's great-grandmother. She was of a wealthy Brazilian family. He gave it to me at the time of our marriage. It has been stolen from my house. You will understand my anxiety as to its whereabouts and I wish to have it returned as soon as possible. I have explained it all to Superintendent Dunn; and that young man over there has written it all down.'

From the corner of my eye, I caught a brief show of emotion on the companion's face. I wasn't quite sure what it was, but it might have been resentment.

'This lady,' Dunn hastened to seize the reins of the conversation, 'is Mrs Charlotte Roxby.'

'I am honoured to make your acquaintance, Mrs Roxby.' Her expression thawed and she nodded at me quite graciously. Alas, I immediately squandered any measure of her approval by asking, as blandly as I could, 'And the other lady?'

'My companion, Miss Chalk!' snapped Mrs Roxby.

Miss Chalk glanced up again, met my gaze, then dropped her eyes to her folded hands on her lap. Now, I thought, that is someone it would pay to talk to. She probably knows all there is to know about the family. I already didn't like Mrs Roxby. Nor would I accept verbatim anything she said. Yes, I would need to talk privately with the companion. But I had one question that needed to be asked immediately.

'May I inquire, ma'am, whether the necklace is normally kept in a bank vault; or is it usually to be found at the house?'

'It is kept in an excellent safe at my house!' she shot back. 'If it were kept in a bank vault, it would have to be fetched from there each time it was required, and returned the next day. I live in Hampstead. The road across the Heath can be lonely. It would be an invitation to highway robbery. It is – was – better kept in my own safe.'

The irony of this last statement was lost on no one in the room. The lady reddened. Miss Chalk looked briefly as if she was enjoying her employer's momentary loss of composure.

'I will acquaint Inspector Ross with the known details, ma'am,' said Dunn frostily, stepping in.

'I expect you to call on me at my home in Hampstead, Inspector, tomorrow at half past two o'clock,' said Mrs Roxby to me. 'You will be able to bring me up to date on your progress in the matter. Thank you, Superintendent Dunn, for your kind assistance.'

With that she left, with the silent Miss Chalk in tow.

'Go and write up your notes for the inspector, Constable!' Dunn ordered Biddle, who fairly scuttled out of the door, clutching his notebook.

'Where have you *been*, Ross?' snapped Dunn. 'That woman has not the slightest respect for rank or procedure! I feel as though I've been court-martialled.'

'I went to call on old Jacobus, sir, as you suggested; with

regard to the jewel thefts that have taken place recently. He denied any knowledge of them, of course. But he knows I'm watching his activities and if he is approached—'

'Never mind that,' interrupted Dunn. He always looked more like a gentleman farmer than a senior police officer. He was of stocky build, with a liking for tweed. His hair was bristly and cut very short and his complexion, normally florid, was at the moment almost apoplectic. 'Let us concentrate for the moment on Mrs Roxby.'

He paused to pick up a portrait photograph. He passed it to me. 'The missing jewellery.'

I studied the photograph. It was of a very young woman laced so tightly into a ballgown I wondered she could breathe, let alone dance. She was wearing a magnificent necklace. It looked heavy and, I imagined, not very comfortable to wear, but it certainly caught the eye. Without all this adornment, I judged the young lady to be of ordinary appearance; and it struck me at once that she did not look happy. True, it is very difficult in a portrait photograph to look relaxed or vivacious. Having to hold the pose for the required length of time usually erases any spontaneity. But there was also resentment in her eyes, staring into the lens.

'The young lady is Miss Roxby?'

'No, she is Miss Gray, the daughter of Mrs Roxby's late brother. She was adopted by her uncle and aunt; her parents having died when she was still a small child. It is a sad story. Apparently, the family was travelling in Italy and the carriage overturned near Turin. The parents were killed. The child, who was travelling in the carriage with her nursemaid, survived, but was left an orphan. She was

brought back to England and the Roxbys, who were themselves childless, took her in.'

'And the nursemaid?' I asked. 'Did she return to England with the child?'

Dunn looked puzzled. 'I really don't know. Does it
matter?'

It had mattered to the nursemaid and any family she
might have had. But there was no advantage in making any
comment.

'Excuse me, sir,' I asked. 'But do we know when the
necklace was taken and why it wasn't locked in the safe?
Were the thieves able to open the safe? That restricts us to
the known cracksmen and narrows the search.'

A mirthless snarl crossed Dunn's face. 'We do, indeed.
It took place at Mrs Roxby's own home, yesterday evening,
during a dinner party that was being held downstairs. All
of the guests are people beyond suspicion. The necklace
was taken from a well-stocked jewellery box, normally kept
in the safe, but for this occasion taken out and left unattended
on a dressing table upstairs. Oh, it's the usual thing!'

'No wonder she's so cross and feels more than a little
guilty,' I murmured.

'She's in a red rage and has no one to blame but herself,'
returned Dunn candidly. 'You will get Biddle's notebook
from him and study everything he's written. I want this matter cleared up, so we can deal with any crime that has been
committed. The sooner the better. We have plenty of other
fish to fry. The lady can be as aggressive as she wants—'

'Excuse me, sir,' I broke in and paused. Dunn only gestured to me to continue. 'How old is her niece?' I asked.

'Seventeen!' snapped Dunn.

'Seventeen and just come out, as it's called, into society. Rather early, perhaps?'

'I have one daughter,' returned Dunn. 'She is twenty-five and married to a clergyman. She never "came out". It wasn't necessary and my salary would not have supported the expense.'

'But Mrs Roxby is wealthy!' I countered. 'So the young woman is tricked out in fashionable gowns and expensive jewels, to be paraded like bait to catch a husband. This photographic portrait has been taken to function in the nature of an advertisement. The hunt is on for a wealthy suitor, preferably of rank, I fancy.'

'Our job,' said Dunn heavily, 'is not to play the Puritan. It is to find and return the jewellery. So go and do it, Ross. Such a haul may well have been broken up into pieces by now.' He slapped the palms of his hands on the desk. 'Did you learn anything of interest during your visit to Jacobus?'

'Nothing to do with stolen items of jewellery. But a couple of other things of interest.' I told him I'd learned that Jacobus owned at least three properties. Also, that he apparently suffered from a form of agoraphobia. 'Never goes out, sir.'

'Well then, where does he keep his money?' murmured Dunn. 'We've not been able to catch him out before. But if we have a cash trail to follow, we may have better luck. When the theft from Mrs Roxby has been investigated, in a week or two, call on Jacobus again.'

But I was to visit the narrow little dwelling in Lime-house sooner than that.

Chapter Three

Elizabeth Martin Ross

'I SUPPOSE,' Aunt Parry had once said to me, 'I *suppose* that being married to a man who holds the rank of detective-inspector at Scotland Yard is a very respectable thing.'

She had not sounded too sure about it. I had told her, yes, it was. I said it because it was true; and not only because it was what she wanted to hear. Aunt Parry likes people to agree with her. Disagreeing with her is simply a waste of time. She never listens to objections of any sort, to her plans, to her ideas, her opinions on any subject. She wants confirmation, pure and simple. If it doesn't come, she simply rewrites the whole conversation in her head. She hears, as it were, what she wants to hear.

I could have added that, although it was a respectable calling, it did not make for an uneventful home life. Ben tries his best, I am sure, to arrive home of an evening in time for supper. He leaves at a regular hour in the morning. But with that also come all manner of interruptions.

That evening Ben had arrived when expected, so it had started well. Bessie, our maid, had just put the soup tureen on the table and bustled back to the kitchen. I ladled out a helping and passed it back. We were in the habit, over the supper table, of catching up on the way we'd each spent the day. Ben's day was almost inevitably more interesting than mine. (He did leave out the gorier bits.) That evening he'd already told me of the missing Roxby necklace. But I also knew that, earlier in the day, he had intended to seek out a dreadful old rogue called Jacobus. I was curious to learn how he had got on. When he'd spoken of him before, I'd had the impression he quite liked this particular villain. He had begun to describe his visit to Limehouse when Bessie had arrived with the tureen. We paused our conversation until she had bustled out of the room again.

'What did Jacobus mean by that exactly?' I asked Ben. 'He might have information or not?'

'Well, my dear,' he replied, 'knowing old Jacobus as I do, it means that if he hears of anyone offering stolen jewellery, and the thief is one he deals with himself on occasion, then he won't tell us a word. He'll want to protect his own business interests. On the other hand, if he hears of the items being offered by a newcomer, someone neither he nor any other receiver of stolen property has dealt with before, or even heard of before . . .'

He paused to sample the soup. 'This is very good. You made it, surely? Not Bessie, I wager.'

'Sh . . .' I glanced at the door. 'Yes, I made it, but don't say anything to upset her.'

'The door's closed. She must know she isn't a very good cook.'

'She's improved immensely!' I defended our only

domestic help. 'And because the door is closed, it doesn't mean she won't hear what's said. She has excellent hearing and she listens.'

'I thought I heard the murmur of voices in the kitchen as I walked through the hall. Has she got a visitor?'

'Constable Biddle.'

'Oh, he's dining at my expense, is he?' Ben muttered. 'He must have run here to arrive ahead of me! Well, keep him away from me. I have already spent an hour reading up his notes and discussing the missing Roxby necklace with Dunn.'

'She must be a very wealthy woman.' I'd been intrigued by Ben's description of the splendid necklace shown in the photograph.

'Very wealthy and, so Dunn tells me, acquainted with some influential people. The late Mr Roxby was a ship-owner, a partner in the family firm. Mrs Roxby herself is of a wealthy family. Don't ask me where Dunn learned that. I fancy someone highly placed has already been bending his ear. Mrs Roxby is the sort who would call in favours instantly. My guess is that the woman aims to marry off her niece to a title.'

'Poor child,' I said. 'Although perhaps she shares her aunt's ambition.'

Ben was looking irritated and perhaps it was time to drop the subject. I concluded with, 'Let's hope Jacobus may hear of something.'

Ben muttered: 'We must hope the piece has not been broken up, the stones removed and the setting melted down for the value of the gold alone. But it is such a distinctive item that I'm afraid that is exactly what will happen to it. Let's hope the thief is an opportunist one, a servant perhaps, who will try to dispose of it intact. Then Jacobus might send word to me.'

'Why would he do that?' I asked.

'Because those who dispose of very valuable items are usually experts, professionals of the highest order. They don't want an amateur blundering about. That could upset the applecart for them all, including Jacobus and any little bit of business he might be engaged in. He'd be suspicious and he might, just might, decide to let the police know. He's a prudent man. He deals with rogues he knows. The amateur finds at once that stealing, say, this emerald necklace, is one thing. Disposing of it is another. Remember, we're talking of a magnificent and distinctive item. That makes it all the more difficult. It won't be easily sold on; and amateur thieves make mistakes. But let us suppose, for argument's sake, that the thief is lucky enough to find a buyer. Well, first of all he won't get the price he'd hoped for. Eventually, he has to settle for what the fence will pay. That leads to the next problem he faces. He can't explain why he suddenly has cash in hand that he didn't have before. If challenged, particularly by the police, he may crumble and confess not only that he pilfered the item in question, but to whom he sold it on. Professional fences like to deal with professional thieves. It's a business.' Ben stared into his soup bowl. 'Dunn is right. I need to go and visit Jacobus again, perhaps in a day or two. But my guess is that it's the work of a ladder gang—'

The door burst open and Bessie appeared with a platter

of boiled beef and vegetables. She set it down on the table and asked, 'What's a ladder gang?'

'Oh, heard that, did you, Bessie?' asked Ben.

'Just as I come in!' our maid told him, unabashed.

'Well, Bessie,' he said. 'Why don't you ask your kitchen guest, Biddle? He'll tell you.'

'About them emeralds, is it?' Bessie swept out with the empty soup tureen and the door slammed behind her.

'You see? She listens!' Ben said triumphantly. 'And what she doesn't overhear, Biddle tells her. She's almost as well informed about any interesting case on our hands as we are.'

'Not from snooping!' I defended Bessie. 'Biddle has probably told her all about it, as you say. And what is a ladder gang, anyway?'

'Professional thieves specialising in country houses. Mrs Roxby lives near Hampstead Heath. It's a lonely spot after dark. The gang picks out its quarry. They bring a long ladder which they secrete in bushes on the property or nearby. In this case, probably on the Heath itself in undergrowth. They wait until the family is at dinner, or has gone out for the evening. They fetch the ladder as soon as it is dark and they have already selected a secluded area. They put it up against the rear of the house, shin up it and force a window. The ladies of the household will have dressed for dinner with care. The jewellery boxes, usually kept in a safe, are all out on the dressing-room tables, awaiting the return of the contents when the family retires for the night. Before that, they will be locked away again.

'Meanwhile, for three or four hours, everyone, family

and servants, is downstairs. The family and guests are chattering away. Perhaps there is music. The staff are working like beavers in the kitchens, making a clatter there. The thief has the upper floors to himself. He helps himself to whatever jewellery is left in the jewel cases, pockets it, retreats down the ladder. He and his accomplices make off, taking the ladder away to hide it until the next job.'

'But would a necklace, like the one missing, be left in a jewellery box? Would not the young lady be wearing it?'

I broke off and frowned. 'No, not unless it is a splendid occasion like a ball or reception. She'd wear something less ostentatious for a simple dinner party.

'So why was this particular necklace taken from the safe? I would have thought it was kept in its own case, not in a box containing other items.'

'That's something I'll have to ask. You see why I like to talk over such things with you, my dear? You're always quick to find a weak spot in a defence. It's also why I don't argue with you!' Ben smiled. 'At any rate, downstairs the house is ablaze with light and full of people. Everyone feels safe. Upstairs it is dark and deserted and no one will go up there until much later when the guests depart.

'The ladder gang runs little risk. Mrs Roxby has no one but herself to blame. Such thieves deal with professional fences and are known to them. Jacobus wouldn't betray them. But the amateur, as I said, is a danger to everyone. His identity is generally quickly known. If he sells the item, he cannot disguise that he is spending more money than he can explain away. Jacobus would happily tell us all about him.'

With that, Ben set about his dinner and I decided it was only fair to let him eat in peace before I quizzed him again. Alas, we were neither of us to finish our meal uninterrupted.

The first sign of what was to come was the sound of a disturbance that seemed to be taking place in our kitchen. I could hear Bessie's voice, and a male voice I recognised as Biddle's, and also another female voice. This one was loud, insistent and rang with desperation.

'Stay there!' Ben rose to his feet, throwing aside his napkin. 'That, if I'm not mistaken, is the sign of trouble!'

It was indeed. The door was flung open and Biddle appeared in his shirtsleeves with a napkin of his own tucked into his shirt collar. He *was* dining at our expense.

'You'd better come, sir!' he panted. 'She's going crazy. Sorry, ma'am!' (This to me with a bob of his head.) 'I don't mean Bessie; she's trying to calm her down. The other one, I mean. She just came bursting through the back door, and she's going on something wild about a murder, or so she says!'

At this point the kitchen door burst open and two female forms tumbled through it into the hall. Bessie recovered her balance first and threw her arms out wide to prevent the visiting woman advancing any further. 'Help me, Walter, can't you?' she demanded of Biddle. 'She's gone mad!'

From behind her, another form surged up, and yelled, 'I want to talk to Mr Ross! Mr Ross, are you there? You got to come with me, direct! He's dead, murdered, and there's blood everywhere!'

'Daisy?' called Ben in alarm. 'Oh, let her in, Biddle!'

To me, he added, 'Sorry, my dear, but I fancy this is an emergency.'

'You're right, it is!' shouted the visitor and burst into the room.

'Good heavens,' I exclaimed. 'It is Miss Smith, is it not?'

I had not seen Daisy Smith since the matter of the murders committed by the River Wraith. Even in this present emergency, I thought she looked more dishevelled than called for, and, for the moment at least, had lost all her old cockney style and boldness. She looked terrified.

'Sorry, Mrs Ross!' she panted to me. 'I wouldn't have come but the inspector was there this morning . . .'

My heart sank. Our evening was to be ruined.

Ben, however, took it calmly enough, for all the news was going to be bad. 'Who is dead?' he asked.

'The old man, old Jacobus! His throat is slit ear to ear!' She drew a forefinger in a straight line across her own throat in illustration. 'Blood everywhere, there is! I never saw anything like it! I ran and told Tom. He sent Quig back with me to see if it was true. Quig came up and he don't get shocked easy, believe me. But he stood there with his mouth open, like he'd been struck with a bolt of lightning. I felt the same way meself!'

Ben was startled enough to demand, 'And you have come all the way here from Limehouse to report to me at home? Good grief, Daisy, you must have been able to find an officer nearer . . .'

'We have, we did! A couple of men, drinking in the tap-room, volunteered to go and get a bobby. They were in luck. There was a regular evening patrol near at hand. But

I knew I had to come and tell you, because you were there this morning! So I come,' concluded Daisy, and without warning she sat down on the floor and burst into tears. 'I liked the old rogue, I swear I did, Mr Ross! I took up him his supper, same as always, pie and mash. I got the key from Tom, the landlord, and I went to take the tray up, but the street door was open. I thought, that's not right! He has his visitors, Mr Jacobus, but they call at the pub first, for Tom or Quig or me to go and let them into the house. He don't like surprises.'

'Who is this Quig?' interrupted Ben.

'The potman at the Keys. Obadiah Quigley is his proper name, only he gets called "Quig" by everyone.'

'I am sorry, my dear,' said Ben to me. 'But I think, in the circumstances, I must go. You too, Biddle. If I don't get to finish my supper, you don't get to finish yours. Bessie, run out and find a cab, a four-seater growler, as there will be three passengers. Tell the cabbie it will be to take us to Limehouse and it will be worth his while to make it quickly!'

Bessie and I stood at the door and watched the growler rumble away with Ben, young Biddle and Daisy Smith. I wondered, should Aunt Parry ask me again in the near future if being married to a detective inspector was a respectable thing, whether I'd be able to answer with the same confidence.

Inspector Ben Ross

I have visited many a crime scene and many a murder one, too. Any murder is horrific. No officer called to a scene

29

ever forgets it. Daisy had rehearsed her story again on the way there, as our cabman drove the growler at perilous speed through the busy streets. I felt real dread in my heart. Biddle, too, was unusually sombre. He sat in the cab silent and, I suspected, nervous. I couldn't blame him.

The streets grew busier and we arrived to find a scene nearing pandemonium. The immediate area was packed with spectators; others stared from all the windows overlooking the scene, as if they were watching a show. The whole scene was lit by bobbing lanterns and a gas lamppost at the corner. I could hear our cabbie swearing robustly as he struck out with his whip at those who pressed too close. He then shouted down to us that he could take us no further. His horse was beginning to panic. Daisy jumped in perilous manner from the rocking cab and scuttled towards the tavern like a mouse making for its hole and safety.

To my relief, I heard myself hailed by Sergeant Morris; and saw his substantial form as he shouldered his way out of the throng towards me.

'You're here quickly, Mr Ross! When we heard about this at the Yard, someone was sent out to find you at home. He must have got there extra fast.'

'I haven't seen him!' I retorted. 'Another messenger came to my house with the news, a woman, but she's run into the tavern, I think. Will no one clear a space?'

'Hey, there!' bellowed Morris. He has a mighty voice and it echoed around the road, seeming to ricochet off the walls. 'Make way!'

He was signalling as he spoke. Two burly uniformed constables arrived and a path was cleared for us to the front door. There, one of them explained they were part of a patrol from the local division. They had been making their regular round when they'd been hailed and told to come at once. There had been a murder. 'That fellow confirmed it,' said the constable. He pointed at Tom, the landlord of the Crossed Keys. He stood nearby and looked shaken.

By him stood another man, one I didn't recognise. I didn't think he could be the potman, Quig. He was a small middle-aged fellow, wearing a foreign-looking overcoat with wide collar trimmed with a fur I couldn't name. It was dense but soft looking and mottled brown, black and cream in colour. He wore a hat with a broad brim; beneath it his face was frightened. Seeing me, and identifying me as someone of authority, he started forward and gasped, 'Please, sir, I know nothing of any of this!'

'Who is this?' I asked one of the local constables, a bulky fellow with a fine black beard.

'This is Mr Overmann, the ironmonger. He has the shop in the building next door, also lives there with his family, sir,' he replied. 'I understand the victim was his landlord.'

'If there is nothing you can tell us now, Mr Overmann,' I said, 'I suggest you go back indoors and stay there with your family. An officer will call on you tomorrow and take a statement.'

'But I know nothing, sir!' he repeated. He was nearly in tears.

'Then you have no reason to stay here. Off you go!'

He bobbed his head and scurried away, the skirts of his distinctive coat flapping and putting me in mind of a bat. I had no wish to frighten him. I guessed he was one of those not long since arrived from Central Europe, and determined to make his way by trade. Such immigrants are often frightened of the police. Not because they have guilty consciences, I knew, but because authority in general has not treated them kindly.

Of Daisy there was now no sign. She must be in the tavern. The smell of the sweat of the crowd, their unwashed garments, the putrid odours of animal dung, of drains and sewers that flowed into the river, and the nauseous stench of Father Thames was unbearable.

'Look here, Constable!' I told the local man. 'There are far too many onlookers. Can't your men clear some of them away?'

'No, sir,' he replied simply. 'They won't go.'

'Ghouls!' I muttered. I turned back to Morris. 'You've seen the body, I take it? It is Jacobus?'

'It's the old fellow, all right. We aren't the only ones who knew of him. Seems he was something of a local character, sir,' Morris went on. 'Highly eccentric, as I'm told, and almost never left the house. These officers from the patrol that was called in say none of them ever saw him. But they knew his reputation. Supposed to handle stolen valuables, but never convicted.'

'I was in the house and speaking with him myself earlier today,' I told him.

And drinking his apricot schnapps. Unexpectedly, I felt a pang of something approaching bereavement. I forced it away. The old fellow had been a crook and I had no sound reason to feel sorrow; and yet . . .

We had reached the door and managed to enter the house. I climbed the narrow old stairway for the second time that day. 'Has the police surgeon been?' I called to Morris, who'd elbowed his way after me. Behind him, I glimpsed Biddle.

'Up there now, sir. You will know him. It's Dr Mackay.'

Indeed, I recognised Mackay from his shock of bright red hair as I stepped into the parlour. He looked up at the entry of new arrivals and saw me.

'Oh, it's you, Inspector Ross.' He sounded relieved.

'Good evening, Mackay.' As I spoke, I looked around me. The room presented a scene of utter chaos. It was as though a tornado had roared through the place. Every piece of furniture seemed to have been ransacked or overturned. The little table I had noticed on my earlier visit lay on its side. Every drawer had not simply been opened, it had been pulled out, and lay on the carpet with its contents. Pictures had been pulled down from the walls. In one corner the carpet had been turned back; and it looked at first glance as if someone had tried to lever up a floorboard before abandoning the attempt. Yet, amidst all this, one thing remained in the same position I had seen it in that morning.

Jacobus himself still occupied his chair. His hands gripped the arms as if he'd tried to lever himself up, but had had no time to complete the movement. His head was tilted back and a great ragged slash had opened his throat. The blood was everywhere. It had soaked into the old man's brocade waistcoat. It had pumped out and sprayed the surrounding room.

'How long has he been dead?' I asked the doctor.

'I would estimate that he died between four and five this afternoon. I might be able to narrow that down when I have made a closer examination of the body.'

I nodded. Bloody footprints had left confused tracks across the carpet, criss-crossing as the murderer failed to find what he sought. At first glance, I guessed them to have been made by one pair of boots, except in the immediate area of the chair where there were a few small prints. The track of these ran in both directions between the door and the dead man; and the retreating prints from chair to door were toe prints, made by a small foot. Daisy, running from the room in panic. She came up to help the old man to bed, saw what had happened and fled. Amongst the debris on the floor was a tray and a dinner plate, smeared with congealed gravy: the remains of the pie and mash she'd brought earlier.

After taking the dreadful news to Tom, by her own account, the potman had been sent to verify her story. But there were no different large prints that might have been his. I guessed the potman had looked through the door, and wisely gone no further in. Fear had not stopped him. Prudence did that. He wanted no suspicion directed towards himself by leaving his own boot prints near the chair. So the majority of the prints had been made by one man, acting alone, and getting progressively more desperate. Or had he found what he wanted? No, or he would not have begun to lever up the floorboard before abandoning the task when he realised it would take him too long.

'The murderer made those tracks while he searched the

room,' said Morris lugubriously. His thinking had been working in tandem with my own. It was an unnecessary comment. But I understood Morris's need to speak, to say anything, and break the horrified silence that had engulfed us all. 'The victim didn't get up and fight his killer. All this mess was made when he ransacked the place.' Morris paused. 'It strikes me, sir,' he began, then stopped.

'Yes, Morris?'

'The perpetrator, if he was bent on theft, doesn't seem to have taken anything, for all his searching. It's possible he did, because we don't know what was here. But there are still plenty of bits and pieces he could have pocketed before he left, if he was just an ordinary housebreaker.'

This was true. Various small items of antique porcelain, and some snuffboxes of fine design and some age, lay among the wreckage. Those had been the old man's private collection and he'd liked to have them where he could see them. A quantity of silver cutlery, too, had spilled from a drawer and lay scattered across the carpet. But yet, something was missing.

'His watch and chain have gone!' I exclaimed.

Morris and Mackay both stared at me.

'He wore a gold chain across his waistcoat, the sort attached to a gold half-hunter, tucked into his waistcoat pocket.'

'Ah!' said Morris, adding: 'make a note, lad.'

I realised Biddle had joined us. He had been lurking by the door. He looked sick as well he might. The smell of the blood alone was enough to make anyone nauseous.

The little room was becoming crowded. Mackay spoke

up, asking, 'Is there anything you'd like to ask me now, Inspector Ross? If not, I'll away and write up my report.'

'I won't detain you, Mackay, but before you go, could you give us an opinion on the nature of the attack? Yes, violent and fatal. But, to my mind, not efficient, if you understand me?'

'Oh, I understand you, and I agree,' returned Mackay promptly. 'The assailant got behind the chair. It was careless of the victim to allow him to do that. Either he trusted his visitor—'

'Jacobus trusted nobody to any great degree,' I interrupted moodily.

'Then the killer moved quickly. The victim is of corpulent build and fairly wedged in where he sits. The killer slashed the throat from behind the chair, perhaps gripping the victim's hair with his other hand, to keep him still. But I agree, it's not an efficient cut. It's more violent than would have been necessary, and it's crooked. My opinion is that the killer wanted to make sure, and was in a panic. The victim's nearly been decapitated, poor old fellow. Even a gamekeeper, dispatching a wounded beast, would make a better job of it than that!' Mackay gave a mirthless smile. 'I earned money, when a boy, helping out at game shoots on estates nearby to where I lived.'

When I stepped out into the street again, Biddle at my heels, a reasonable space had been cleared in front of the house and was being guarded vigilantly by local officers. This did not mean the crowd had dispersed. If anything, beyond the cleared area, it was more numerous. The news was still spreading. A throng now waited patiently to see the body removed and driven away. We made our way to the Crossed Keys and walked into the now empty public bar. Anyone who had been drinking in there earlier would now be out in the street. None would wish to be interviewed by the police. This didn't mean they were guilty of any crime; just that co-operation with the Law went against any principles they had. They had left behind them an atmosphere heavy with the odours of tobacco and ale, mixed with that of unwashed bodies and a general staleness.

Tom, the landlord, Daisy and a third person waited for us. The one I didn't know I guessed to be Obadiah Quigley, known as Quig. The potman was immediately noteworthy as being almost square in build. He was not tall, but very broad, with powerful shoulders and long arms that hung by his sides motionless. His head, jutted forward, sat on a very short neck and his small dark eyes, set close together, fixed me with as much expression as two glass marbles. Biddle seated himself discreetly at a table to one side and opened his notebook.

'Well, now, landlord,' I addressed Tom, 'perhaps we could have your surname.'

'Mullins,' he said. He made no attempt to add anything. This interview was to be conducted by me and it was down to me to ask any questions I might have. He would reply, but not volunteer any information not directly put to him.

'Where is the key to the house next door usually kept?' I asked.

He glanced towards the bar and pointed to a bare hook on the wall behind it. Anyone who distracted the landlord or Quigley at a busy time could slip behind the bar and take the key. As a system, it was anything but secure. I wondered if Jacobus had realised how easily anyone might obtain the key to his front door.

'Where is the key now?'

Mullins put his hand in his pocket and withdrew a large key and handed it to me. 'Daisy took it down to open up the house, when she took him the supper tray.'

'I will take charge of them now,' I said.

Mullins shrugged. 'I got no need of them.'

'Are there any other keys? Duplicates?'

He shook his head. 'Not here.' His voice was low pitched, hoarse and held no hint of the Irish descent suggested by his surname.

Perhaps not here, but surely elsewhere? For the time being, I let it go. I would quiz Daisy later. Daisy herself sat at a nearby table with her hands clasped before her and watched Biddle as he wrote. I wondered if she herself had had any schooling. I suspected not. She did not turn her gaze towards me and that, I knew, was deliberate. She trod a delicate path. She had a room here, in the attics above our heads. She did not want to lose it or her job as a cleaner, also, probably, glass- and bottle-washer. This was how she lived now. I wondered as to her relationship with Tom. I sensed that she was at least a little afraid of him. She had also had a dreadful shock, discovering the body.

'When Miss Smith came to tell you that Mr Jacobus was dead, did you go yourself to check that this was true?'

'No,' said Tom. 'I had a house full of drinkers. I couldn't leave the bar. I sent Quig.'

'And when Quig returned to confirm the truth of what Miss Smith had said?' I asked.

'I still stayed here.' His gaze challenged me. 'I couldn't do much else, could I? I asked a couple of the regulars to go and find the police patrol. It passes by of an evening at about that time.'

Now, that was interesting. If the murderer had been aware that the regular police patrol would be on the scene before long, he might not have attacked his victim just when he did. I would have to make sure that none of the local constables forming the patrol had noticed anyone hurrying away from the spot.

I glanced at Biddle to make sure he was writing this down. I needn't have worried. Biddle, the tip of his tongue protruding between his front teeth, was doggedly covering the pages of his notebook. I knew him well enough to be confident he wouldn't leave anything out. But this was an important point. I turned my attention to Quig.

'Now, then, Mr Quigley!' (He looked wary and clenched his fists, not in a threatening way, but rather in a nervous reaction to attention being turned directly to himself.)

'Perhaps you would tell me exactly what you did when you went to the scene with Miss Smith. Everything you saw, even something that may appear trivial. Don't leave anything out.'

Quig opened his mouth and the voice that came out contrasted strikingly with the landlord's growl. It was surprisingly high pitched It didn't suit the general appearance of the fellow. 'I went on my own. Daisy, she didn't want to go back and see it again.'

'I gave her a glass of brandy,' interjected Tom. Daisy glanced up and nodded.

'I went upstairs and looked through the door. I saw Mr Jacobus sitting there in his chair with his throat slit.' Quig raised one broad, grimy hand and drew a blackened fingernail across his own throat. 'Covered in blood.'

'And what did you do next?'

'Came back here to tell Mr Mullins it was true.'

'You didn't go into the room where Jacobus was?'

'You gotta be joking!' Quig's high voice rose a notch.

I wondered if he had a singing voice and, if so, whether he was a counter-tenor.

'I wasn't going anywhere near him! B'sides, how did I know for sure the killer had left? He might've been on the floor above, or hiding down on the ground floor in the room where Mr J kept his antiques and pictures and all that sort of junk.'

Even Quig knew rubbish when he saw it. But he was right. The killer might well have still been on the premises, especially if he was seeking something; and the state of the murder scene suggested he had been looking for something.

I turned back to Tom Mullins. 'How often did Mr Jacobus have a visitor? If the key was kept here, you must know.'

For the first time, Mullins looked a little uneasy but he masked it well and quickly. 'I wasn't the only one with a key.'

Now, this was something! 'Who else?' I demanded.

He hunched his shoulders. 'Overmann, the ironmonger, he has a key, I reckon. And the old man himself, he had a key.'

As I knew the latter was true, I must make sure that the deceased's pockets were well searched, in addition to his room, to find the personal key the old man had kept. And if all this were correct, there were at least three keys to the house in the keeping of three different people.

'As Jacobus kept a key of his own,' I speculated, 'then from time to time he must have left the house himself. No one need be any the wiser.'

'Not often,' said Tom. 'He didn't like being among people. He reckoned there were diseases to be caught, brought in on the ships that dock along the river. They come in from all over the world, carrying all sorts of strange illnesses along with their other cargo. Cholera and the bubonic plague, those were what he was most afraid of, so he told me once.' He paused. 'My point,' he continued, 'is that anyone wanting to visit him didn't have to come here for a key. He'd knock at the street door, Mr Jacobus would look out and, if he was expecting him or it was someone he knew, he'd throw down the key.'

A look of triumph flickered briefly in Tom's eyes. 'So, it wasn't just down to me who went in and out of his house. You reckon I let the murderer in, do you? Well, I didn't, not necessarily.'

There came a clatter of hooves from outside in the street and a black, windowless van was driven past, the crowd falling back in respect. A few men took off their hats. The body was being taken to the morgue. It was getting late, I was tired and I had not eaten my supper, apart from the soup.

'Someone will come back tomorrow and speak to you again,' I told the three of them. 'There will be a guard on the front door of the murder house, twenty-four hours round the clock. There is no chance, I suppose, that you know who might be the next of kin?'

The question took all three of them by surprise and they looked at one another. Daisy was moved to speak at last.

'He never had no family,' she said. 'Or if he did, he never spoke of them. Not them that is living now, I mean. He used to talk about his ancestor sometimes, come over with the Dutchman and his army.'

'William of Orange?' I asked.

All three of them nodded in unison like a set of automatons.

'That's him!' squeaked Quig. 'He was uncommon proud of him.'

Chapter Four

IT WAS the early hours of the morning before I arrived back home. The nearby railway terminus at Waterloo was already astir. Indeed, I knew it had been active all night, for a mainline rail station never fully sleeps. The timetable may not have yet come into force, and passengers not yet arrived, but all night long the station had been preparing for the day ahead. Waiting rooms and other public areas had to be cleaned. The restaurant had to be restocked. Trains that had parked at outlying stations chuntered to each other as they were slowly moved alongside platforms to await the first passengers. Freight, including mailbags, was being loaded. The sky above it, already beginning to lighten with the dawn, was further illuminated by the gaslighting of the station concourse. But our house was dark and quiet when I let myself in. I took off my boots to creep upstairs, hoping not to wake Lizzie. She heard me, as she always does. She stirred and her voice, heavy with sleep, asked, 'Was it very bad?'

'Yes,' I replied as quietly. 'Bad enough.'

'I'm sorry,' she replied. 'You liked him.'

'Yes, I liked the old rogue.'

★

Sadly, too few hours later, I found myself back at Scotland Yard, in Dunn's office.

'I propose to return to Limehouse today, sir,' I told him. 'I'll be taking Sergeant Morris and Constable Biddle with me. Between us, we should be able to cover the ground thoroughly; and hope to find a witness who noticed something unusual, or a stranger in the vicinity of the house before the murder. I shall talk to the tenant of the other adjacent property owned by Jacobus. That's the ironmonger, Overmann. He is a nervous fellow and if anyone suspicious had been lurking about, I think there is a good chance he'd have noticed him. He did deny he knew anything the moment I arrived on the scene last night. But that I fancy was an automatic response. His great wish would be not to become involved. But I also think he is basically an honest man and he wouldn't hide any knowledge deliberately.'

Dunn looked, I fancied, momentarily shifty. 'Do as you wish, Ross, this morning. But don't forget that Mrs Roxby is expecting you in Hampstead at two thirty this afternoon.'

'But, sir!' I exclaimed. 'Surely you are not putting someone else in charge of this murder? I must have been one of the last people to see Jacobus alive! Besides, there are other officers who are more experienced than I when it comes to investigating jewel thefts. I have long experience of murder inquiries—'

'Don't argue, Ross!' he interrupted wearily. 'I am not taking you away from investigating this foul murder. But if you are there this morning, then Morris and Biddle can continue for the rest of the day. Sergeant Morris is a very able and experienced man. Tomorrow, I will put you back in charge of the murder, never fear. But Mrs Roxby is expecting you this afternoon.' With more energy, he concluded, 'And she will kick up the devil of a fuss if I send someone else!'

Oh, yes! I fumed silently to myself. Someone very senior has given instructions to Dunn. We are not to upset Mrs Roxby!

'And am I to be running back and forth between Limehouse and Hampstead until both these crimes are solved?' I knew I sounded angry. I didn't care.

'No, no, of course not! I shall explain to Mrs Roxby . . .' Dunn faltered and rallied. 'I'll put Reynolds in charge of recovering her missing jewels, after you've called on her today. You need not be troubled with it again, after you return from Hampstead. Oblige me, Ross, if you will, in this.'

'The Roxby business will turn out to be the work of a ladder gang, mark my words,' I muttered. 'Why can't wealthy householders take more care of their valuables?'

'They think,' said Dunn, 'that with a house full of guests and servants running around everywhere, every room blazing with light, they are safe.'

'Don't they know such robberies have happened to others?'

'They don't think it will happen to them!' snapped Dunn. 'I'd be obliged it you'd stop raising objections, Ross.'

'Am I to go alone to visit the lady?' I asked stiffly.

'No, no, I'll send Sergeant Wood with you.' Dunn made an appeasing gesture and added, 'You may hire a conveyance

45

to and back from Hampstead and reclaim the cost from the Yard.'

'Thank you, sir,' I said.

It was the very least he could do and he knew it. But I had one more request. 'The only item we know so far is missing from the murder scene is the victim's watch and Albert chain. The watch is a gold half-hunter, and the chain also gold, and heavy. Perhaps word could be passed to the constables on regular patrols in all areas, that they might inquire of any pawnbrokers in their area whether anyone pawns or offers for sale such a watch and chain within the next week or two? With a description of the customer?'

'Watch and chain? It is generally the first thing to be pawned when someone is hard-up,' retorted Dunn. 'We shall be inundated with reports of such items from every pawnbroker in London. Each one, no matter how many we receive, will need to be carefully investigated. We do not have an endless supply of men to send on such speculative errands.'

Well, he was probably right. But it was worth a try.

'I think it's the thing to do first, sir.'

'Oh, very well,' muttered Dunn. 'Get over to Limehouse and see what you can find out. But don't get so carried away that you are late for your meeting with Mrs Roxby at Hampstead this afternoon!'

So I returned to the narrow little house where the murder had taken place and, while Morris and Biddle made inquiries among other houses and businesses in the immediate area, I paid a call on the ironmonger.

I found him alone. He was standing behind the counter of his shop when I entered. He looked up quickly at the jangle of the bell above the door, but his smile of welcome faded quickly as he recognised me. I told him I'd be obliged if he'd close his business so that we could talk uninterrupted. He hurried to bolt the door and turn the sign in the window to read 'Closed' to anyone who might be in urgent need of a box of nails.

I waited, taking a good look around me and noting that he sold a good deal more than nails. Much of the stock might have been found on the premises of a ship's chandler. Besides hatchets and saws, other miscellaneous tools, buckets and watering cans, rolls of chicken wire, skeins of rope, letter boxes, door handles and hinges, and tins of paint and lamp oil, the visitor could also purchase canned meat. It is something I have always been careful to avoid. It is considered to be safe now, but earlier scandals have put me off the product. However, what took my eye in particular was a display of knives of various design, some of them large, others small, and general-purpose clasp knives. I was standing before this when Overmann returned from the entrance door and stood patiently beside me, with his hands folded. He wore an apron and woollen sleeve protectors.

'You sell a lot of knives?' I asked him, careful to keep my tone conversational.

'Yes, sir,' replied the shopkeeper. 'A working man needs a good knife to carry about with him. Every housewife needs a good set of knives in her kitchen.'

'Sold any lately?'

Overmann considered the question. 'I sold a penknife

to a clerk the other day, three pocketknives, and two larger knives to seamen off the ships.'

He probably did quite good business overall, I thought.

'Do you sharpen knives?' I asked.

'Oh, yes, sir, I have a knife-grinding machine over there, in the corner. A knife is no good if it isn't sharp!' It then occurred to him that a knife had been the murder weapon. Hurriedly, he added, 'I have never sold a knife to any man who looked like a criminal. If any suspicious person came in and bought a knife, I would inform the authorities.'

'I believe you also keep a key to Mr Jacobus's house?'

He turned paler, if that were possible. 'Yes, sir, in case of fire, you understand.'

'You have never used it to enter the house for any reason? Don't be alarmed. I am not accusing you of anything.'

'I had an arrangement with Mr Jacobus.' Overmann hesitated. 'Once a month I called on him to pay him the rent money, for this place.' He waved a hand to encompass our surroundings. 'He was a good landlord. Now he is – he is gone, I don't know . . .' Desperation showed in his eyes. 'We have made a good life here, my wife and I.'

'I understand. I must ask you to give me the key. Also, I would like to speak to your wife.'

'The key, of course! But my wife speaks very little English . . .' He paused. When I did not add anything further, he sighed and said resignedly, 'I will bring her – and the key.'

He left through a door at the back of the shop. I heard the faint murmur of voices and he returned, accompanied by a small woman of much younger appearance than I had expected. But then I realised that Overmann himself was probably only in his late thirties. On the previous evening, in the gloom, he had appeared older.

Mrs Overmann fixed me with apprehensive brown eyes and bobbed a curtsy. Then she put a hand into the pocket of her apron and withdrew a large door key. She handed it to her husband who, in turn, handed it to me in a ceremonious way, and made me a stiff half-bow.

I felt absurdly that I were part of some civic ceremony, the opening of a new public library or a workmen's institute.

'Thank you. Would you ask Mrs Overmann if she has noticed anything unusual lately? Anyone taking an interest in the house next door, for example?'

The Overmanns exchanged a few words in their unknown language. The husband turned back to me. 'No, sir. She does not go outside into the streets very much and never alone. There are some men out there, from the ships, who look dangerous to her. We come from a small place, a village only. Everybody there knows everybody else . . .'

And here they might just as well have stepped off the boat on to the surface of the moon, as the soil of England.

I put the key in my pocket. 'Thank her, please.' I found myself making a half-bow to Mrs Overmann similar to that her husband had made to me when handing me the key.

His little wife blushed and bobbed another curtsy.

'Please, sir,' he said, 'may I continue to do business here in the shop? I do not know to whom the building now belongs, who will be our landlord in the future.'

'I can't tell you that. I don't know, either,' I confessed. 'I think you can continue for the moment. After that, lawyers may be involved.'

They had come across Europe and worked hard. Now they faced everything being snatched away from them. He had paid the rent to Jacobus personally. I thought again about the untidy murder scene, the abandoned search. Someone had rightly suspected that the old man had money hidden about the place.

In the doorway of the back room from which Mrs Overmann had come appeared the form of a small child, a little boy, who gazed at me as if I'd come from a different world. Perhaps, in a way, I had.

'I will trouble you no longer,' I said to the ironmonger. 'Please feel free to open up your shop. I can't speak for the future, but you have been paying your rent until now, so . . .' At this point I ran out of words and merely gestured around me.

'Thank you, sir,' said Overmann.

Wood and I hired a growler to take us all the way to Hampstead, wait for us there, and bring us back to central London. It was an old but capacious and comfortable vehicle; and I suspected it had once been a private carriage. The cabbie was very pleased to take our fare. It promised him an easy day. He would be driving out of London's crowded streets, where all the various carts, omnibuses, private carriages and vehicles plying for hire disputed the road. This without taking account of pedestrians trying to cross the streets, costermongers' carts piled with produce, the numerous accidents and disputes regarding who had the right of way. There was also the need, as soon as he had set down one fare, to find another.

Sergeant Wood, too, cheered up; and that is saying something, for by nature he is generally a lugubrious fellow. He has a long, narrow face, sallow complexion and large dark eyes that survey his surroundings as though he not only sees the material evidence provided, but something else, an unseen world, chiefly manifested in the possibility of crime and mischief, lurking everywhere. At times I have thought that Wood might make a very good undertaker. I could imagine him standing, hands clasped, by the side of a coffin, gazing mournfully at the deceased, and speculating on the journey the departed soul might be making.

He also has a penchant for mint-flavoured humbugs. These he rolls around his mouth so that they rattle against his teeth as if he had a mouthful of marbles. If anything spoiled the prospect of the trip into cleaner air and more open space, it was the thought of being shut up in the growler with him. But he is an experienced officer, several years of service behind him. As I have already indicated, it has left him without illusions regarding human nature. Wood is inclined to think the worst of everyone. It is a trap into which, as a police officer, it is easy to fall.

On our way to Hampstead I was able to tell him all I knew about Mrs Roxby. He listened, sitting with his bowler hat on his knees, uttering a grunt from time to time and crunching the humbugs. When I'd finished, he observed, 'They should've kept their valuables locked up all the time.'

He and I were at least in agreement on that.

'There is a companion living in the house. Her name is Miss Chalk. I need to speak to her also, and alone, if Mrs Roxby will allow it of course. She wants her jewellery returned; but not that we should learn the secrets of her family. The lady is extremely annoying; but she is not a fool.'

'So why didn't the Roxby female take better care when she had strangers coming to dine and the servants were all busy downstairs?' objected Wood. 'Do you know what I've observed in people with money, Mr Ross? They believe everyone must respect them, but thieves don't, do they? They are what I call natural targets, people like this Mrs Roxby.'

Neither was Wood a fool, I thought, and was suddenly pleased that, since I couldn't have Morris, I at least had someone competent to assist me.

'See what the staff have to say,' I told him. 'They always know the family scandals and secrets. Make a friend of the cook. That's always useful.'

We were crossing the Heath now; its open prospects pleasing to the eye, its clean air almost exhilarating after the smoke and stink of the city. The Roxby property was a substantial one, standing back from the road and Heath, in well-kept gardens stocked with a variety of trees worthy of an arboretum. One might think oneself in the country and yet the great, sprawling metropolis was so near, ready to swallow up wrongdoers of all kinds and hide them in its unlit alleys and shadowy courtyards. A property like the Roxby mansion would be a ladder gang's delight: an opportunity for ill-gotten gains, with routes to escape in all directions across sparsely inhabited heathland.

Wood was thinking the same, because he muttered, 'I wonder this sort of robbery hasn't happened to them before.'

The gates had been left open ahead of our expected arrival, so we bowled through in fine style and drew up before the portico. Our cabbie was sufficiently impressed to climb down from his perch and open the door of the cab for us, as though we were regular arriving guests.

We were not in the ordinary run of visitors, but we were expected and, as we approached the door, it was opened by a butler who eyed us with some disfavour.

'You gentlemen will be from the police?'

I had never heard the term 'gentlemen' spoken so much in a way that implied the opposite.

Behind me, Wood muttered, 'Hullo! Should we have gone to the back door?'

Well, we were both used to cool receptions. Nobody wants the police at the door.

'Mrs Roxby is expecting us!' I said firmly to the butler. 'I am Inspector Ross. This is Sergeant Wood.'

He stood back to admit us and, as we passed by him, he called out to the cabbie, 'If you are to wait, you may take your horse and vehicle round to the stables.'

That wasn't out of consideration for the horse or the driver, I thought ruefully. It was so that the shabby hackney carriage should be out of sight. Wood was probably right and the butler would have preferred us not to present ourselves at the front door.

'Sergeant Wood,' I said firmly to the butler, 'would like to interview the staff. I will speak to the family.'

The butler gave me a venomous look and, in a smooth tone, replied, 'Certainly, sir, come this way and I will announce you.'

Mrs Roxby had obviously given some thought to which room should be used to receive our visit. We were not paying a social call. Rather cleverly, I thought, she had instructed the butler to show us into what had clearly been the late Mr Roxby's study. It was to the rear of the house, a little dark, perhaps because it did not receive the afternoon sun, but comfortably furnished. There was a large and splendid desk of, I guessed, French design. There was also an impressive chesterfield sofa of the sort favoured by gentlemen's clubs, and two large leather-covered armchairs. The room smelled faintly of tobacco. A pair of paintings on the wall above the desk were of clipper ships. Roxby had been a shipowner I remembered. Perhaps those two vessels had been the basis of early successful ventures. He'd done well, because a third painting, larger and set above the fireplace so the visitor couldn't miss it, showed a steamship. Of particular interest was a large and solid metal safe, painted green. Valuables such as the emerald necklace, together with important documents, would normally be kept in that. But on the night of the dinner party, the necklace had been taken from its place of safety and left unattended on a dressing table. I couldn't ignore this fact, and it remained only partly explained. It was like hearing a wrong note struck mid-tune on a piano. I made a mental note to request that the safe be opened and thoroughly examined.

'Inspector Ross, madam, of the police!' intoned the butler. He had been watching me with fishy disapproval in his cold eyes. He knew I was taking mental notes. Perhaps he feared the staff would be blamed in some fashion.

'Thank you, Ventham,' said the lady.

Mrs Roxby and Miss Chalk were both seated on the chesterfield. The dimensions allowed a clear gap between the two of them. Miss Chalk, plainly attired in a dark green gown with a high neck, looked impassive and stared past me, appearing fascinated by the clipper ships. Without her hat, her hair could now be seen to be a mousy brown, drawn back in a severe style and secured in a bun. She was completely overshadowed by her employer, Mrs Roxby, who was resplendent in violet silk bedecked with a double necklace of pearls, and pearl earrings. She wore her hair piled up and mostly covered by an elaborate widow's cap, with long lace streamers, such as worn by her Majesty Queen Victoria. She managed to convey wealth, good taste, her bereaved status and an awareness of fashion. With a gesture of her hand worthy of our gracious Queen, she indicated I should take an armchair.

'*Don't upset her!*' had been Dunn's parting instruction to me. I had every intention of disobeying it. She was not in charge of this interview, and neither was Dunn. I was.

'Thank you, madam,' I said and sat down.

'You have made some progress, I hope, in your inquiries?' she asked.

'We are spreading the word among the jewel fences known to us.'

'Fences?' asked Mrs Roxby with a slight frown.

'Receivers of stolen jewels and other valuables, ma'am. Several of those gentlemen have been in the business for some time and are known to us. However, I must stress that, even if we recover some of the emerald necklace, we may not be able to recover it intact. Nor is it certain we shall recover any of it. We may track down the thieves.'

'But if you find the thieves,' she objected, 'surely you will find my missing property?'

'They may no longer have it, ma'am. Indeed, it is fairly certain that they don't. It will have been passed on and it may have been broken up.'

'Broken up?' exclaimed the lady in horror.

'Such a distinctive item cannot be left intact and recognisable. May I ask whether the jewellery is insured?'

She didn't like that question. 'It is, naturally. But I don't want the value in money, I want the necklace returned intact! It was a gift to me from my late husband, an heirloom in his family, and has great sentimental value.'

It always does, I thought unkindly. *I dare say the late Mr Roxby expected you to take better care of it!*

Aloud, I said, 'I should like to see the actual location from which the necklace was taken. From this house, obviously, but from an upstairs room, I believe.' I turned my attention to Miss Chalk. She abandoned her study of the clipper ships and looked at me rather quizzically. 'Perhaps this lady could accompany me?'

Mrs Roxby hesitated but thought better of making any objection. 'Go along with the inspector, Chalk!' she ordered.

Miss Chalk rose to her feet and proceeded towards the door. 'This way, Inspector Ross.'

The butler, Ventham, was lurking in the hall. It wouldn't have surprised me if he'd been listening at the door. I wondered why he wasn't supervising Wood's examination of the staff. He watched our ascent of the staircase. When we'd reached the upper landing, and I glanced back, he had gone. *He can't follow me,* I thought. *So, he's gone back to check on Wood's activities below stairs.* The unfortunate fellow had his work cut out, trying to keep track of both the police officers who'd invaded the house.

We emerged from the main staircase into a long gloomy corridor. The gas mantles projecting at regular intervals from the wall had not yet been lit. But I was able to discern to the left, at the far end, a curved iron banister. This I guessed must guard access to a spiral stair used by the domestic staff about their duties. Miss Chalk turned to the right and led me to a door which she opened and then stood back, allowing me to enter ahead of her.

We were in a well-appointed bedroom with many feminine touches by way of frills on the furniture legs and lace curtains at the windows, in addition to heavy damask drapes. An unexpected, but charming, item was a well-loved rag doll, propped on a little chair in the corner. It made me feel sad for a moment. It had been so short a time since the doll had been carried everywhere by its owner.

'This is Miss Gray's room?' I asked. My guide nodded; and indicated that I should continue through a door leading into a dressing room. Here she gestured towards a table with a heavy lace skirt, laden with items necessary for a lady to look her best. The little room also contained a cheval mirror in a gilded frame.

'This is where the jewellery boxes were left while the family and guests were downstairs dining?'

'That is so,' said Miss Chalk, breaking her silence. I understood what the pattern of any conversation we might have would be. She shared the same attitude towards official questioning as Tom Mullins, albeit in a more genteel way. She would answer direct questions. She would not volunteer anything else.

If I were correct in suspecting the activities of a ladder gang, there was no window in this tiny room large enough to allow a thief to climb through. I went back to the bedroom and crossed to one of two windows there, overlooking the rear of the house and, I guessed, the garden. I drew aside the net curtaining.

I was right. It was an attractive garden; the area I looked down on was laid to lawn, dotted with the rhododendrons so popular for some years now. But right in the middle was a venerable oak tree. Its size indicated its great age and I guessed it was older than the house. Once it had stood on open heath. Its spreading branches had sheltered travellers, making their way to and from London. It may have sheltered a highwayman or two, in the previous century. Now it bestowed its shade on a long wooden seat set beneath it, and occupied by a young couple engaged in spirited conversation. I opened the window and leaned out.

They heard the sound and both looked up quickly and, I fancied, guiltily. The young lady I identified at once as Miss Gray. But such an animated Miss Gray! So unlike the emerald-wearing, sulky young woman in the photograph

I'd been shown. She had been laughing, but as soon as she realised she was observed the smiles vanished. The young fellow with her looked up too. I judged him in his mid-twenties, with dark curling hair. He had also been laughing but when he saw me, he scowled.

I closed the window and turned to Miss Chalk. 'That is Miss Gray, I think. Who is the young man with her?'

'That is Mr Henry Roxby,' said Miss Chalk, breaking her Trappist-like silence. 'In the family he is called Harry. He is the son of Mr Jeremy Roxby, the younger brother of Mr George Roxby, now deceased, who was Mrs Roxby's husband.'

'Is Mr Jeremy Roxby still alive?'

'Yes,' said Miss Chalk.

'And also in the shipping business?'

'The brothers were in partnership. Mr Jeremy Roxby has been the head of the firm since his brother's death. That is to say, for some years now.'

'So does Mrs Roxby own shares in the company?'

Miss Chalk was becoming restive. 'Yes, but she takes no part in the running of it.'

'What about Harry Roxby down there? Does he take an active interest in the family business?'

A flicker of emotion crossed Miss Chalk's hitherto impassive features. 'No. He hasn't the brains for it!' She glanced back down towards the garden. 'Besides, he likes enjoying life too much.'

'You don't like him?'

'My personal opinion of Harry Roxby is neither here nor there.'

'Young ladies might find him attractive; I dare say?' I observed as mildly as I could.

'If you mean Bella Gray,' snapped Miss Chalk, 'she's known him all her life. They were childhood friends. I hope she would not be so foolish as to entertain romantic notions about him. He would make a terrible husband. Besides, Mrs Roxby has other plans for her niece.'

'A title, perhaps?'

'Why not?' replied the companion, fixing me with a challenging stare.

It appeared Miss Chalk shared her employer's hopes for Miss Gray. That didn't surprise me. But I was a little taken aback that she had expressed criticism of Harry Roxby. Did this mean that Mrs Roxby shared this view of the young man?

'I should like now to go into the garden and examine the ground beneath the windows!' I told her briskly.

'Whatever for?' asked Miss Chalk, showing genuine curiosity at last.

'The marks of a ladder, of course.'

'I've already had the gardener take a good look,' she said. 'And check that his shed has not been broken into or any implement removed.'

'Like a ladder?'

She nodded. 'He tells me there is no sign of intrusion or disturbance.'

'You are astute, I fancy, Miss Chalk!' I told her. 'And would make a good detective yourself.'

'Inspector Ross,' she replied. 'Dependent on my position in this house as I am, I have learned not to rock the

boat, as they say. Any more questions will have to be asked
by you, in your official capacity.'

'I quite understand,' I told her.

We left the house and went into the garden from a pleasant little morning room on the ground floor, exiting
through open French windows. I had avoided returning to
the study, as I wanted to avoid alerting Mrs Roxby to my
progress, and had requested Miss Chalk to show me out of
the house as discreetly as possible. Now, outdoors again, it
was really difficult to believe we were not in the countryside. The air was clean. Leaves rustled, birds swooped and
fluttered by. Harry Roxby and Isabella Gray had fallen
silent, seeing there was a new arrival. He leaned towards
her and whispered something in her ear. For a moment she
looked alarmed, before hiding her face from me behind a
little fan. *He has told her I am a police officer*, I thought.

I chose to ignore them and instead took my time to look
along the flowerbeds by the walls. As Miss Chalk had told
me, there were no marks that could have been made by a
ladder, or any footprints. On the other hand, if there had
been any, the gardener could have raked them smooth.
While I was doing this, I knew I was still being observed
closely by the couple seated by the tree. I set off purpose-
fully towards them, the companion following on my heels.
They remained seated until I had reached the spot. There,
Miss Chalk informed them who I was (as if they didn't
already know). Harry Roxby rose to his feet and faced me
with ill-disguised hostility.

Miss Gray surveyed me over the fan with large pale-
blue eyes. It was a Chinese fan, I noticed, painted with a

scene showing lovers fleeing to safety from guards sent in pursuit by the girl's angry papa. Willow pattern! I thought. Memory can strike at unexpected and inappropriate moments. Now, in the middle of an investigation and in Mrs Roxby's garden, I thought of my late mother and my childhood home. It had been the dwelling of a miner's family, its contents practical without luxuries. But my mother had had one prized possession: a large meat plate showing just such a willow pattern of blue-and-white design. That plate had never been used for joints of meat. Our family budget had not run to such good dining. It hung undisturbed on the wall, except when it was taken down, from time to time, to be dusted. In the absence of pictures, it was the only ornamentation hanging there. I found myself wondering now what had happened to that plate. I had left home to seek my fortune in London. I had joined the police force. My mother had died not long after I travelled south. Her death had left me with a sense of guilt that had never gone away. I had travelled home only to bury her. By then, new occupants lived in the house. The furniture had been sold to pay the doctor. I never knew what had happened to the willow-pattern plate. Nor, come to that, did I ever discover what happened to my mother's wedding ring. The old woman who had come in to care for my mother as she lay dying declared ignorance.

I was abruptly brought back to the here and now by the voice of Miss Chalk, slightly raised, as though she had noted my drifting attention.

'Inspector Ross!' she announced briefly, by way of introduction, indicating me with her hand for the benefit of the young couple. 'Mr Henry Roxby, Inspector!' she added to me, then hesitated. 'And Miss Isabella Gray.'

'I am here about the theft of the necklace,' I said bluntly. 'You probably already know that. I am very sorry, Miss Gray, that you won't have such a splendid article of jewellery to wear to parties from now on.'

Miss Gray folded the fan and set it down on the rustic bench she shared with young Roxby.

'I didn't like it,' she said frankly. 'It was very old fashioned and uncomfortable to wear. My aunt wanted me to wear it at the dinner party that evening; and it was brought out of the safe for that reason. But I absolutely refused, and left it on the dressing table. I wore something else. She was very cross about that at the time, and when it was discovered to be missing, well, you really can't imagine what a fuss she made.'

I could imagine it, very well. But this answered Lizzie's question, and my own concern, as to why the necklace had been taken from the safe to the dressing room.

'It is not Bella's fault!' said Harry Roxby loudly.

'It certainly isn't!' she declared. 'How was I to know a thief would creep into the house? I am sorry it has been stolen, of course. But I don't care a bit whether or not you are able to get it back, Mr Ross.'

By now, my expectations of Miss Gray had made a complete turnabout. I had thought, having only seen her in the ball-gown portrait and peeping at me over the Chinese fan, that she might be shy, and perhaps sulky. But she spoke with confidence and spirit.

'I think it is unlikely that it will be found in the state in which it was taken,' I told her apologetically. 'I believe it will have been broken up into its component parts. So, to confirm, the jewels were taken from the safe with the others, and left in plain view in the dressing room?'

She nodded. 'You must think us very careless, Inspector Ross.' She managed a weak smile.

'It was certainly unfortunate,' I agreed.

'Look here!' snapped Harry. 'You're not going to blame Bella – my cousin – for this, are you? I told you, it's not her fault. My aunt Roxby is a bully, I don't care who hears me say it. She kept telling Bella to wear the wretched necklace when Bella had made it clear she didn't want to.'

'I am not in the business of apportioning blame, Mr Roxby. I am investigating a theft.'

We had all failed to notice the approach of Mrs Roxby from the house. Suddenly she was there, red with fury. 'What is the meaning of this, Inspector Ross?'

'I am conducting my inquiries, ma'am,' I said as mildly as possible. 'I have to speak to everyone who was present that evening. Perhaps I could have a list of your dinner guests?'

'I do not intend to countenance your troubling my guests! They have nothing to do with this. They are all above suspicion.'

'Nevertheless, any one of them might have witnessed something of interest. I shall need a list before I leave this afternoon.'

'Chalk!' She turned on the luckless companion. 'Write out a list of names for the inspector.'

'Yes, Mrs Roxby. I have already done it.'

The lady reddened. 'Why? I had not asked you to do so.'

'I thought it very likely that you would, before Inspector Ross left.' Miss Chalk seemed unruffled by her employer's anger.

Mrs Roxby turned her fire back in my direction. 'Chalk will give you her list before you leave. But, if you wish to speak to Miss Gray again, I'd be obliged if you would consult me first. I would wish to be present.' She paused for breath.

Time to let her know that I didn't take orders from her. 'I am afraid I am a police officer investigating the theft you yourself reported. That is what you asked the Yard to do. I am doing it. I don't see any impropriety in my actions, in any case. A member of the family has been present . . .' I indicated Harry Roxby. 'And also Miss Chalk.'

'You should have sent word to me, Chalk, about this!' Having failed to rattle me, she turned again on the unfortunate companion.

'Please don't blame Miss Chalk,' I said quickly. 'I asked her to show me to the area beneath the bedroom windows, to see if there were any marks of a ladder. By chance, Mr Roxby and Miss Gray were in the garden, so I took the opportunity to speak to them.'

'Were there any marks of a ladder or footprints or anything?' asked Harry Roxby keenly.

'No, sir, the soil appeared to have been raked clean.'

'Oh, right,' he muttered. I thought he looked relieved, but perhaps that was only my suspicious mind.

'I will return to London now, ma'am,' I said to Mrs Roxby. 'And make my report to Superintendent Dunn.'

'If you come back,' said Mrs Roxby icily, 'kindly inform me of what you intend to do while on my property. Incidentally, why has that other officer been sitting in the kitchen all this time, eating cake and chatting to the maids?'

'Been getting on well in the kitchen, I believe, Wood?' I asked as we rolled back towards the city centre.

'Very good cake,' said Wood. 'Pleasant woman, the cook. The butler looked in on us. He didn't like to see me sitting there talking to them all. But he couldn't do anything about it. The maids fancy the young lady and young Mr Roxby are sweet on one another. Mrs Roxby doesn't like that. The cook said to me, privately like, that she didn't blame the mistress for not wanting Miss Gray to be getting "silly notions", as she called it, about her cousin. Harry Roxby is a bit of a wastrel, the cook reckons. Nice young chap, but Mrs Roxby wants Miss Gray to do better. How about you, Mr Ross? How did you get on?'

'An interesting afternoon,' I told him. 'Oh, and Wood . . .' I took Miss Chalk's list of the dinner-party guests from my pocket. 'These people were all present at the dinner on the night of the theft. You can spend tomorrow morning calling on them. They will all be utterly respectable and it will be a waste of time. But they will be expecting someone representing the police to ask them for their personal experience on that night. They will be disappointed and mortally offended if no one comes. And when you've done that, you can ask around discreetly concerning Harry Roxby. Just what does he get up to, eh?'

★

'Well, Ross, how did you get on?' was also Dunn's question when I looked into his office on my return. 'You didn't upset her?' he added anxiously.

'I think I worried her, sir,' I told him frankly.

Dunn leaned back in his chair, squinted at me, rubbed his hand over his bristly head of hair and invited, 'Go on.'

'Something is amiss in that family. It is not just this robbery that has made them all so jittery. The lady is defensive, the niece would be glad to have seen the last of the necklace, and the nephew is worried enough for all of them. The companion is a clever woman and may know more than she is saying.'

'The jewels are insured?' Dunn asked, after a pause.

'Yes, sir.'

'And the loss has been reported to the insurers?'

'Not yet, I believe. She is insisting she wants the necklace returned. In any case, I fancy this is not a straightforward case of an attempted fraud. Something else is going on, and I can't work out what it is.'

'Did you see the safe in which the necklace was normally kept?'

'Yes, it is in the study. It is a large, heavy piece, made of steel, and free standing. It could not be moved without great effort and difficulty. A team of men would be required. A skilled cracksman might be able to open it, but he would take time. Otherwise, an explosive would be needed, and the process would be audible, even in a household where a dinner party was taking place. When Mrs Roxby spoke of valuables kept in it as more secure than if they had been kept in a bank in town, since they would have to be transported across the Heath, when required, she was probably right. For it to be stolen as it was, it had to be removed from the safe first.'

'Meaning that the ladder gang, if one was responsible, was extremely lucky to find the necklace left unattended on a dressing table.'

'Yes, sir.'

'I don't like it!' growled Dunn. 'Too damn convenient.' He tapped his fingers on his desk. 'To whom did you speak, other than the lady, the niece, the nephew and the companion? What did the companion have to say?'

'Miss Chalk is the soul of discretion. She excels in speaking in code. She is also clever, as I said.'

'And the niece and the young fellow you mentioned?'

'Mr Henry Roxby, known in the family as Harry. He was deep in conversation in the garden with the young lady, his cousin, when I spotted them from an upstairs window. We already know that "cousin" is a courtesy term in this case. The relationship is circumstantial rather than by blood. Miss Gray is the daughter of Mrs Roxby's deceased brother. Harry Roxby is the son of the late Mr Roxby's brother, Jeremy. The Roxby brothers were partners in the shipping company and the surviving brother now runs it. Mrs Roxby holds shares in the company; but takes no active part in the day-to-day business.'

'And Harry Roxby? Is he active in the company?'

'I gather from Miss Chalk that he's not. I fancy he is something of a wastrel and, in Miss Chalk's opinion, not suited to serious business. But she may be prejudiced on account of the girl. Wood learned from the servants that there may be a romance between the "cousins", calling them that for the sake of convenience. Miss Chalk doesn't approve, I think. I am sure Mrs Roxby wouldn't! If Miss Chalk and her employer are united in anything, it is believing that Miss Gray should make a very good marriage, with the prospect of a title.'

Dunn snorted derisively. 'What's the girl like?'

'A pleasant enough young woman with a naïve charm, as I believe it is called. Not pretty exactly, but attractive, more so than in that photograph. She has spirit.'

Dunn's eyebrows rose alarming and nearly disappeared into his hairline. 'You have a sophisticated turn of phrase that surprises me, Ross!'

'I learn these things from my wife, sir. I think it's how Lizzie would describe her. I don't know about a romance. The young people are very close friends; such was the impression I had. But then, they have known one another since childhood. They share confidences, yes, but I'd say no more than that without further proof. Also, my conversation with them was in the presence of Miss Chalk. When Mrs Roxby discovered us talking together, she was furious. I am afraid I have upset her, but it is difficult to do otherwise. Perhaps, when Inspector Reynolds takes over, he may make a better fist of it than I have.'

'Hum!' muttered Dunn thoughtfully, and in a way that made me apprehensive. 'It seems to me you've done very well so far, Ross. I am reversing my decision to hand it all over to Reynolds. I'll leave this case in your capable hands.'

'But what of the murder investigation in Limehouse?' I exclaimed in dismay.

'Oh, you can keep an eye on that, too. Sergeant Morris can safely be left in charge of the day-to-day running of the inquiries. It will probably turn out to be some sort of sordid underworld crime, a falling-out among thieves, eh? Old Jacobus always did play one side off against another. The danger in walking that kind of tightrope is that you can fall off very suddenly, with catastrophic results, eh, Ross?'

Elizabeth Martin Ross

We had finished our dinner and sat before the fire. I could see Ben was tired and I didn't want to quiz him at length. But he wanted to talk over his day, as we usually did, particularly the part about his visit to Hampstead.

'It is very unfair of Superintendent Dunn to make you work on both cases,' I said.

'Morris can probably manage in Limehouse, Dunn's right about that. But I admit I am more interested in who killed the old fellow on the very day I had called on him myself than I am in the Roxby necklace. That woman is a harridan. If her niece stood up to her in refusing to wear the necklace at the dinner party, when ordered, then my respect for Miss Gray increases. The young lady didn't like the piece, of course, and said so, frankly.'

'Mm,' I replied. 'You say that when Miss Gray spoke of the jewellery, she used the past tense. "I *didn't* like it" instead of "don't like it"; and "it *was* very old fashioned" instead of "is". 'She seems to accept the jewellery is lost; and she doesn't expect to see it again.'

'I did say to her that, probably, it has been broken up by now, and the stones may have been dispersed,' Ben admitted. 'I told Mrs Roxby the same. The lady wouldn't hear of such an outlandish idea. Miss Isabella, in the popular phrase, couldn't care less!'

'I suppose that explains it,' I agreed. 'Only let us suppose that Harry Roxby, who has shown no interest in joining the family firm, and must depend on an allowance from his father, is in need of money. Isn't that what Sergeant Wood's chat with the kitchen staff suggested? He can always go to his father for an emergency amount, I dare say, if the situation becomes extreme. But one can easily imagine the unpleasant and embarrassing scene that would follow. Jeremy Roxby must already be disappointed that his son has no aptitude for business. I think Harry would have to be at his wits' end before he faced his angry parent. He might be tempted to devise some harebrained scheme to raise some money.'

'You have a suspicious mind, Lizzie, but so do I!' replied Ben, managing a smile. 'The last thing I did today before setting off home was to give instructions to Sergeant Wood. Tomorrow morning he is going to be very busy. He is to call on all the guests at dinner on the night of the burglary. After that he is to start discreet inquiries about young Harry. Perhaps, if the sergeant discovers some interesting information, I may find a reason to approach Jeremy Roxby directly. In any case, it would be interesting to hear what the head of the Roxby shipping line thinks about the robbery. The necklace was a family piece and he can't be happy that his sister-in-law has lost it.'

Chapter Five

Inspector Ben Ross

LIFE IS full of surprises, and mishaps, and the following day held several. In the early hours it had begun to rain and had settled into a steady downpour by the time I set out. Bella Gray and Harry Roxby would not be able to sit spooning in the garden today, if that was what they had been doing.

My progress was delayed within minutes of leaving home, when I discovered Waterloo Bridge to be blocked. Originally this had been caused by a spillage of a load of vegetable sacks. It had come about when the horse pulling the cart had fallen in the shafts. It is sadly not unusual to see a wretched, overworked and poorly fed animal collapse.

It was being encouraged to rise with kicks and blows, but it clearly couldn't. Several hessian bags had split open. Potatoes, carrots and onions bounced around us, kicked aside or squashed underfoot. Efforts to get the poor animal up on all four hooves continued unsuccessfully; and the decision was taken to cut it free of the traces. It now staggered upright, but stood trembling, with head hanging and in no state to continue.

This incident effectively blocked Waterloo Bridge, and roads leading to it, until the cart could be manhandled to one side. Even then, onward progress was impeded. In addition to the crowd of pedestrians and vehicles which had built up while waiting for a clear route ahead to be made, would-be travellers, fearful of missing their trains from the station, had decided to abandon the hackney cabs they travelled in. Together with their baggage, they struggled to get across on foot. Also, word had spread of unexpected bounty, and numerous urchins had appeared from the surrounding streets. They were busily gathering up the spilled produce and stuffing it into their ragged shirts, while the driver of the cart did his best to catch them and retrieve what he could. Eventually a path for pedestrians was opened up, and immediately blocked again. Those trying to cross from this side of the river met with those coming towards us from the far side. They soon faced each other like armies in battle, each refusing to give way. Minor scuffles broke out, and London's army of thieves and pickpockets, alerted by some telegraph system of their own devising, were soon profiting. Three constables arrived and did their best. I myself arrested one nimble-fingered fellow who had just extracted a wallet and handed him over to one of the uniformed constables.

At last I was able to battle my way across, but onward progress continued slow due to the density of the crowds and the ever-increasing heaviness of the rain. Finally I reached the Yard, divested myself of my wet coat, and presented myself in Dunn's office.

'Where have you been, Ross?' he demanded.

'I am sorry to be late, sir, but there was an accident on the bridge—'

I was not allowed to finish. 'I don't care!' snapped Dunn. 'What are your plans for today? *Progress*, Ross, I expect progress from all my officers in their inquiries. I don't expect everything to grind to a halt because it's raining!'

I abandoned any explanation. 'I have sent out Sergeant Wood, firstly to interview the dinner guests on the night the necklace was taken. There are only a few of them and I doubt it will take Wood very long. After that, he is to make inquiries about young Roxby,' I told the superintendent. 'That may take longer, depending on what Wood turns up. This is just so that we don't overlook anything, you understand. I am not suggesting the young fellow is involved in the theft of the necklace, so there may be nothing to find out. But I'd like to know how he supports his way of life. Probably his father makes him an allowance. But I dare say Jeremy Roxby would like his son to enter the family business; and, so far, he's shown no interest in doing so, according to Miss Chalk.'

'I see,' returned Dunn thoughtfully. 'Papa threatening to cut off, or reduce, his allowance, you think?'

'Such things happen, sir, I believe. While awaiting Wood's report on his calls on the Roxby dinner guests, I'll go over to Limehouse and see how Morris is getting along there.'

Dunn was already waving me out of the room. But I was delayed yet again from leaving for Limehouse. Bad temper at the top trickles down through the ranks. It is as infectious as measles. This time it was Inspector Reynolds who was out of sorts. He is a burly figure with a permanently disgruntled expression. He seems to expect to find trouble everywhere. (He has been a police officer for a long time, so it is understandable.) Now, seeing me emerge from Dunn's office, he waylaid me to demand, 'See here, Ross! Who is in charge of this emerald necklace business, you or I?'

'It seems I am – again!' I told him.

'You're welcome to it,' grumbled Reynolds. 'I have more than enough on my hands. I don't want to find out that Dunn has changed his mind again! There were two bur-glaries last night in Mayfair; and a couple setting out to dine were held up by a gang of ruffians and relieved of their valuables. The press is having a field day, accusing the police of being unable to do anything about it; and the commissioner is furious, declaring we must make some arrests soon. Wood tells me you suspect this robbery in Hampstead to have been the work of a ladder gang.'

'Yes, I do – or at least, it was my first thought. Now I am not so sure.'

Reynolds held up a hand. 'Don't burden me with your new theory. Just don't let Dunn pass it all back to me again.'

I was getting angry myself. 'I've got a murder in Lime-house to solve. I'd like to get over there before this afternoon. It's already midday!'

'Old Jacobus, I hear!' said Reynolds. 'Well, at least I can cross him off my list of jewellery receivers.'

My route to Limehouse was still not without its delays. It takes more than rain to deter London's pedestrians; and the pavements were as busy as usual, with almost all encumbered with umbrellas. Many of those were wielded

without due care and attention and often quite danger-
ously. Spying a cab that had just set down a fare, I hailed it,
and jumped in ahead of a cross-looking traveller with a
portmanteau. Each man for himself and I was on duty.
That didn't mean I'd be able to reclaim the fare from the
Yard, but it meant I'd get to Limehouse faster and dry.

I arrived to find an unexpected scene of activity before
the door of Jacobus's quaint little house. A heated argument was in progress, accompanied by raised voices, wild
gestures and flailing umbrellas. It had already attracted
sightseers, as any new activity in a London street does, and
if it had not been so wet there would have been more. I
tried to assess in my own mind what was going on, before I
was near enough to be drawn in. Of the players I recognised, Morris was already there, accompanied by Biddle
and by the black-bearded local constable I'd met on the
night of the murder. The three of them were barring access
to the front door. Trying to gain entry to the building were
three other people, unknown to me.

The newcomers included a couple I guessed must be
husband and wife. Both were of generous build and clad in
black. The man wore a silk hat with a black ribbon tied
round it. The lady, also in deepest black, wore a mourning
bonnet with a face veil attached. It had been turned back
so that she could argue her case better with Morris. Something about her chubby features was familiar. The third
newcomer was a small, sharp-eyed man with a professional
air. The leather document case he carried added to this
impression.

'Mr Ross, sir!' exclaimed Morris with undisguised relief

when he saw me. 'It's good that you've come. There's been a development, sir.' He indicated the stout couple. 'Mr and Mrs Perkins, from Leeds.'

The Perkins duo turned their hostile gaze on me. The small man with the document case stepped forward and announced loudly, 'Josiah Haynes! I represent the family.'

Ah, a solicitor. But the family? Whose family?

'I take it you are a senior officer?' added Haynes, peering at me closely.

'I am Inspector Ross,' I told him. 'I am in charge of this case.'

'He won't let us in!' interrupted the woman in the mourning weeds, and brandished her umbrella at Morris. 'It's unheard of. It's despicable!'

Her husband added, 'The officer won't let us have the key!'

'I haven't got the key!' roared the exasperated Morris. 'All keys to the property are at the Yard. The house is the scene of a serious crime – murder. There will be no unofficial access to it until all inquiries are complete. We are conducting these in the neighbourhood; and you are obstructing us. We are not obstructing you!'

'Scandalous!' declared the lady. 'I don't believe it. Someone here must have a key. And it is imperative that we be allowed to enter!'

She was alarmingly agitated now and I feared some kind of a medical incident. As it happened, I had brought the key with me and it sat in my pocket. My intention had been to search the house again, to see if there was any kind of evidence we'd missed. Whoever had killed Jacobus had turned at least one room, the scene of the murder, upside down. But that didn't mean he'd found what he sought. At any rate, I wasn't about to let a group of strangers rampage around the property.

Mr Perkins was eyeing his agitated wife with concern and now begged, 'Calm yourself, my dear.'

She had run out of adjectives for the moment. Bosom heaving, she pointed at her consort, and panted, 'Tell them, Wilfred!'

'We are within our rights,' said her husband with a shake of his head. 'Go on, Haynes, tell them!'

When faced with an insurmountable obstacle, pass the problem to someone else, I thought.

'It is necessary for us to enter the premises,' said the solicitor, taking advantage of the invitation thrust upon him, and Mrs Perkins's lack of breath. He had been waiting patiently for his clients to run out of invective. 'Because a list of all the contents must be made, before anything can be removed by other parties.'

'I've told them they can't go wandering around the place, moving things. It is the scene of a horrid murder and we haven't finished with it,' repeated Morris obstinately. 'And I haven't got the key!'

'They're obstructing the police,' declared the black-bearded local officer, not wishing to be left out of proceedings. 'Higgins, sir,' he added. Presumably this was his own name.

'But the house belongs to me now!' Mrs Perkins almost yelled with replenished energy. 'These policemen are obstructing us!'

A dreadful suspicion entered my mind. The solicitor, Haynes, confirmed it.

'Mrs Perkins is the daughter of the deceased, Jacob Jacobus, Inspector. The will has yet to be proved, but when formalities are complete the bulk of the estate will go to her, as the lady correctly states. She is the principal heir.' He lifted the document case on high, and placed a hand on it in a Napoleonic gesture. '*The will!*'

'Yes, it is! And my birth and baptismal certificates; and my parents' wedding certificate. But we haven't the key and he won't let us in!' stormed Mrs Perkins. She flung an accusing finger at Morris.

'Biddle,' I ordered, turning to him. 'Wipe that expression off your face. Go into the tavern and ask the landlord, Tom Mullins, if he has a small private room we can use. I think it would be a good idea to shelter from this rain. Tell him we'd like a fire lit, and for someone to fetch us all coffee.'

I turned back to the newcomers. 'There is no need for us all to stand out here getting soaked. Have you come down from Leeds today?'

'We arrived about two hours ago,' said Mr Perkins. 'We had to collect Mr Haynes on the way. We have taken rooms at the Railway Hotel and left our baggage there. The news came as a terrible shock. We were sent a telegram. It arrived just as we sat down to breakfast about eight this morning; and we wasted no time. Fortunately, the railway runs an excellent service between Leeds and London.'

'Then I am sure your wife would like to sit down. My deepest sympathy, Mrs Perkins, on your sad loss.'

'I should think so too!' snapped the large lady. She then decided that a show of grief might be expected, so produced a black-edged handkerchief from about her person and sniffed loudly into it. 'My poor papa!' she moaned.

'Don't take on, Maggie,' begged her husband.

Biddle reappeared, beckoning, and we progressed in stately manner into the Crossed Keys, leaving Constable Higgins, the local man, to guard the house.

'This public house is, I understand, part of the estate,' said lawyer Haynes quietly to me.

He had not spoken softly enough to prevent Tom catching his words.

'Here!' The landlord gripped my sleeve and demanded in an urgent undertone, 'Are those the new owners?'

'May well be, Mr Mullins, when formalities are completed. I have no further information,' I told him.

'Strewth!' muttered Tom. More loudly, he invited, 'This way, lady and gents! I've made the snug available.'

We proceeded into a cramped little den where we found Daisy, on her knees before the hearth, doing her very best to get a fire going. So far, she had managed only to cause the fuel to emit a good deal of smelly black smoke. As a young boy I began my life in the mines; and whatever was in that grate, it wasn't best sitting-room coal.

'Faugh!' cried Mrs Perkins. 'We shall all be suffocated!'

'It'll be all right, missis!' called out Daisy. 'When I get it going. There you are, see?' A feeble flame flickered into life and some shreds of charred newspaper floated into the air. 'Be really cosy in a minute.'

In an attempt to distract Mrs Perkins from the discomfort

of the smoking grate, I said unwisely, 'The young woman busy lighting the fire is Daisy Smith. Besides working here in the tavern, she took care of your late father.'

Mrs Perkins was holding a handkerchief to her face; but snatched it away now to exclaim, 'Took care of him! How, pray?'

Daisy scrambled to her feet and came over to where Maggie Perkins sat. 'Bless you, yes! I went in, got him out of bed and helped him dress in the morning, took him in his dinner from the pie shop, and went back and put him to bed at night.'

'Wilfred!' cried Mrs Perkins, clutching her spouse's arm.

'Calm yourself, Maggie!' he begged.

'That – that trollop . . .' Words failed her and she pointed at Daisy.

'Oy!' snapped Daisy. 'I'm respectable I am. I was once in the business of obliging gents, when I was younger, but not now. So there!'

'I assure you, Mrs Perkins,' I hastened to add, 'that Daisy is now reformed and a respectable working woman. What is more, it was she who discovered your father – er – deceased . . .'

In the background I spied Constable Biddle. He appeared to be controlling himself with some difficulty. He met my eye and sobered.

'Yes, that's right,' confirmed Daisy. 'And I ran all the way to tell Inspector Ross here. Oh, and I am very sorry for your loss, ma'am. He was a nice old feller. Not everyone thought so, but I did.'

'Thank you, Daisy,' I said hurriedly.

At that moment a diversion was provided by the arrival of coffee, carried in by Quig and a lad I supposed to be from the coffee shop. The sight of it seemed to cheer everyone up. I took the opportunity to draw aside the solicitor, Haynes, and ask, 'Who sent the telegram informing the family of the death?'

'Mr Perkins is in the woollen cloth trade and travels down to London from time to time on business. One of his business acquaintances here, accustomed to receive the earliest editions of the press, read of the murder and knew Mrs Perkins formerly to have been Miss Jacobus. He took it upon himself to send a telegram. It was a great shock to my clients; and causes considerable inconvenience to myself.'

'Quite so. I gather they, or your office, held the will?'

'We held the will. It was drawn up some years ago and only modified once, two years ago, in a codicil. The late Jacob Jacobus and his wife were estranged, you should understand. Mrs Jacobus died several years ago. But he wished to provide fairly for his daughter, though he hadn't seen her for some time. For the sake of her late mother, she always avoided direct contact with him.' Haynes cleared his throat. 'I think there was some scandal . . . I don't know the details.'

Well, the old man was a crook, I thought, but didn't say. Not something a respectable cloth merchant would want known.

'Thank you, Mr Haynes.' I glanced at the others who had all begun drinking their coffee. They had been joined by Mullins, the landlord, who was busy telling Mr and Mrs

Perkins how well he ran the Crossed Keys, allowing no dis-
orderly behaviour or strong language, and making a steady
profit. Quig was outside in the street, turning away any
customers who tried to come in. Frustrated and curious
would-be drinkers milled about outside the entry demanding to know what was going on.

I drew the solicitor towards the door of the room. He
understood and followed me into the deserted public bar.

'I urge you to persuade your clients to return to the hotel
for the time being. The room in which the fatal attack took
place is a hideous sight, spattered with blood and in considerable disorder. The lady should not see it as it is now.
We, the police, need to search it again ourselves. If it is
necessary to remove any item, it will be entered in our
records and kept safely by us. Nothing will be lost. Any evidence will only be retained until such time as there is a
trial.'

'Do you know who did it?' asked Haynes bluntly.

'No, we don't. But the late Mr Jacobus kept some dubious company.'

Haynes thought for a moment. 'Mr and Mrs Perkins are
particularly concerned that works of art and antiquities
stored in the house should not be removed before being
listed. The late Mr Jacobus was a dealer.'

'Nothing will be removed without your being informed.'
I paused. The solicitor, once detached from his clients,
seemed a sensible fellow. 'If you care to put Mr and Mrs
Perkins in a cab and send them back to the hotel, I can take
you into the house for a brief look round, if you wish. It will
give you a general idea of the contents.'

'I'll consult with them,' said Haynes.

Thus, it turned out a little later, a weeping Mrs Perkins was helped into a cab, and, accompanied by her husband, rolled off back to their hotel. I produced the key and pushed open the door of that narrow little dwelling. Morris, Biddle and Higgins formed a solid barrier on the pavement outside, so that the curious crowd couldn't see anything. This frustrated them and they jeered.

'I rather thought at least a senior officer such as yourself must have the key on his person,' said Haynes drily as he followed me inside. Almost immediately, he exclaimed, 'Oh, my G—!' He dragged out a handkerchief and pressed it to his nose and mouth.

The smell of the blood assaulted the nose as soon as we were in the narrow entry. It was accompanied by a faint but persistent buzz of flies. It would be best to show Haynes round as fast as possible. He must already be regretting his earlier request to be admitted.

'This ground-floor room holds the deceased's stock in trade. That is what he called it himself,' I said.

Haynes cast me a sharp look, removed his improvised mask and asked, 'You knew him – or of him – before his death?'

'Yes, I knew him.' I confessed. 'We often have reason to make inquiries in the antiques trade. We get to know those whose business it is. Also, this is quite the open season for burglary.'

'Quite!' said Haynes after a moment. The man was not a fool. He understood what I meant.

He walked into the ground-floor room, glanced round

it, and came back. 'Listing all that should be straightforward. In view of what you have just said, I dare say the police may wish to verify the origins of the contents.'

'We have no reason to suspect anything in there to be stolen. Jacobus often invited me to browse the contents. He wanted me to do so, in fact.'

'Bit of a rogue, was he?' asked Haynes. 'I don't expect you to answer that, Inspector Ross!'

We began our climb to the first floor. The odour of blood grew stronger. Flies in the stairwell assaulted our faces as we reached the landing.

'You're sure about this?' I asked him. Haynes had turned even paler and had replaced the handkerchief over his nose. 'You're not going to faint? I wouldn't blame you, if you did. But I'd like due warning.'

'I have seen death before!' he said tersely. 'And Jacobus is not still there, I take it?'

'Good heavens, no,' I assured him. 'The corpse is at the morgue.' A thought struck me. 'It's customary for a relative to identify the body . . .'

'I'll discuss it with the family. Would the husband do? Though the wife would not see her father, I believe Wilfred Perkins would call on his father-in-law whenever business brought him down from Leeds to London. He knew him well enough.'

But how well had *I* known the late Jacob Jacobus? I was beginning to wonder. Perhaps hardly at all.

'You do not need to go into this room, unless you wish,' I said. 'You can see it all from the doorway here. Besides which, a police photographer will be coming later on today, with his apparatus, to make a record of the scene. Cleaning will remove the bloody footprints which are important to our investigation. So it's necessary that the photographs are taken first.'

Haynes nodded, but took one step over the doorsill, pressed the handkerchief to his mouth and nose, and stared around the area. Then he stepped back.

'There is considerable disorder,' he said, sounding shaken. 'Was there a struggle, do the police think?'

'No, we believe the attack was sudden and brutal. The victim hadn't even the opportunity of getting up from his chair over there, or defending himself. The chaos of the contents occurred when the murderer made a search. We don't know for what, but probably cash. The only item we know already to be missing is the watch and chain the victim habitually wore across his waistcoat. We are making inquiries among pawnbrokers.'

'What has happened over there by the wall?' asked Haynes suddenly. 'Someone has turned back the carpet and attacked the floorboards by the look of it.'

'Yes, but the search – that is what it was – was either interrupted or was taking the killer too long. He fled before he managed to lift the boards.'

Haynes looked briefly into the bedroom and attic; but he was now obviously anxious to be out of the house.

'I'll report to my clients,' he said, when we stood outside again, in the street. He seemed in a hurry to leave. I guessed he was feeling somewhat ill. 'I think I can safely say they will not want to see inside the house before the – the blood and so forth is cleaned away. I will ask Mr Perkins if he is

87

prepared to identify the body.' He hesitated. 'You have your procedures, Inspector, and I respect that. But I do feel that the bloodstained carpet, furniture and walls, if not cleaned soon, will render the atmosphere in there impossible for anyone who needs to go in.'

'It will be cleaned, under police supervision,' I assured him. 'I'm hoping Daisy Smith can be persuaded to do it, if paid enough. She was the woman lighting the fire.'

'I think I can safely say the cost will be borne by the estate, if there is any problem,' said Haynes. 'Only, I beg of you, have her do it immediately.'

We made arrangements to meet the following morning for the sad business of identifying the body. Haynes promised to have Wilfred Perkins there, and I was reasonably sure that he would keep his side of the arrangement. Perkins was a businessman and would understand that if the will was to be settled, formalities must be dealt with first.

'As for Mrs Perkins,' said Haynes. 'I think it best she waits at the hotel. She won't like being left alone for a couple of hours; but in my view there is no alternative.'

'There is perhaps something that can be done,' I offered. 'If you think the relatives would agree, my wife would be willing to go to the hotel, as my representative if you wish, and sit with Mrs Perkins until her husband returns from his sad duty.'

'It might be a very good thing,' said Haynes. 'If Mrs Ross would be kind enough to help.'

'I'm sure she would,' I told him, merrily committing Lizzie to the task. 'Before our marriage, my wife was companion to a lady; and became accustomed to dealing with all manner of crises.'

I didn't add that anyone who could manage Aunt Parry could deal with Maggie Perkins. I watched the cab carry the solicitor away; then went to find Morris and receive his report. That didn't take long.

'We've knocked on all doors, and visited all the places of business, in the surrounding area. No one saw or heard anything suspicious,' said Morris glumly. 'Around here, no one ever does.'

I returned to the Yard, wrote out my report on the events of the morning and, having first established that Superintendent Dunn was out of his office, went in and left the report on his desk. I did not particularly want to encounter Dunn again that day, unless it proved absolutely necessary.

I received a visit myself in the late afternoon. Sergeant Wood returned from making his inquiries about young Roxby. Wood has a talent for moving very quietly and without apparent effort. His lanky, lugubrious form materialised before me now in a fashion that would have been disconcerting, had I not known of it and had advance warning by way of an odour of mint humbug. I fancied he looked less gloomy than usual. This encouraged me to hope he had something of interest to tell me.

'Well, how did you get on?' I asked. 'Are you going to tell me Harry Roxby has a weakness for wine, women and song? Or is it the card tables?'

'Horses,' replied Wood. 'Racehorses, to be precise, and

prizefighting. Together with the company that goes with it. Well known among "the fancy", is young Mr Roxby. It's as good a way to lose money as is cards, I suppose. Chief difference being it takes place outdoors. Well, some of the boxing bouts are staged indoors; but mostly they take place in out-of-the-way corners of the countryside, on account of the real mix of followers the sport has. He keeps varied company, you might say. There's wealthy young ne'er-do-wells like himself. Also, there are some clever rogues who know how to make money out of 'em.'

I mulled over his words and the inescapable conclusion to which they led me. 'If Harry is running short of money, and daren't go to his father because he's probably been warned by him before, well, he might have had a wild fancy of organising the theft of a very valuable piece of jewellery. Let us say, an item normally kept locked away, but that is conveniently much paraded of late. The reason being that it's frequently to be seen around the neck of his cousin, Miss Gray. But, Wood, if Miss Chalk is correct, Harry would need help in organising such a theft, because he, to quote the companion, "hasn't the brains for it".'

'He could find it among the rougher element who share his sporting interests, goes without saying,' agreed Wood, anticipating my line of thought. 'He'd be running a risk, though. Putting himself in danger of being blackmailed later.' Wood cleared his throat. 'One other thing, Mr Ross.'

'Well?' I encouraged him.

'I'm not the only one making inquiries about Harry Roxby on the quiet.'

'Aren't you, indeed! Who else is interested in the young man?'

Wood almost smiled. Not quite, because I've never seen him actually smile, but very nearly, so I knew he was pleased with his day's work.

'Finding that out took a bit of doing,' he told me confidentially, leaning towards me and enveloping me in a mist of mint humbug.

I really must have a word with him about that. An officer is not supposed to eat on duty, anyway, and as the humbugs appeared to constitute a regular part of Wood's diet, it must count as 'eating'.

'The snooper wanted his name kept out of it, but from the extent of the inquiries, the number of places he'd visited and people he'd spoken to, well, it had to be someone professional,' he concluded.

'A private inquiry agent!' I exclaimed. 'Well, hiring one of those costs money. Have you yet been able to establish who the agent is?'

'I don't know yet who hired him,' Wood told me. 'But from odd snippets of information I picked up here and there, I reckon the private inquiry agent in question is our old friend Sam Morgan.'

'Morgan?' I exclaimed. 'I didn't know he was still in business. He must be over sixty.'

'And has learned his trade! There's nobody working in that line who is better.' Wood nodded his approval. 'It's my belief people are off their guard when they talk to him. They tell him things they wouldn't tell a bright young fellow. A great pity he never joined the regular police force. I wasn't able to run him to earth today. I reckon word has got back to him that I'm asking about him, so he's scurried for cover. But I'll smoke him out tomorrow, don't worry about that.'

'Well done, Wood!' I told him.

Once again, Wood looked as if he might smile, but he didn't. His face isn't used to it. I believe the muscles must have forgotten the knack.

'My dear,' I said to Lizzie when I arrived back home that evening. 'I hope you have not made any plans for tomorrow, because I have a confession to make. I have arranged for you to make a visit. Of course, I will quite understand if you feel you don't want to do it.'

Lizzie's expression brightened. 'It's a case!' she exclaimed. 'You want my help!'

I explained about Maggie Perkins. 'I confess, I never imagined old Jacobus had any family. He never mentioned any. I don't recall any framed photographs in his room. Mrs Perkins had not seen her father for years. But her husband used to call on Jacobus whenever business brought him to London. To him falls the unpleasant task of identifying the body. While that grisly task is taking place, it would help immensely if you'd be so good as to comfort the daughter at her hotel. You know, just talk to her, draw her out. She may well know nothing. But you will be doing a good deed, in any case, and who knows?'

Chapter Six

Elizabeth Martin Ross

RAILWAY HOTELS are, by their very nature, places of transit. The guest list changes frequently, many staying only overnight. There is little need to provide more than a bed and reasonable breakfast. Few people would choose to spend the day relaxing in the parlour. A sign above the door declared that to be the room in which we sat. It was a joyless place, in need of a fresh coat of paint and offering little comfort. Even the aspidistra atop its stand before the window looked depressed, as if it had given up hope of its leaves ever being wiped clean of dust. Maggie Perkins was waiting for me there when I arrived. She did not appear hostile; but she was wary.

I introduced myself and suggested we ask for tea. It seemed to me to be as good a way of breaking the ice as any.

'We don't drink tea in the middle of the morning in Leeds,' said Mrs Perkins, 'or not in our house, at any rate. But if that is what you fancy . . .' She spoke as though I had suggested gin. 'Had you far to come, Mrs Ross?'

'From just the other side of the river,' I told her. 'Our house is near to Waterloo Station.'

'Noisy, no doubt?' asked Mrs Perkins.

'We are accustomed to the sound of the trains.'

The tea was brought by a glum, middle-aged waitress who asked if we wanted cake.

'I couldn't face it,' said Maggie Perkins promptly. 'I had the breakfast.'

I told the waitress no cake was required.

'Just as well, we'd have to send out for it,' was the reply. 'It'd probably be half an hour or more before it arrived.' With that the waitress plodded away.

It was time to take control of the conversation. 'I am very sorry for your loss, Mrs Perkins,' I told her. 'I never met your late father myself. But I believe my husband visited him on several occasions and enjoyed his conversations with him.'

She sniffed. 'Visited him on his inquiries into criminal matters, no doubt!' she snapped. 'You don't need to beat about the bush, Mrs Ross. My late father often dealt with reprehensible people; and he led my poor mother a terrible life. And now Perkins has to go and identify his body. I couldn't do it, of course, because I was seven years old when I last saw Papa.'

She tilted forward in a stiff fashion that suggested formidable corsets. 'I want you to understand, Mrs Ross, that my dear mother took her marriage vows very seriously; and would not have left him in ordinary circumstances. Though his general behaviour gave her ample cause! However, her own father, my grandfather, who was a respected cloth merchant in Leeds, fell ill. He was a widower and had no one to care for him. My mother returned to Leeds, taking me with her, in what was intended as a temporary measure. However, my grandpapa's condition worsened, and, to cut the story short, my mother never returned to London. I must emphasise that my late father was in agreement with this; he made her a regular allowance, including an amount for me. He had probably made other domestic arrangements by then.'

Mrs Perkins added bitterly, 'I was not surprised when Inspector Ross introduced us to the woman who had been looking after him, the cleaner from the public house. She was just the sort of woman my father had always liked, or so is my understanding.'

'But your husband did call on Mr Jacobus whenever he was in London?'

'Oh, yes,' Maggie Perkins sniffed. 'He thought it right. I am an honest woman, and I am well aware one should find at least one good thing to say of the departed. So I should tell you that when we married, my father settled a generous sum on me.'

'A dowry!' I exclaimed.

She frowned briefly. 'You could call it that, I dare say. He was very Continental in his ways, Mother always said. And he gave us a wedding present of a very handsome long-case clock.'

'I understand,' I said, 'that an ancestor had come to England in the entourage of William of Orange, in 1688.'

'Oh, that,' said Maggie. 'Anything is possible. Mother always thought there was a good chance that was true.

Though you couldn't believe everything he said. He was given to flights of fancy, was how she put it.' She eyed me. 'I suspect you are not a Londoner, Mrs Ross.'

I told her I was not, not by birth. My father had been a medical man, with a practice in Derbyshire. He had been a widower, and I ran his household until his death. I'd then come down to London to be companion to a relative by marriage, an aunt. 'My father was generous to others and, as a result, when he died, I was left obliged to find a position,' I explained.

'Well, then, my dear Mrs Ross.' Maggie Perkins unexpectedly smiled, though sadly. 'You have the consolation that your papa was a respected, good man, even though he left you poor. My father was a rogue, but it seems, according to Mr Haynes, that he has left me rich through his ill-gotten gains.'

'And you have no good memories of your father?' I asked. 'From the time when you were very young? Nothing you can recall?'

She sat for a moment and then suddenly said, 'His half-hunter watch and chain! He wore the gold chain across his waistcoat, and the watch itself was hidden in a little pocket. I do remember sitting on his knee, and being fascinated by it. He allowed me to open and shut the hinged cover that protects the dial. Being only three or four years old at the time, I thought it like a little door, with a window in it. He told me he had taken it in payment for a debt owed to him, though I'd no idea what a debt was. I imagined it to be some object and they had swapped, as little boys do with marbles. But then, he had so many stories. My mother once said, much later on, that he was the master of invention!'

She sighed. 'It is ironic that the one item we know has been stolen, so far at least, is that watch and chain. Inspector Ross told Mr Perkins so. I should like to have that watch and chain returned to me.'

'I am so sorry,' I told her. 'It is a precious memory. Perhaps it will be recovered.'

'It is very vexing,' she declared with a return of her former indignation. Then she added, 'And the scandal of it all! How am I to explain it to my acquaintances in Leeds? Not one of them has ever had a relative who was *murdered*! It just doesn't happen in respectable families, does it? They will be talking of nothing else; and when we return, we shall have to face it all. It may even affect the business. Poor Perkins. Even now, as I sit here drinking tea, he must be staring down at my father's lifeless corpse.'

Inspector Ben Ross

Wilfred Perkins was able to identify his father-in-law's body, so that was one unpleasant task done. However, it is one thing to gaze down at a deceased relative, laid out neatly, washed and clothed, on his own bed or in a coffin. It is another to look at the lately departed prone on a marble slab, naked and with a towel draped over the throat to hide the slash. Poor Perkins took it very badly. He swayed and I thought he might faint, but he warded off my support. When we led him outside into the street, however, he couldn't hide his distress. It took Haynes and me some time to rally him.

'Dreadful, dreadful!' he moaned, mopping his brow. 'Such a savage attack! It hardly seems that any human being can behave in such a way. It is as if a wild animal, some savage beast like a lion perhaps, had seized his throat to pull him to the ground.'

'He wasn't pulled to the ground, Mr Perkins. He remained seated in his chair throughout!' I said briskly.

It might have sounded insensitive to remind him, but in my experience once an embellished image takes root in the brain, it is sometimes difficult to dislodge. I had to stop any flight of fancy in its tracks, or Wilfred Perkins might return to the Railway Hotel to inform his spouse that her father had wrestled with his attacker, trying to fight him off, and had been slashed numerous times with the knife. I have known many witnesses embellish the truth to an extraordinary degree; and then stick to their version because they have succeeded in convincing themselves. The plain reality was bad enough.

'He needs a brandy,' said the solicitor bluntly to me.

'No, no, my wife . . . she is a member of the Temperance League!' protested the unfortunate Perkins.

'She's not here!' snapped Haynes, dismissing this as a quibble. 'And she would not wish to have you faint in the street.'

So we bundled him into the nearest respectable-looking establishment and Haynes asked for brandy, one glass only.

'And you other gentlemen?' the waiter asked.

'I am on business,' declared Haynes.

'And I am on duty,' I added.

'Right you are,' said waiter. 'You gents been over the road at the morgue, have you? I'll bring the other gentleman a double.'

When we eventually returned to the hotel, we found Lizzie and Maggie Perkins chatting confidentially, quite like old friends.

At the sight of Wilfred's pallid countenance, however, Mrs Perkins rose to her feet and declared, 'Dear Mrs Ross! I thank you sincerely for your company and your kindness. I hope we may meet again before we return home. But now I must take care of my husband.'

With that, she marched Perkins away, with a grip on his arm that would have befitted an arresting officer.

'Thank you for your help, Mr Haynes,' I told the solicitor.

'We shall certainly meet again,' he returned. 'My thanks to you, Mrs Ross.'

We left him there and crossed to the station where cabs were waiting. I directed the driver first to take us to our home, to set down Lizzie, and then to take me back to the Yard.

'I feel very sorry for Mr and Mrs Perkins,' said Lizzie, as we rattled through the streets. 'Respectability means so much to both of them. I am very much afraid that when they return to Leeds, some of their acquaintance may avoid them. And I do so hope, Ben, that you are able to retrieve the stolen watch and chain. It is the only good memory of her father that Mrs Perkins has.'

'A very difficult woman. I think Haynes will have his work cut out trying keep her calm,' I said.

But Lizzie shook her head. 'I wouldn't call her difficult, or no more than many others in her situation would be. I would rather judge her to be frightened. You are used to dealing with murder, Ben, and so am I by now. But neither she nor her husband will ever have encountered such a thing. They don't know what to do. For them it is a scandal that threatens to blow their lives apart.'

'Well,' I told her, 'that may be so. The unfortunate Perkins took the viewing of the corpse very badly. But the solicitor, Haynes, seems alert. They will be well advised.'

I had a visitor awaiting me on my return to the Yard. Sergeant Wood was standing guard over him at the door of my office. He greeted me with, 'I told you I'd find him, Mr Ross, and I have!'

I was slow to change the direction of my thinking. 'Whom have you found, Wood?'

'Why, Sam Morgan, the private inquiry agent, as he likes to call himself. I put him in your office, and waited here by the door so he couldn't slip out.'

The unwilling visitor rose to his feet as I entered. He was a small, grey-haired, sparely built man, wearing a suit of tweed and well-polished brown boots. He carried a bowler hat of the kind favoured by gamekeepers. His complexion was weather tanned like fine Spanish leather. I could well understand how, if he had been making inquiries among the followers of horse racing and prizefighting, he stood a good chance of learning something. No one would have wondered at his presence in such company, or taken him for anything other than a retired groom or game-keeper. If anyone had thought he was after any information, it would be about form or that race meeting's favourites.

'Well, Mr Morgan!' I greeted him. 'I am surprised to learn you are still in business. I'd have thought you might have retired.'

He shook his head sadly. 'I can't afford to, Mr Ross! Besides, what would I do with so much time on my hands? I like talking to people, that's the truth of it; and they seem happy to talk to me. So, why not earn a little money by it?' He gave me a wicked grin. 'Much like yourself, I dare say, Mr Ross, or Mr Wood over there. We have been born with curious minds, and you can't go against nature.'

'So then, sit down, Sam, and tell me what you have learned about Henry, known as Harry, Roxby, while you have been talking to people. Let us begin by you telling me who has engaged your services. Who is interested enough in young Roxby to pay you to follow him around race meet-ings and prizefighting bouts?'

Morgan tilted his head to the side and fixed his bright little eyes on my face. He was working out how much to tell me and, as I expected, he began by admitting nothing at all.

'Well, here's the way of it, Mr Ross. To tell you the truth, I've been curious about him on my own account. Again, there is no particular reason, other than my own nature. It's a weakness. I can't help but take an interest in others!' He beamed at me. 'I'd seen the young fellow around and asked who he was. Nothing very particular.'

I sighed. 'Sam, I am a very busy man. I have more than one matter to investigate, and there are only so many hours in the day. As an officer of the law, it is my duty. But I am also paid for my efforts, and that, in turn, supports myself and my dear wife, and pays our household bills. I do not work for free and, Sam, neither do you. What is more, I have just come from viewing the corpse of a murder victim at the morgue; so don't try my patience. Let us have no more nonsense. Who is paying you to spy on Harry Roxby?'

Morgan turned his bowler hat crown downward and stared intently into the interior, as if the maker's name had become in some way meaningful. 'I must confess, I have a client who asked me to, well, check on how the young man spends his free time. Young Mr Roxby has a good deal of free time. I never had any when I was his age. But my father was a coachman.'

'And Mr Jeremy Roxby is a shipowner.'

His bright gaze flickered in my direction. 'Such is my understanding, Mr Ross. I am not saying, mind you, that Mr Jeremy Roxby is my client.'

'Your discretion does you credit, Sam. But I need to know. Is your client Jeremy Roxby?'

Morgan frowned. 'That would be to betray a professional confidence, Mr Ross! I would need the permission of any client before I divulged his name.'

'Not when it is a police officer who is asking you. Let me see, perhaps we can approach the answer by a different route. If the client is perhaps not Jeremy Roxby, could it be the widow of his brother, Mrs Charlotte Roxby?'

Morgan looked reproachful. He frowned and shook his

head, as if I'd committed some faux pas. 'I very seldom accept work from a lady, Mr Ross! They always expect so much and in such a short time. They don't appreciate how long it takes to find out anything, the finesse required, the many obstacles there are to overcome in any inquiry. They can cut up rough about settling the bill.'

That description of a lady client's expectations pretty well described the attitude of Charlotte Roxby, so I understood what he meant, and sympathised.

Morgan sighed. 'Besides, ladies don't need the professional services of hard-working individuals such as myself. They learn all they want to know from their friends, at tea-parties, and while playing games of whist. To my knowledge there isn't a lady who is unwilling to pass on the latest scandal to her closest friend, in the strictest confidence, mind you. So what need would any of the fair sex have of me?'

'Then it is Mr Jeremy Roxby? Come along, Sam. I, too, have inquiries to make and mine are official.'

Morgan sighed and grudgingly gave in. 'Mr Jeremy Roxby is the gentleman who has engaged my services. But more than that I cannot tell you, Mr Ross, without the express permission of Mr Roxby. An inquiry agent, such as myself, must have a reputation for discretion, for loyalty, for not blabbing what he has learned to anyone, including the police. If I did that, none of 'em would pay; and my professional reputation would go straight down the drain. I am frank, Mr Ross, because you know that for a fact as well as I do. The clients come to me because they don't wish to involve the police, there! No offence!' He smiled apologetically.

'I am not offended, Sam, if you play fair with me. Now then, would you be so kind as to inform your client that I should like a word with him. I am happy to meet him anywhere convenient to him and to me. He does not have to come to the Yard, nor would I wish to cause any gossip by asking for him at his place of business.'

'I will convey your message to the client, Mr Ross. May I leave now?'

'Yes, yes, Mr Morgan.'

Sam leaped to his feet and almost ran out of my office.

'Quaint old fellow, isn't he?' observed Wood. 'But sharp, very sharp. Will he do it, do you think? Pass your message to his client?'

'Oh yes, he'll do that, Wood. He needs the goodwill of the police, or we could easily make his life very difficult. Let's wait and see what happens now.'

For the rest of the day, however, nothing happened to prevent me writing up my report on the morning's visit to the morgue, and the afternoon's quizzing of Sam Morgan. This time, I was unable to avoid handing it personally to Superintendent Dunn and answering his questions.

Dunn tapped his fingers on the surface of his desk and sat silent for a moment or two. Then he looked up and asked suddenly, 'This private inquiry agent, Morgan, isn't he a little fellow, dresses like a gamekeeper in his Sunday best?'

I turned my gaze towards the window to avoid staring at Dunn's own tweed suit. 'That's the man, sir.'

'Good heavens, I remember him, of course! But I'd have thought he must be long retired.'

'So did I, sir.'

'What does Mr Jeremy Roxby want to be hiring some-one like that for? Has he no confidence in the police force's professional ability?'

'I don't know. I shall find out, sir.'

Dunn leaned back in his chair and squinted at me. 'What do you make of all that, Ross?'

'Until I have spoken to Jeremy Roxby, sir, I am trying to keep an open mind.'

'Very laudable, I am sure,' returned Dunn in a dry tone. 'Do you have any opinions about this Roxby business that you would like to share with me? Something perhaps not in the reports you have taken to leaving on my desk when I'm out of the room?'

'Only a feeling I have that there is something amiss in that family. But I don't know what it is. It may turn out no more than a story we've heard before about a prodigal son, in this case, young Harry.'

Thankfully Dunn seemed satisfied with that, and dismissed me with a curt instruction to keep him informed.

Thus I was able to leave the Yard and arrive home at a reasonable hour. That is quite a rare event in my life; and I was grateful for it. I was blissfully unaware that things were about to take a turn for the worse. But such is the life of a police detective: always to be on the scene after the event, and unable to foresee what will happen from one day to the next.

Chapter Seven

THE SURPRISES began at breakfast-time the following day, before I had even left home. We had heard a rumble of wheels outside in the street, followed by a knock at the door and voices in the hallway.

'Stay there, my dear,' I told Lizzie. 'I'll see what it's about.'

But I hadn't the time. Bessie appeared with a rack of toast in one hand, the other hand held out to indicate a visitor.

'Here's Miss Nugent!' she announced.

Nugent was Mrs Parry's long-suffering personal maid. Her appearance meant a message from the lady.

Nugent herself appeared at that point, in a cape and an odd little hat with a feather in it. 'Good morning, Inspector Ross, and Mrs Ross,' she stated. 'I am very sorry to disturb you so early. But madam has sent me with a note for you, Mrs Ross, and wanted you to read it before you made any plans for the day.' She withdrew a small mauve envelope from her pocket and handed it to Lizzie with some ceremony.

'Good heavens!' exclaimed Lizzie. 'What on earth has

happened now?' She took the proffered envelope and opened it. 'Oh, she wants me to take tea with her this afternoon. Well, I can do that, I suppose. I have no other plans. But I wonder what she wants. Nugent, have you any idea?'

'No, Mrs Ross.' Nugent hesitated. 'I believe there is someone, a lady, she wants you to meet.'

'Don't go!' I warned Lizzie. 'This is one of Mrs Parry's plots. She wants something of you.'

'Does she, Nugent?' Lizzie asked.

'Madam does not confide in me,' returned the visitor stonily.

'It's all right, Ben, I'm sure.' Lizzie folded up the note and returned it to its mauve envelope. 'We've only just returned from Hampshire. She can't want to make another journey so soon.'

'Don't be so sure!' I turned to the messenger. 'Does Mrs Parry have some intention to travel? You would surely know that, Miss Nugent.'

'Oh, she doesn't want to go out of London again for the time being.' Nugent shook her head and the little feather in her hat quivered. 'She found the visit to the New Forest very tiring. She is still recovering. I'll tell her to expect you, then, Mrs Ross? At four o'clock.'

'My dear!' I warned, when the messenger had left and Bessie had returned to the kitchen. 'Mrs Parry wants something. And it involves this mysterious person she wants you to meet.'

'I shall be on my guard,' my wife promised.

There was nothing more I could do. I reached Scotland Yard without any mishap that morning: no rain, no accident on the bridge or anywhere else, no encounter with Reynolds, thus no late arrival to displease Superintendent Dunn.

Towards midday, Sergeant Wood appeared. For once he was not rolling boiled sweets round his mouth. His whole demeanour, in fact, was more professional and alert.

'There is a gentleman here who wishes to speak to you, Mr Ross,' he said. 'This is his card.' He handed me a small white rectangle.

I had expected further developments after the interview with Sam Morgan. But this was even quicker than I'd anticipated.

'Show Mr Jeremy Roxby in, Sergeant,' I said.

The man who entered my office was tall, and still slim in build despite being, at a guess, in his mid-fifties. He was well dressed and carried a cane with a carved ivory pommel. He would, I guessed, be accounted handsome, certainly when younger. He still had a luxuriant head of hair, as did his son now. Young Harry's hair was dark. Jeremy Roxby's hair had silvered, but in that way that lends distinction to a man's appearance. His eyes were grey and his gaze sharp. He looked what he was: a successful, wealthy man of business. A formidable opponent, I thought to myself. One would need to be both alert and cautious in dealing with him.

I was not the only one to think so. Behind the newcomer, Wood stood practically at attention.

'Mr Roxby,' I greeted him, 'it is very good of you to call. I take it Sam Morgan has reported to you that I had spoken to him. I was prepared to meet you at any place of your choice. I appreciate you coming here. Please, sit down.'

Roxby flicked the tails of his coat and sat down, his crossed palms resting on the ivory pommel of his cane.

'Mr Morgan,' he said, 'was somewhat embarrassed when he confessed to me that, despite his experience and caution in making the inquiries I'd charged him with, the police had realised what he was about so quickly. And to identify him, too! I fancy you have caused Mr Morgan to "lose face", as the Chinese so cleverly describe it.'

The least I could do, on Sam's behalf, was speak up in his defence.

'Morgan is one of the best in the business when it comes to private inquiry agents, Mr Roxby. But he's been around for several years and we do know him.'

Roxby listened to this speech, his face giving no clue as to his feelings. I imagined his attitude at board meetings of the shipping line must be similar. As for doing business with him, that must call for the utmost alertness on the part of others concerned. He wouldn't, in the popular parlance, miss a trick. Now he inclined his head, then drew a deep breath.

'This is a somewhat embarrassing situation for me, Inspector Ross. I must be frank and confess it. I was not best pleased when I learned that my sister-in-law had been here at the Yard, demanding investigation into the loss of a piece of family jewellery. She had not told me of her intention. If she had, I should have advised her strongly to leave it to me. But she is a determined lady, and sometimes headstrong.'

'You wouldn't have involved the police? Not reported the theft?' I asked.

110

His grey eyes assessed me. 'It would have been reported, of course, both to the police and to the insurers, if necessary. But the circumstances are not so simple. I don't know how much you already know. The company was founded by my great-grandfather. He married the daughter of a wealthy Brazilian family. Her dowry provided a basis on which the company was able to expand rapidly. But you may know that?'

'I have been told something of it,' I admitted.

'The necklace holds considerable significance for our family. Its loss is a severe blow. We want it returned, it's as simple as that. We don't want its monetary value from the insurer, we want the necklace itself. Roxby wives have traditionally been presented with it at the time of their marriage into the family and the firm. But it has always been clearly understood that it was not an outright gift. It would be presented to the wife of the eldest Roxby son, when he married. To my future daughter-in-law, should my son marry. In turn, when the time should come, and always assuming that Harry and his wife will one day present me with a grandson, a new generation of Roxby brides will wear it. It has always been looked upon as a kind of mascot, a bringer of good luck in business. While it remains in the family, we'll thrive.'

'Well, I can understand all that, Mr Roxby, but two questions leap to my mind,' I began.

He raised his eyebrows. 'And they are?'

'Forgive me, but your wife . . .?'

'I am a widower, Inspector Ross. My wife did not survive our son's birth.'

'I am very sorry and apologise for any distress.'

He inclined his head. 'You were not to know; and your question was understandable. You have a second question?'

He had succeeded in disconcerting me. But I had to continue. If it meant 'putting my foot in it' for a second time, so be it.

'I had supposed, mistakenly no doubt, that when Miss Isabella Gray marries, Mrs Charlotte Roxby would give the necklace to her. She has already insisted on the young lady being seen wearing it.'

When he replied, his voice, so far smooth and courteous, was steely. 'The only circumstances under which that might happen would be if my son married Miss Gray.'

'And is that . . . possible?'

'Anything is possible in theory, but that doesn't make it practical. Were such a union suggested, I would oppose it. She is not the bride I would wish for him. My sister-in-law knows very well that she holds the necklace in trust. It is not for her to decide how to dispose of it.'

Clearly he was not about to offer any explanation of his rejection of Isabella Gray. I could hardly ask. I therefore turned my questions in a slightly different direction. 'Forgive me, but why did you hire Sam Morgan to follow your son about and report on him to you?'

He flushed and the grey eyes were like polished flint. 'I am concerned about how my son spends his time and the company he keeps. Are you married, Inspector Ross? Have you children?'

'I am married but, sadly, my wife and I are childless.'

'Children are a joy when they are in the nursery, Inspector, and a constant source of worry once they are out of it.' Roxby glanced over his shoulder towards Wood. 'The sergeant will have told you what kind of company my son has been keeping. But I mean to put my house in order. I will say no more. It is a private, family matter.'

It would be foolish to quiz him further and make an enemy of him. But I had to remind him of one distressing fact.

'You are aware, Mr Roxby, that it may not be possible to recover the necklace intact? It may already have been broken up.'

He leaned forward and the knuckles gripping the head of the cane were white. 'It must be found intact. It is unthinkable that it be destroyed! It is a talisman for the house of Roxby and must be recovered in such a condition that it can, if damaged, at least be repaired. I am ready to pay a considerable sum for its return.'

'And you have let that be known, sir?'

'I have! It is the reason I am very displeased that Charlotte decided, without consulting me, to come to the police. I would have, what is the expression? "Spread the word", is that it? Morgan might have been able to help me do that. He has numerous contacts.'

'It is. It would be a dangerous thing to do, Mr Roxby. You could set yourself up to be swindled, blackmailed, cheated in so many ways. Was that another task you entrusted to Sam Morgan? To spread the word around the underworld that you would pay for its return?'

But our interview was at an end. He rose to his feet. 'I have said all I have to say on the matter, Inspector. I bid you good day!'

He walked briskly out with a startled Wood scurrying along behind him.

I went along to Dunn's office to report the visit. The superintendent listened attentively and then observed, 'You can be sure Roxby doesn't like us prying, as he would see it, into his family's private concerns. That sort of successful man does not like mere employees of the state, like us, to meddle in his affairs. A good number of them still resent the police being given any authority to inquire into their private business, as they see it, enter their homes, if necessary, and ask questions of their family members and domestic servants. I can well believe he is furious with his sister-in-law for coming to us, with or without informing him beforehand.'

'But he himself has employed a private detective, Sam Morgan, to pry into his son's affairs!' I pointed out.

'Is it that you cannot or will not understand, Ross? Yes, he *employs* Morgan, just as he *employs* the clerks at his company's offices, or the cook and housemaids at his private house. As a taxpayer, I dare say he feels he employs you and me. That we act without consulting him first, and ask questions he doesn't wish to answer, that, to him, is the height of impertinence. Unfortunately for him, he can sack his cook, but he can't sack you and me. Thus, his influence and freedom of decision are limited by the very existence of the police force. We are an irritant and he can't order us to go away. Don't upset him any further, Ross, whatever you do.'

I still felt impelled to defend myself. 'I hope I haven't upset him at all! But his family, one way and another, is causing us quite a lot of trouble at the moment. We are supposed to protect the public against those who would commit serious crimes. We are not here to sort out the domestic tiffs within a wealthy family. At this time of year, when we are so busy, all of us have enough to do.'

Dunn sighed. 'Privately, Ross, I agree with you. Professionally, we have been asked to recover stolen property – and find out who stole it in the first place. I agree that Mr Jeremy Roxby must be discouraged from taking private action to recover the missing jewels. But if he wants to pay a private investigator to follow his wastrel son around London, that's his business, and none of our concern. We should all remember that wealth does not necessarily make for happiness.'

I did not mind discussing a case and listening to the superintendent's views on that. But I had neither the time nor the inclination to listen to a sermon.

'As you say, sir!' I agreed, and took myself off.

I did not escape altogether scot-free. Inspector Reynolds was coming up the stairs as I made to descend them. He stopped, looking up at me. 'Found your emeralds yet, Ross?'

'Not yet,' I told him.

He surveyed me thoughtfully. 'Any idea yet what's become of them?'

'Not a clue,' I told him frankly.

'Hm,' said Reynolds. 'I'm also on the trail of a couple of significant burglaries, as you know.'

'Good luck!' I wished him, and made to pass him on the stairs. But he had something to add.

'I've been asking around the usual informers and fences about the missing items I'm trying to track down; and heard a few rumours. Nothing about your emeralds, though.'

'Give it time!' I was losing patience. He was a bulky fellow and I couldn't get past him if he didn't give way.

'Nothing at all,' he repeated. 'Rather odd, that, don't you think?'

He recommenced his upward climb. I gave way to him, and watched him walk off down the corridor towards Dunn's office. Going to make his report, I guessed. But he had left me thoughtful.

Elizabeth Martin Ross

Before Ben and I married, when I had been living in Dorset Square as companion to Aunt Parry, Bessie had also lived there, as the lowliest member of the household staff. When we married and set up our own household Bessie came with me to be our maid of all work. Because of this, whenever I visited Aunt Parry I was in the habit of taking Bessie with me, so that she could renew her acquaintance below stairs. Ben had warned me to be cautious on today's visit; and I had every intention of it. But for Bessie it was an outing and great fun. She prattled all the way there and when we arrived disappeared down the basement steps almost before I had time to ring at the front door.

'A pleasure to see you, Mrs Ross!' Simms, the butler greeted me.

'Thank you, Simms. Mrs Simms is well, I hope?' His wife was the cook.

'Thank you, madam. She is in very good health.' He made to usher me up to the first floor, where Aunt Parry had her sitting room and was accustomed to hold her tea parties. But I detained him.

'A moment, Simms! I believe another lady is expected.'

'She has already arrived, Mrs Ross.'

'Is it likely I'll know her?' I asked cautiously.

'It is a Miss Gray,' said Simms, adding in a low voice, 'a very young lady.'

I managed, just, not to show my astonishment and followed Simms up the staircase, thinking that Ben had been right to warn me that Aunt Parry had some unexpected purpose. Perhaps I should have pleaded some indisposition and not come. But it was too late. However, forewarned is forearmed, as they say. And, I admit, I was curious to meet Isabella Gray. But how Aunt Parry could possibly know her was a mystery. And what purpose could be served by my meeting her, I couldn't imagine.

'Elizabeth, my dear!' cried Aunt Parry when I was ushered in by Simms. 'Here you are at last. Now we can have tea.'

She was sitting by the hearth, resplendent in royal-blue silk. Somehow, despite the beaming smile, she had managed to suggest that I was late. I was not; and it irritated me. However, being annoyed with Mrs Parry served no purpose. I stooped to kiss the powdered cheek she turned towards me.

'I hope I find you well, Aunt Parry?'

117

Ann Granger

'Much better, I am pleased to say. I am recovering from
that exhausting trip you took me on to the New Forest.'

I had not taken her. She had taken me. The entire
expedition had been her idea and at her insistence, and
arranged by her.

'Now, my dear,' she continued. 'Here is someone I
would like you to meet. This is Miss Isabella Gray. She is
the niece of a friend of mine, Mrs Roxby. Mrs Roxby and I
share an interest in the pastime of whist.'

Ah, so that was how it came about. But it still didn't
explain why I'd been invited here this afternoon to meet
the young woman.

She was, indeed, very young. The expression 'scarcely
out of the schoolroom' came to mind. She was not a con-
ventionally pretty girl, but the bloom of youth lends its own
attraction. She was expensively dressed in mauve-striped
taffeta, with ruched trim, and with what I judged to be
French lace at the neck. A confection of artificial flowers,
masquerading as a hat, topped her elaborately curled hair.
I remembered Ben's description of the photograph he had
been shown; and how he had spoken, with disapproval, of
Mrs Roxby's insistence on her niece being launched into
society for the 'Season'. Seeing the young woman now, I
was put in mind of one of those elaborately dressed dolls
that dressmakers used once to send around the country,
displaying the latest fashions. Their hope had been to
attract new custom. Mrs Roxby's aim was to attract a
wealthy, preferably titled, match for her niece. It struck me
that in her methods Mrs Roxby was no better than a pro-
curess. The child, for she was little more, did not look

118

happy. She seemed anxious. Without warning, she spoke, and her light, almost childish tones made the situation she had been thrust into even more desperate.

'I am very pleased to make your acquaintance, Mrs Ross. I must ask you to forgive me if this meeting comes as a surprise. My Aunt Roxby recently held a whist afternoon at which Mrs Parry was present.'

In the background, Aunt Parry nodded and beamed.

'My aunt spoke of the efforts being made by the police to recover an emerald necklace that was stolen recently from the house, while we were all at dinner downstairs. She said that Inspector Ross was in charge of the case. To everyone's great surprise, Mrs Parry then told us that the inspector was a family connection, through his marriage to you.'

I tried not to think how Ben would have reacted on hearing himself described as a 'family connection'. But really, it was too bad of Aunt Parry to behave in this under-hand way.

'So,' continued Miss Gray, 'I asked Mrs Parry if she would be kind enough to arrange an introduction for me – to you, that is, not to the inspector.'

It was all I could do not to blurt out, 'Why?' Instead, I said cautiously, 'I am very pleased to meet you, Miss Gray. But I play no part in any investigation carried out by Scotland Yard. I don't think I can help.'

At that moment, the tea tray arrived. I think both Miss Gray and I were grateful for the interruption. It allowed us both to plan our next moves.

'Oh, it's not about the necklace!' exclaimed Miss Gray,

seizing the initiative as soon as Simms was out of the room and we'd had time to eat a muffin apiece. 'The necklace is a horrid thing, very heavy and old fashioned. It means a great deal to the Roxby family because it was created for the wife of the firm's founder. She was a Brazilian lady and a great beauty. There is a portrait of her in the boardroom of the company. It shows her wonderful dark eyes and black hair. The necklace is shown in the portrait and it must have looked splendid on her. But it never looked right on me. I don't have the complexion for it. I am too fair. My Aunt Roxby is very upset at its loss; but I don't care a bit. I never liked wearing it and she would insist so.'

'Come, come, my dear,' interposed Aunt Parry. 'I am sure you looked very well when you wore it. But I do understand that it is far from being a modern piece. Young people do so like modern fashions. It is only natural. I have some very fine pieces bought for me by my dear late husband, when we married. But I suppose they look old fashioned now. Perhaps a younger woman might not like them.' She cast a speculative look at me. 'Although they could always be remodelled.'

Miss Gray had been looking increasingly impatient during this speech. 'I am sure they are very nice,' she said. 'But they probably are out of fashion now, as you say. The Roxby emeralds are even more so, because they were made a hundred years ago.'

Aunt Parry looked startled, probably not at the age of the Roxby necklace, but at Isabella's blithe agreement that the contents of Mrs Parry's own jewel case were dated and unlikely to attract a modern wearer.

Miss Gray had turned back to me. 'It is not about the necklace itself that I want to speak to you, Mrs Ross. Well, not directly, but it does influence everything, or its being stolen does. It's really about my cousin, Harry Roxby, that I'd like to explain to you, if you would be kind enough to allow me.'

'A very dashing young man, I believe,' said Aunt Parry, recovering from the setback of Miss Gray's dismissal of her jewellery. 'But perhaps a little, um, wild.'

Isabella Gray was not to be distracted again. She kept her eyes fixed on me with an imploring look that I found very unsettling.

'I felt I could not let the opportunity slip to meet you. Someone has to speak up for Harry! I have always looked on him as an older brother. We spent so much time together as children. He never knew his mother. She died of a child-bed fever. I didn't have a chance to know my parents, either. They perished in an accident while travelling in the Italian Alps. I was in the carriage, with my nurse. She was heroic, so I've been told. She wrapped her arms around me, protecting me from the impact, and I was saved. She was not, alas. I was but eighteen months old at the time. I am sorry to say I really don't recall it at all. I wish I did. It's not often one has such a dramatic start to one's life and it would be nice to have some memory of it. But I don't remember a thing.'

She drew a deep breath. 'Anyhow, it is being orphans that has drawn Harry and me together, or so I have always believed. Although he has his father, of course. But he saw little of him while he was growing up, because Uncle

Jeremy – I call him that, although at times I think he doesn't really like it – is a very formal sort of man. Now, I know Harry sometimes keeps unwise company. He can be a little foolish, I admit. To be frank, he is often rash and doesn't seem to realise at all how his behaviour looks to others. He doesn't do anything *wrong*. He is completely honourable. But he hasn't got a head for business!' She finished her speech abruptly.

'Ah . . .' murmured Aunt Parry. She, I knew, had a very good head for business.

'And that makes Uncle Jeremy very cross.'

'Mr Jeremy Roxby is the present head of the family shipping line,' explained Aunt Parry. 'I dare say his son is expected to follow in his footsteps, so he would like to think he is a serious young man.'

'Harry can be perfectly serious when he wants to be,' Miss Gray defended him. 'But that's not as often as his father would like. Can you believe it, Mrs Ross? Uncle Jeremy has engaged a *private detective*, who has been following poor Harry about wherever he goes.'

'That does seem a little extreme,' murmured Aunt Parry.

'He is a funny little man, Harry says. He hadn't realised who he was, not at first. How should he? But people Harry knows recognised this detective, whose name is Morgan, and they warned Harry. They pointed the man out to him. After that, Harry was very aware of him, and looked out for him. Sure enough, wherever Harry goes, to sporting events and the like, this little man Morgan turns up there too. Harry is inclined to find it amusing. I've told him it's serious, but he won't listen. It isn't funny, Mrs Ross, really it is not. It is very vexing! Sometimes I could box Harry's ears, I get so angry with him. But that would do no good, because he'd find that funny also. I have no one else to turn to. So,' she concluded, 'I have turned to you!' Her voice trailed away like an engine running out of steam.

Time for me to step in. 'But what help or advice do you think I can give you in this, Miss Gray?'

'Oh, I haven't finished yet!' she said impatiently. 'It gets worse.'

Aunt Parry brightened and showed increased interest. My heart sank. Now what?

Miss Gray leaned forward to impart a new confidence and Aunt Parry did the same, except that she only inclined, being too stout and well corseted to actually bend at the waist.

'You will find it hard to believe, but last night Harry found out that his father intends to go to Scotland Yard today *and speak to Mr Ross*!' Miss Gray sat back and waited for my reaction.

'About the necklace?' I was finding it a little difficult to keep track of all this.

'*No*, about this man, Morgan! Well, perhaps about the necklace too. But the awful thing is, somehow – Harry and I have no idea how – the *police* found out that Uncle Jeremy had engaged a private detective. They already knew all about this man, it seems. He is quite notorious. They wanted to speak to Morgan about Harry. They actually sent an officer to escort Morgan to Scotland Yard; and Inspector Ross quizzed him. He wanted to know why the private detective was following Harry! What I would like to know is, why should it be of any interest to the professional police? Are they suspicious of poor Harry? I know Inspector Ross met Harry just the other day, in Hampstead.'

'Did he?' asked Aunt Parry, surprised.

Miss Gray turned to her. 'Oh, yes, when he called to see Aunt Roxby. The inspector wanted to be shown the room from which the necklace had been taken. Miss Chalk – she is my aunt's companion – took Mr Ross upstairs. He looked out of the window and saw Harry and me in the garden. So he came down and outside and began to talk to us.' She turned back to me. 'Oh, he was very pleasant and polite. But then Aunt Roxby appeared on the scene and she was neither, neither pleasant nor polite I mean.'

'I really don't know—' I began, but she swept on. She really was a child with a story to tell; and it had to bubble forth in an unstoppable stream of narrative.

'When Mr Ross spoke to Morgan, the private detective, he asked him who had engaged his services. I have this from Harry, who has now found out all about it. Uncle Jeremy, of course, had sought out the private detective; and Morgan told Inspector Ross so. And if you want *my* opinion, in engaging Morgan to follow Harry, his own son, like this, well, it is absolutely wrong. I am quite shocked that Uncle Jeremy should do such an underhand thing. It is hardly the action of a gentleman.'

In the background, Aunt Parry uttered a faint sound of protest at this criticism. But as she had been avidly following every word Isabella spoke, she did not actively intervene.

124

'What I – and Harry, too, of course – would very much like to know, Mrs Ross, is why should Inspector Ross be interested in how Harry spends his time?'

'Really, I—' My attempted interruption was again ignored, swept aside by her passion.

'Morgan reported back to Mr Roxby that he had been called to the Yard. And today, Harry has learned from his father's secretary that Uncle Jeremy intends to go to Scotland Yard and speak to your husband. He may already have been there. Oh, it is intolerable! Poor Harry hasn't done anything!'

I managed to get in a reply at last. 'Perhaps no one is suggesting that Harry has done anything wrong,' I suggested. 'Perhaps it's more a matter that Harry hasn't, in the eyes of his father, done anything right.'

She was young but quick to take my meaning. 'Oh, you mean Harry should be working in the firm! Learning all about the shipping business.'

'Yes, I do mean that, Miss Gray. It is quite understandable. His lack of interest and fondness for spending so much of his time on frivolous pursuits must worry his father. Sooner or later, your cousin Harry, whether he likes it or not, will find himself responsible for business decisions. He would do well to learn all about the shipping line now.'

'This is true, my dear Miss Gray,' Aunt Parry now spoke up in support. 'My late husband insisted I understood his business because he knew very well that, in all likelihood, I should one day have to sign documents, make decisions about all sorts of things. He was much older than me, you see. He did not like to think that I should be left with responsibilities I didn't know how to manage. There are so many rogues about.'

Isabella Gray swept all these quibbles aside. 'You don't understand! I admit, Harry wagers money on horse races and prizefights, and all manner of things that men like to call sport. Unfortunately, he generally loses. I've told him he is a noodle, but he doesn't pay any heed to me. He has had to appeal to his father to pay his debts. Uncle Jeremy says he won't do it any more. Not unless Harry "buckles down", that is the expression he uses.' She hesitated and tears filled her eyes. 'So poor Harry has been left owing money; and now that horrid old monstrosity of a necklace has disappeared and, and . . .'

'My dear child!' cried out Aunt Parry. 'Do not distress yourself. No one will accuse your cousin of having any part in the theft of this jewellery. Why, the very idea is impossible! Have a piece of sponge cake.'

Isabella picked up a slice of cake and stared at it despondently. 'They haven't yet, but they will. Won't they, Mrs Ross?'

Oh dear. How to reply? Honesty is the best policy. 'It's not impossible, Miss Gray.'

'You see? So, you will speak to Mr Ross, won't you? And explain to him why poor Harry can't possibly have anything to do with it.'

To my great relief, and I think to Aunt Parry's also, Simms reappeared at that point to announce that the carriage had arrived to take Miss Gray home to Hampstead.

When she had left, Aunt Parry asked me cautiously, 'And will you speak to Mr Ross?'

'I shall have to tell him I've met Miss Gray, and what she says. He'll probably find out sooner or later, anyway. And I should warn you, Aunt Parry, that Ben will be very displeased.'

'Whatever for?' asked the lady serenely. 'She is a charming child, don't you think? And she is so very worried about young Roxby, her cousin.' Here Aunt Parry sighed in a theatrical manner. 'What it is to be young and in love!'

Whatever could one do about someone like Mrs Parry? She would pursue her own view of events, whatever objection anyone else might make. The best I could do was to try to find out how much she actually knew about the whole Roxby affair. 'Do you really believe Isabella Gray to be in love with her cousin Harry? That was not my impression. It is possible to love someone dearly without actually being in love.'

'Oh, my dear Elizabeth!' She threw her pudgy hands in the air. 'Isn't it quite obvious? I dare say he's a very attractive young man and, after all, she is very young and has had little opportunity to meet anyone else.'

'She's having a good deal of opportunity at the moment,' I argued. 'Her aunt is parading her round London society with a view to her meeting any number of eligible young men.'

'Now, Elizabeth!' Aunt Parry said reproachfully. 'I don't think that is quite a nice way of describing it. I have noticed before, my dear, that you sometimes have a very – very blunt way of describing things. I dare say it comes from being married to a policeman. I am sure that Mrs Roxby is anxious to do the very best for her charge.'

If she thought me blunt, then I would be blunt. 'What sort of woman is Mrs Roxby?'

'Oh, well, I only know her from card parties, you understand.' Aunt Parry put her head on one side and considered the matter. 'I would say she is very capable, observant, and quick witted. She is an excellent card player! Now then, if you be so good as to ring for Simms, we can have some fresh tea.'

It is no use telling a man bad news when he is hungry. Therefore I waited until after our dinner that night. I did not have to find a way to broach the subject, because Ben asked me openly.

'Well, and what did Mrs Parry want?'

I recounted my tale, and waited for him to explode in rage.

'Meddling old bat,' he said disrespectfully, but accurately, of Aunt Parry.

It was quite a mild response and I was surprised. 'You must be cross, Ben. I really had no idea, until I arrived in Dorset Square, what it was all about.'

To my further surprise, he laughed. 'Old Sam Morgan is a shrewd bird. He said that ladies rarely engaged his services to find out information. They found it out very well for themselves over tea and whist. He was right!' He looked at me and raised his eyebrows. 'Is the girl in love with young Roxby? I have met the pair of them together, you remember, in the garden at the house in Hampstead. I had the impression that they were discussing something until I arrived on the scene. I might almost have judged them to be conspirators. But I could have misread the situation completely. I know nothing of young people like them. How close would you judge them to be?'

I picked my words carefully. 'I have *not* seen them together, as you have, Ben, and you may be better placed than I am to form an opinion on that. I would only say that she is certainly very fond of him. He was her childhood companion; and I believe she looks upon him as an older brother. She was orphaned at a very young age, still an infant, and has no other siblings. They are doubtless very close. That is not the same as being "in love". Aunt Parry would have it differently.'

'How far would she go in her devotion to the young wastrel? Let us say, just for the sake of argument, that he confessed to her how desperate he is for money to settle his debts. She has made no secret of how much she dislikes the Roxby emeralds. He might have suggested to her that there was an opportunity for him to get his hands on a lot of money: and for her to free herself of the obligation to wear a piece of jewellery she hates.'

'Ben!' I gasped. 'You are not suggesting that Isabella Gray took the necklace and gave it to Harry, so that he could dispose of it somehow for cash?'

'It disappeared, very conveniently, from her dressing table, where she left it in full view.' He smiled with a touch of sadness. 'I am a police detective, my dear. I have become accustomed to believe almost anyone capable of almost anything! "Love is a powerful motivation", as old Jacobus told me at our last meeting. And the young can be impetuous, if that's the word. They seldom think the world will see their actions as seriously wrong. They are accustomed to being forgiven, because everyone loves them. But not everyone loves them as much as they love themselves; and the world in general won't forgive them. It is something a very young person like Miss Gray has yet to learn.'

I argued the opposite cause. 'But even supposing, for the sake of this discussion, she did take the necklace? It would be such a harebrained thing to do, I can scarcely imagine it. But yes, she is young, and at that age one is tempted to do all manner of foolish things. What could Harry do with it? He would have to realise its value somehow, get money for it. You told me yourself how difficult that is for the amateur thief. He could hardly walk into a reputable jeweller's shop with it and sell it to them.'

'No, he, or someone on his behalf, would have to take it to a fence.' He leaned back in his chair. 'Even to someone like the late Jacob Jacobus.'

I stared at him in dismay.

Chapter Eight

Inspector Ben Ross

SOMETIMES POLICE work is an unexciting business, a matter of routine, of countless interviews, reviewing of evidence, painstaking construction of a case. It is much like building an edifice of playing cards. Like a house of cards, a case can suddenly collapse and one must begin all over again. Looking back on the investigation I conducted at this time, I am astonished how many surprises each day produced. Who would appear in my office today? I sincerely hoped it would not be Isabella Gray, come to plead her ne'er-do-well cousin's innocence – and her own. I would have to make some discreet – very discreet – inquiries about the pair of them. It was important I make these inquiries first. Then I should have some facts at hand before I faced the delicate task of dealing with impetuous youth.

Towards mid-morning Sergeant Morris appeared, looming up in the doorway looking mightily pleased with himself, like a genial giant.

'You look like the bearer of good news, Morris,' I told him. 'I certainly hope so.'

'Well, now, Inspector Ross, sir,' replied Morris, 'I do believe we might be getting somewhere at last with the Limehouse murder.'

I put down the pen I held in my hand to exclaim, 'You've found a witness!'

'Not in Limehouse, sir, and I doubt we ever shall, but perhaps even better, if things turn out right. We might have found the missing half-hunter watch and gold Albert chain.'

'*What?*' I cried out in an undignified way.

'You recall,' began Morris, 'that you asked that all officers on regular beats make inquiries of pawnbrokers of whom they know? As to whether anyone had come in, in the days following the murder, wanting to sell or pawn such a watch and chain?'

'Yes, yes! Don't keep me in suspense!'

'A constable in the Covent Garden area, doing as he was ordered and inquiring of pawnbrokers, was shown a watch that had just been brought in. Of course, it might not be the one belonging to Jacobus,' warned Morris. 'But I believe you have seen the item in question and you might recognise it. Or at least you might be able to say it's definitely not the one, and we can start again. I have it here.'

He produced a box and took out a gold half-hunter watch with the chain, though this was now separated from it. He laid both items ceremoniously on my desk. 'Well, sir, any luck?'

I leaned over the watch and studied it and the chain carefully. 'I can't be sure. I only ever saw Jacobus wearing the missing watch. I never handled it. It certainly looks very similar. Where is this pawnbroker?'

'I've got him here. Just a moment.' He disappeared briefly and reappeared, ushering in a small, neatly turned-out man with dark hair and a luxuriant moustache.

'This is Mr Giovanni Carlotti. Mr Carlotti has a pawn-broker's business in Covent Garden. This is Inspector Ross,' Morris added to the newcomer. 'Tell him what you've told me.'

Bearing such a name, I expected Mr Carlotti to have a marked Italian accent. Instead, I heard myself addressed in a voice indistinguishable from any other in Covent Garden. 'I'm a law-abiding man, I am, Inspector Ross,' he said.

'Thank you for coming forward, Mr Carlotti,' I replied.

That pleased him. He smiled cheerfully and nodded. 'Expected me to sound a bit different, I dare say?'

'Er, well, given your name . . .'

'My grandfather came from Naples,' explained the visitor. 'He set up a fruit and veg stall in the present market. That was still a new building then, and very fine. But my father was the one who had an eye for an opportunity to improve general circumstances. Oh, the fruit and veg market is a good living! But it's very hard work and it puts a man under a lot of stress. So when a suitable shop property became available near the market, he decided to leave the fresh produce and go in for pawnbroking. You see,' Carlotti leaned forward confidentially, 'you don't have to rise with the dawn and stand about shouting your head off, while watching like a hawk for those thieving ragamuffins. Swarm all over the place, those kids do. Plus, you don't have to worry about unsold produce being left on your hands to go bad.'

'Well then, sit down, Mr Carlotti, and tell me how you acquired this watch and chain,' I invited him.

This was clearly going to take some time. Mr Carlotti held centre stage with a leading role and he was going to make the most of it. He needed no more urging, but pulled out the chair opposite me and settled himself down in a way I recognised as that of a man preparing to embark on a saga. He folded his hands on the desk surface and, supported by his forearms, pushed his head so close to mine that I instinctively recoiled.

'It's like this, Inspector Ross. You may be aware that the working man sets great store by sending off his nearest and dearest on their final journey with a really good funeral. Proper casket, mourners all turned out in black, a good crowd in the church and at the graveside, and a proper tea afterwards, with ham sandwiches and cake, and a drop of ale for the men.'

I had no idea where this was going, and it seemed to have no relevance to the reason he was there, so I opened my mouth to protest. But he held up his hand to stop me.

'What has this got to do with a watch and chain, you will be wondering.'

'Yes,' I told him frankly. 'I am.'

'There is one obstacle to the working man in question laying on a good do, and it's having the money to pay for it. He hasn't got it. Now, what does he do?'

'Please tell us,' I begged.

'Get on with it! The inspector is a very busy man!' growled Morris.

Carlotti was oblivious to our impatience. 'What he does,

gentlemen, is come into my shop – or another like it – and either pawn or sell something he has in the house, usually something that's been in the family for a few years. A very popular item is a watch, better still a watch and chain. I've had any number come into my shop over the years. Usually, it's belonged to an elderly relative. Sometimes it's even belonged to the deceased. Paying for his own funeral, as it were. The family are sorry to let it go, but it's a matter of self-respect to make a good show on the day.

'So when a fellow walks in yesterday morning with just such an item – that one there . . .' He pointed at the box containing the half-hunter and Albert chain. 'I think nothing of it. His father-in-law has died, he tells me, and there is no one else to bury him. His wife is very upset. She doesn't want her dear old dad shovelled into the ground with no more ceremony than the family dog. Well, like I was saying, it's a tale I've heard many a time before. I had no reason to doubt it. I asked him, did he want to pawn or sell? He says, he wants to sell. He needs the best price he can get; and he doesn't want to pawn it, because there's no way he's ever going to be able to redeem it. I gave him a very fair price for it, and off he went quite happy.'

Carlotti leaned back and sighed. 'Bless me, but this very morning a Peeler walks in – beg pardon, a constable walks in. I recognised him. He walks that beat regular. Making inquiries, he says, as to whether I've been offered a half-hunter watch and perhaps a chain to go with it, within the last forty-eight hours. You could have knocked me down with a feather. "Why, officer!" says I. "I had just such an item brought in yesterday morning." Then he asks me, very polite, if I would mind coming down to the station to report it officially, bringing the watch and chain along with me. That took me aback. I asked him if I was being arrested, because if it was stolen property, I didn't know it was! Had no reason at all to suspect it. "No," says he, "it's possible evidence in a case of horrible murder that's being investigated in Limehouse; and every constable is inquiring of every pawnbroker on his beat." So, to cut a long story short . . .'

Morris, standing behind him, rolled his eyes towards the ceiling.

'That,' said Mr Carlotti, 'is how I come to be here now, sitting in front of you.'

The abrupt way Carlotti wound up his tale left me speechless for a second. But I managed to ask, 'The customer who came in with this watch, can you describe him? Too much to hope he gave a name, I suppose?'

Carlotti shook his head. 'Ah, no. If he'd pawned it, of course, I'd have entered his details in the book, against his coming back to redeem it. But just buying it, cash, no need to ask his name.'

'Then, can you describe him?'

'Now, there's the thing,' said Carlotti confidentially, leaning forward and preparing, I thought with dismay, to embark on another long yarn. 'He looked like a market porter, so that's what I thought he was. I see a dozen just like him going past my shop every day. Not a tall fellow, but very strongly built. Really powerful shoulders and arms, he had, like he was used to carrying heavy loads. His arms were very long, too, I noticed.'

I sat up at that. 'How about his voice?'

'Oh, that was something you'd remember!' Carlotti told me. 'Very high pitched it was, really squeaky.'

I explained that we needed to retain the watch and chain, for the time being at least, but that he would be given a receipt.

'I'm going to be out of pocket on this, I suppose,' he observed, as he tucked the receipt away in his pocket.

'It may turn out not to be the one we're interested in, in which case it will be returned to you, Mr Carlotti. We have now to try to identify it for certain, you understand. Thank you again for coming in.'

'Well, Morris,' I said to him when Carlotti had left. 'Are we thinking of the same man? Long arms, powerful build, squeaky voice?'

'The potman at the Crossed Keys!' said Morris.

'Just so. We need to have a word with Obadiah Quigley, known as Quig. But before we do that, we have to hope that Mrs Perkins can identify the watch as belonging to her father. She told my wife that the one happy and clear memory she has of her papa is of sitting on his knee and playing with the watch. Let's hope the Perkinses are still at the Railway Hotel. Send Biddle over there immediately, in a cab, and have him bring them back here. If they aren't at the hotel, but haven't paid their bill and left, then tell Biddle he's to go at once to the solicitor's offices. He gave me a card, I have it here.' I fished in my waistcoat pocket and luckily found the card still there. 'His name is Haynes, you'll recall. I need him to bring his clients here at once!'

★

137

Biddle located Mr and Mrs Perkins, not at their hotel, but at the offices of Mr Haynes, with whom they were in conference. Haynes insisted on coming along too, so my office was rather crowded.

'Do you know who murdered my poor papa?' demanded Mrs Perkins. (This same 'poor papa' whom she had steadfastly refused to visit when he was alive.)

'I wish I could say that I did, but as yet I do not. I am afraid, Mrs Perkins, that detective work proceeds step by step. Eventually, we have to be satisfied we have a case that can be put before a judge. Is that not so, Mr Haynes?'

'It is!' said Haynes firmly. 'Can't be rushed.'

'Yes, my dear,' said Perkins unexpectedly to his good lady. 'It is no use trying to hurry the inspector. This is Scotland Yard! The whole tragic matter is in the very best hands. Mr Ross will get there in the end, but we must allow him to proceed at a professional pace.'

'Thank you, Mr Perkins.' I was not sure that his speech had been altogether complimentary. But I credited Perkins with intending it to be a vote of confidence; even if it didn't altogether come out sounding that way.

I also had a strong suspicion that Haynes had had a word with Wilfred Perkins, and stressed that he had to keep his excitable spouse as calm as possible. Unfortunately, I was about to produce the half-hunter and chain for identification. I feared the combined forces of Wilfred Perkins, Mr Haynes and myself would not suffice to keep the lady under control.

'I believe I told you that we were making inquiries of

pawnbrokers regarding the missing watch and Albert chain belonging to the late Mr Jacobus.'

'Ripped from him as he lay dead!' declared Mrs Perkins. To her husband she added crossly, 'Yes, yes, I am perfectly calm, thank you!'

I met the eye of the solicitor, who pursed his lips and shrugged. I wondered what had been the atmosphere at the conference he had been having with them both when Biddle interrupted it to bring all three to the Yard.

'One of the pawnbrokers had indeed lately received such a watch and chain, and has handed it over to us. I would be grateful if you would examine it carefully. Take your time. I am aware, Mrs Perkins, that you were a child when you last saw the half-hunter. But you, Mr Perkins, have visited Mr Jacobus over the years and must have seen it on those occasions.'

'Oh, yes.' Perkins nodded. 'I remember it very well. He always wore it.'

Now for it. 'This is the item in our possession.' I produced the box and took out the watch and chain, laying them on the desk.

All three of my visitors leaned forward and stared down at it.

'Has it a dent in the back of the case?' asked Maggie Perkins suddenly. 'I do recall, there was a dent in the back of the case. I don't know how it got there. I know I played with it but I don't believe I was responsible.'

I turned the watch over. There was indeed a slight dent in the back of the gold case.

'It is Papa's watch!' shrieked Mrs Perkins. 'Wilfred! I am going to faint!'

This was to be avoided at all costs. There followed ten minutes during which a glass of water was fetched and Wilfred hunted in his wife's capacious handbag for her smelling salts.

While this was going on, Haynes asked me, 'May I examine the watch? I acted for the late Mr Jacobus in matters regarding his properties. I have seen the item. I should stress that I know nothing of the antiquarian business he claimed to be in. His property holdings are all above board and legal.'

That didn't mean I wouldn't be making further inquiries about them later. However, in the meantime, I was happy for him to examine the watch and chain.

Unexpectedly, he produced a jeweller's loupe from his pocket and peered at the watch through it. 'I cannot swear to it being the same one; but it is extraordinarily similar. Mr Perkins, would you care . . .?'

He handed the loupe to Perkins, who abandoned his efforts to rally his wife in order to peer closely at the watch himself, before declaring, 'Yes, yes, it does indeed appear to be the same one. To be my father-in-law's.'

'Let me see it again!' demanded Maggie Perkins, suddenly perfectly sensible. 'Yes, I am sure of it. That is my dear papa's watch!'

'Has the pawnbroker been able to give you the name and address of the customer who pawned the items?' asked Haynes.

'The customer in question wanted to sell the watch and

chain outright and, unfortunately, the pawnbroker did not record his name. But we have a very good description of the man in question, and we think we know where to look for him. More than that I can't say at the moment.'

'That pawnbroker,' said Haynes to me very quietly, 'needs checking on. He had no business buying such a valuable article from a casual caller without some proof of the customer's identity.'

'I agree, Mr Haynes, but in this case, if it is the watch and chain we seek, I suspect the customer would have given a fictitious name and address anyway. Also, the pawnbroker in question came forward freely in response to inquiries. That is something we would want to encourage.'

When the solicitor and his clients had left (Mrs Perkins weeping into a small square of material edged with black lace), I summoned Morris.

'We now have reasonable cause to question Obadiah Quigley. So let's be off to the Crossed Keys and see what we can find out!'

On our arrival in Limehouse, we might have thought ourselves in the middle of a thunderstorm. Barrels of beer were being delivered from the brewery. The dray and its patient horses waited while the draymen unloaded and rolled the barrels towards the opened flaps giving access to the ramp down into the cellar. Each barrel made a deafening sound as it rattled and bounced down into the darkness below. I wondered the horses did not take fright; but supposed they were used to it. The draymen were aided by a familiar figure, short, brawny and broad shouldered, with long arms.

'There's our man,' muttered Morris.

As yet, Quig hadn't noticed our arrival. Tom Mullins, who stood nearby, supervising the delivery and ready to sign it off, had noticed us, I was sure. But he saw fit to ignore us for the time being. We were spotted, however, by Daisy Smith, who stood outside the tavern door, watching the barrels career down the ramp. She was carrying a bucket and looked more dishevelled than before as well as generally out of sorts.

''Ullo, Mr Ross!' she greeted me sourly. 'I done it.'

'You've cleaned the carpet?' I guessed. I had left a key to the property at the local police station for this purpose.

'Yes, I have, with that Constable Higgins, him with the big black beard, standing over me all the time. Blessed nerve of him! Was I likely to pinch something? Anyway, the carpet is pretty well cleaned but it's wet, so don't go trampling all over it, you and the sergeant there!'

Constable Higgins himself appeared from the direction of Jacobus's house. 'All done, sir, and I've locked up again. I've got the key here. Do you want it back?'

'I'll take care of it!' growled Morris, taking the key and putting it in his pocket.

'Thank you, Daisy,' I said to her. 'I'll see you are paid for the work.'

'Obliged!' said Daisy briefly. 'Only don't ask me to do something like that again.' She took herself off.

'That was unpleasant work,' observed Morris. 'She's earned her money.'

Mullins was signing the receipt for the beer. The draymen climbed back on to their seat and the driver whistled to his horses. The dray rumbled away. Quig was closing the cellar flaps. At last he stood up and turned to go back into the tavern. At that point, he saw us.

He knew why we were there, of course he did. He must have hoped he'd got away with selling the watch, but he knew from the expressions on our faces that he hadn't. For a moment, I wondered if he would run. It would have served him nothing and, realising that, he abandoned the instinct and merely stood, shoulders hunched, and head lowered, his fists clenched as I'd seen previously when official attention turned on him.

'Got your cuffs there, Constable?' Morris asked Higgins.

'Yes, Sergeant!' Higgins was surprised, but reached for the handcuffs.

'Then put 'em on that fellow there. Obadiah Quigley, you are under arrest for theft.'

Quig sat staring at us sullenly. Since his arrest, he had not said a word.

'Well now, Quigley,' I began. 'You recently sold a gold half-hunter watch and chain to a pawnbroker in Covent Garden. This watch . . .' I opened the box so that he could see the watch and its chain lying in it.

'No, I never did,' growled Quig.

'The pawnbroker can identify you. He is on his way here at the moment.'

Quig was sweating, the beads pearling on his forehead. There was the sound of voices outside in the corridor.

'Ah,' I said. 'Here is our witness now, I believe.'

The door opened and a constable showed Carlotti into the room. The pawnbroker took one look at our prisoner and declared, 'That's him! No mistake!' He then addressed Quig directly with, 'Oy, you, what do you mean by coming into my place of business and selling me stolen goods? I got a reputation to maintain, you know! And where's the money I paid you for it?'

'If you hadn't gone squealing to the police, you'd still have the watch and the chain!' countered Quig.

'I'm an honest man!' shouted Carlotti.

'No, you ain't! I wouldn't have taken the watch to you if I'd thought you'd hand it straight over to the law! I was told you never asked questions,' added Quig. 'People told me you could be trusted. Well, no one will be trusting you no more. Word will get round that you peached! You can depend on it. You want to watch out!'

'Don't you threaten me!' stormed Carlotti. 'I got a blameless record in business!'

'All right, Mr Carlotti, thank you for your help,' I told him.

When Carlotti had been ushered away, Quig spoke again sullenly.

'I never killed the old man!'

'As yet, you are not being accused of murder. You are being accused of robbing a dead body,' I reminded him.

'Exactly!' squeaked Quig. 'He was dead, wasn't he? He didn't want the watch no more. No good to him. I didn't know he'd got family, did I? No one knew. He hid away in that house like a big old spider, waiting for people to come to him. And they did come! But him, he never went out, or hardly ever.'

'Just tell us the circumstances in which you took the watch,' I ordered. 'When did you take it? It must have been very soon after the murder; because when the police, including myself, arrived on the scene, the watch had already been stolen.'

It was slowly dawning on the potman just how much trouble he was in. By his own faulty logic, the watch had been available to anyone who took possession of it. The owner was dead. It was not known that he had any relatives with claims on his property. If he, Quig, had not taken it, someone else would. He'd realised, of course, that authority might not agree with this deduction. But authority, in Quig's world, was there to outwit.

I was interested in his claim that Carlotti had been recommended to him as someone who would buy without asking too many questions. It chimed with Haynes's suspicions. On the other hand, Carlotti had come forward the very next day, when told that the half-hunter was being sought urgently in a case of murder. Stolen property: well, Carlotti might turn a blind eye and purchase that. But evidence in a murder case? No, definitely not. Especially as he had probably already heard the name of Jacobus, and of his gruesome death.

Quig was watching me with his sharp little eyes, working out what was now best for him to say.

'It's just like we told you already,' he began.

'Who are "we"?' growled Morris, and I signalled to

Biddle, sitting patiently with his notebook and pencil. He made ready to write down Quig's statement.

'Tom Mullins, Daisy and me. Well then, the day old Jacobus got his throat slit, Daisy went to take the old feller's dinner tray up to him, same as usual. She did it every day. She came rushing back into the Keys to say she'd found him horribly murdered; and the whole room spattered with blood. She was in a fair old state and nothing would have made her go back. So, Tom, he says to me, "You go on up and take a look, before I go looking for the police." All right?'

'The story so far is all right. But you've yet to get to the important part. You are claiming that Mullins, the landlord, sent you to verify Daisy's claim about the murder.'

'Reasonable enough,' explained Quig. 'You don't want the police poking their noses in—' Even Quig's slow brain realised these were not well-chosen words. He changed what he had been about to say. 'Tom didn't want to trouble the police, if it was all Daisy's imagination. Ask Tom himself, he'll tell you the same. She was hardly making any sense. Kept on about the blood and horrid murder and the room being ransacked. You got to admit, it's not something to just take on trust. You got to check it's right.'

He stopped again, peering at us to assess just how his tale so far was being received.

'Keep going!' ordered Morris.

'I didn't like Tom telling me to go and take a look. But I didn't have much choice. I went over to the house – Daisy had left the door unlocked when she'd rushed out. Anyone might have gone in and helped himself to that watch and chain! Anyhow, I went up the stairs, looked into the room – cor!' He dragged out a dirty rag from his pocket and mopped his head. 'You never seen anything like it. Well, I'd never seen the like! It was just as she'd told us. Old Jacobus still sitting there in his chair, just as always, except that his throat had been cut; and blood had sprayed out everywhere. The room had been turned over, that I could see, all the drawers emptied. But the old chap's watch and chain were still on his waistcoat. That did seem odd to me, I admit,' added Quig with a frown. 'Because if it had been me as killed him and searched the place, I'd have taken the watch.'

'You did take it!' Morris reminded him.

'Well, yes, I took it *afterwards*!' argued Quig. 'But I didn't take it before. It wasn't me searched the room and it wasn't me killed him! Well, I didn't want to hang about there. Tom was waiting for me to come back and, besides, I didn't know where the killer was. He might've been upstairs in the bedroom. He might've been hiding anywhere ready to jump out. Of course, I knew he'd probably scarpered. Anyway, there was the watch and chain in full view. It seemed sort of meant that I should have it. It'd only be the work of a minute to take it. So I stepped out of my boots, and I tiptoed across the carpet, taking care to step in the footprints already there. I snatched the watch and chain, stuffed them into my pocket, went back the way I'd come, put on my boots and hurried on back to tell Tom. It was true, what Daisy had told us.'

Quig fell silent. 'I give way to temptation,' he added unexpectedly. 'I was tempted by the devil. I didn't know

147

any better. I never had any education. I'm a poor man. What'd you expect me to do?'

I knew it would be useless but I had to try to make him face the reality of what he had done. Perhaps in the form of a story? 'Look at it this way,' I began, 'let us suppose you owned a gold signet ring.'

'Where would I get a gold ring from? Here!' added Quig suspiciously. 'Am I going to be accused of stealing something else?'

'No! Listen, I'm trying to explain something to you. Let us suppose you have a gold ring – something you've inherited, perhaps.'

'I never had no family. I was a foundling, a workhouse brat. How could I inherit a gold ring?' argued Quig.

'Just pay attention, can't you?' I was getting exasperated and wished I hadn't embarked on an attempt to explain why he was in such trouble. 'Let us pretend, right? You are working as usual at the Crossed Keys one day, unloading beer from the brewery, as you were this morning. A full keg is dropped on your head and down you go, dead as mutton on the pavement. A crowd of people gather round you. One of them spots the ring, and he manages to slip it off your finger and pocket it. You don't think that's right, do you?'

'It's what I'd do,' said Quig simply. 'So would most folk, I reckon.'

There was a crazed logic in this, I had to admit. But it wouldn't help Quig before the magistrate. 'Can you read and write?' I asked resignedly.

'I just told you, didn't I?' retorted Quig with a pained

look. 'I never had schooling. How can I be expected to read and write?'

'Then the constable will make a fair copy of your statement, it will be read back to you, and you can sign it.'

'Can't write!' countered Quig. 'How many times I gotta tell you?'

'You can make your mark and I will witness it.'

'You can witness anything; how do I know what I'm making my mark to?' argued Quig. Unlettered he might be, but like nearly every arrested suspect I'd ever met he wanted to avoid going on record.

'That's the recognised procedure, Quigley. Now then, you said something earlier that interested me.'

'Oh? What?' Quig frowned ferociously, as he tried to recall what he'd said, and where, if anywhere, he'd let slip more than he'd needed to.

'You described the victim, Jacobus, as sitting in his house like a spider, waiting for people to come to him. You added that they did come to him. Well now, who came? How did they gain access to the house?'

Quig cocked a wary eye, chewed his lower lip, and finally admitted: 'Sometimes they came to the pub and asked for the key. Of course, neither Tom nor me would've given it to just anyone. We would have asked the caller's business first, and whether the old man was expecting him. Sometimes Mr Jacobus would have sent us a message through Daisy, letting us know he was expecting a caller. Sometimes, we'd be none the wiser about his callers. They'd knock on the street door and wait for the old man to look out. If he wanted to see 'em, he'd throw down a key. He had a lot of private business, the old feller, stuff he wouldn't have wanted anyone to know about.'

'What did they want, these visitors?'

'How should I know? I just told you, it was private business!' A look of cunning entered his mean little eyes. 'The day the old chap was killed, *you* came yourself, Inspector Ross! You were there that very morning, and went up to visit him. Daisy, she come back from washing down his staircase and told us you were with him.'

'She was passing the word that the police were about,' muttered Morris.

'She was no more than making conversation!' countered Quig loftily. 'Anyway, you was there, Inspector Ross, wasn't you?'

'I was, Quigley. We have reason to believe that Jacobus sometimes acted as a receiver of stolen property, in particular items of jewellery.'

'Well, I never!' Quig shook his head, his mien sorrowful.

'So you don't know anything about that? Never heard a whisper?'

'Of course not. Cross my heart and hope to die!' declared Quig, making a clumsy sign of the cross over his waistcoat.

'Tell me, did you happen to notice whether Jacobus had any other visitors that day, either before I came, or after my visit?'

Quig thought about answering. But he needed our goodwill. 'All sorts used to come and go,' he said at last. 'Some of them real swells.'

'Swells?' I asked.

'You know, dressed very smart. There was one young

fellow there, the day before the murder, it was. I'm sure of it. He was really something to look at, he was! Dark hair and well dressed. He didn't have the look of someone who had ever done a hard day's work in his life. Thought a lot of himself, I reckon. Walked with a bit of swagger, turned the girls' heads, I expect.' Quig fell silent, watching me cautiously.

There is a sensation which I experienced now, and had experienced before, when working on other cases. I would find it hard to describe, a tingling, maybe, like a mild electric shock. There is something else! I thought. But he's not sure whether to tell me. Whatever it is, it's important. He knows it's important. He is toying with the idea that what he knows might be valuable to someone else, other than the police.

'And on the day of the murder? Apart from me.'

'Nah!' said Quig firmly. 'We were very busy that day. I didn't have time to stand about outside in the street, watching.'

'If you remember anyone else,' I said casually, 'tell us straight away.'

'Of course I'd tell you!' squawked Quig with an unconvincing expression of virtue on his unlovely countenance.

'And Quigley! Don't be foolish. This is a case of murder. If you know anything at all that might be of interest to the police, you must tell us.'

'Can't be foolish, can I?' he countered. 'Sitting in a police cell, waiting to be took up before the magistrates.'

I wasn't so sure.

'Well, Inspector Ross,' said Morris, when we were alone.

'It always gives one great satisfaction when solid, routine police work turns up trumps.'

'It does, Morris. But if this hadn't been a murder case, I wonder whether Carlotti would have produced that watch so readily?'

'Probably not,' said Morris, with the tone and air of a man who had seen the human condition with all its flaws.

'There is something he is not telling us, Morris.'

'Carlotti, sir?'

'No, the wretched Quigley! It is *why* he's not telling us that worries me. It makes me think it might be something of real significance; and he thinks it might be worth his while to hold on to his knowledge. It is fashionable now to talk of criminal tendencies; and spout a lot of nonsense about the shape of people's heads, or noses, or some such stuff. If Quigley is holding on to some information, it is because he hopes to make use of it. The shape of his skull doesn't come into it.'

'Well, Ross,' said Dunn later. 'You have managed to recover the missing watch and chain taken from the Limehouse murder victim. Let us now hope you have equal luck in recovering Mrs Roxby's emerald necklace.'

'As to that, sir, perhaps I should tell you that it's possible Mrs Roxby does not own the necklace outright.'

'What do you mean?' Dunn pushed his head forward and squinted at me. 'Explain yourself! She came here and reported the jewellery missing – to me, in person. She claims it belongs to her.'

'Well, it seems possible, sir, that it is, in fact, a family heirloom and belongs, as it were, to the family.'

Dunn scowled. 'It's not part of the Crown Jewels, is it?'

'Er, no, sir. But Mr Jeremy Roxby has been to see me; and he tells me that the necklace has been in the family since his great-grandfather's day. By tradition, it is given to the bride of the eldest son, on her wedding day, and worn thereafter until such time as the son of that union marries – or, as Mrs Roxby does not have a son, until Mr Jeremy Roxby's son marries. Then it will be presented to that bride, held in trust and worn by her, as it is now held in trust by Mrs Charlotte Roxby, before it was stolen, that is. She doesn't own it outright.'

'Extraordinary!' said Dunn. 'I never heard of such an arrangement.'

'I believe,' I told him, 'such a practice is not uncommon in the nobility. Some jewels are regarded as family property. The wife of the current holder of the title wears them until the next generation to inherit the rank marries.'

'The Roxbys aren't titled, are they?'

'No, sir, but that is how Mr Jeremy Roxby explained it to me.'

'Ah!' exclaimed Dunn, as someone who has found the solution to a problem. 'Then, if Jeremy Roxby's son marries Miss Gray, the necklace will be given to Miss Gray after the wedding, to wear until such time as the next marriage, which would be that of their eldest son! Wouldn't that solve the problem? Surely Mrs Charlotte Roxby wouldn't object to the necklace being given to her niece, whom she's raised as a daughter?'

'It might, sir, but Mr Jeremy Roxby is unwilling to accept the idea of his son marrying his cousin – courtesy cousin – Miss Gray. He would almost certainly oppose it vigorously.'

'Why?' asked Dunn bluntly.

'He did not divulge that to me. However, I think it possible that he doesn't much like his sister-in-law, Mrs Charlotte Roxby. I'd go so far as to say he actively dislikes her. There may be more to it than that, I don't know. I suspect some acrimonious past history.'

The superintendent considered this. 'I respect your judgement, Ross. We have both met Mrs Charlotte Roxby and know her to be a difficult woman. What kind of man is Jeremy Roxby? I know he's a successful man of business, runs a shipping line, all that. But, as a person?'

'I would not want him as an enemy, I'll be frank,' I admitted. 'But he was perfectly civil when he came here. I had the impression that he maintains a true fatherly affection for his wayward son. But the young man has tested his father's patience to the limit. He has, I've been told, refused to pay any more of his son's debts.'

'Who told you?' snapped Dunn, suspicion in his voice.

'My wife accepted an invitation to tea with her godmother, Mrs Julia Parry. Mrs Parry is acquainted with Mrs Roxby.'

Dunn's complexion was turning an unnatural shade of purple. 'Are you going to tell me, Ross, that Mrs Roxby was present at this tea party?'

'No, sir, but Miss Gray, Mrs Roxby's niece, was there.

You recall, she was pictured actually wearing the emerald necklace in the photograph—'

'I know she had been parading the wretched necklace around London!' exploded Dunn. 'She might as well have been advertising it. You also know how I feel about Mrs Ross becoming involved in detective work.'

'Yes, sir, but I must stress that when my wife accepted the invitation to take tea, she did not know that Miss Gray would be there. It is embarrassing.'

'So it is from Miss Gray, via Mrs Ross, that we know Roxby is refusing to settle his son's debts?'

'Yes, it is,' I admitted. 'That is to say, I had deduced it already. It's natural that he does not like his family's private relationships dragged into public view for all and sundry to discuss. Personally, I am beginning to suspect that this loss of the necklace threatens to reignite old quarrels.'

Dunn was silent for a few minutes. He steepled the tips of his fingers and frowned. 'Ross!' he said eventually. 'I don't like this one bit. You realise, don't you, that it is possible that Mrs Roxby, having realised that Jeremy Roxby would oppose any marriage between his son and Miss Isabella, has secreted the necklace away, thus avoiding the obligation to hand it over to any other young woman?'

'I am bearing it in mind, sir.'

'Damn awkward business,' grumbled the superintendent. 'I want this necklace matter cleared up as soon as possible. And if it does turn out to be the case that Mrs Charlotte Roxby has misrepresented the facts, then I shall insist she is charged with making a false statement and wasting police time.' He waved a hand towards the door, dismissing me. 'See to it, Ross!'

'I'll do my best, sir.'

'Oh, and Ross, my compliments to your wife.'

'Thank you, sir. I'll pass them on.'

I look forward to going home at the end of the day and spending the evening with Lizzie. Sometimes we discuss a case I am working on. At other times, I set all thoughts of criminal matters aside, clearing my brain and giving such deductive powers as I have a good rest. If I'd been hoping to do that on this particular evening, I was out of luck.

The first delay was due to my running into Reynolds again. He was also setting off home and appeared in cheerful mood. He hailed me with, 'Found your emeralds yet, Ross?'

'Not yet,' I admitted. 'I shall, I am confident of it.'

'It takes patience to track down stolen jewellery,' he told me consolingly. 'Your trouble, old chap, is that you spend too much time consorting with murderers. Murderers are clumsy fellows compared with jewel thieves.'

'Are you volunteering to take over the inquiries from me?' I snapped. 'With your knowledge of the ways of jewel thieves?'

'Good Lord, no! I've got enough on my hands. Don't take offence. Enjoy your evening!'

Enjoy my evening? I did not even have the chance to eat my dinner in peace.

'I should warn you that Daisy is here again,' Lizzie told me as I divested myself of my coat. 'She is in the kitchen, talking to Bessie. She's very upset.'

'She hasn't discovered another murder, I hope?'

'No, it's all about a gold watch and chain.'

I groaned. 'Am I not to sit down at my own dinner table?'

The answer came immediately. I had been heard in the kitchen. The door from kitchen to hallway was thrown open; and Daisy stood there, arms akimbo, in full battle mode.

'Here!' she demanded. 'What have you done with poor Quig?'

'He has been arrested for a theft he admits to committing. He took Jacobus's watch and chain from the body.'

'Well, we need him at the Crossed Keys. We're busy. Tom Mullins has sent me to ask, when can he have Quig back again?'

'That is no longer in my hands. He will be up before the magistrate in the morning. When the magistrate has heard the case, and depending on the decision, it may or may not result in the matter going before a judge. I doubt very much you will see Quigley for a while. Robbing a dead body, removing evidence, disposing of it by selling it . . . Come, Daisy, you know such things can't be ignored.'

'It's not like robbing a living person,' argued Daisy. 'The old man was dead!'

'He has an heir, a daughter. You know that now. You've seen her and spoken to her. She is very anxious to have the watch returned. It has sentimental value for her. What is more, under the terms of his will, as I have been informed, it is now hers. Theft is theft, Daisy, and it's no use arguing about that. Perhaps you should consider Mrs Perkins's feelings.'

'Why didn't she ever come and see him, then,' asked

the truculent Daisy, 'if she's got these sentimental feelings? We never had any idea he had any family. He never spoke to me about daughters or anyone else. And she wasn't very polite to me when I told her how I looked after the old man. She never thanked me.'

'I believe his son-in-law did visit him from time to time,' I told her.

Daisy sat down without warning on a lower tread of the staircase. She rested her forearms on her knees, scowled up at me, and demanded, 'If you mean that tubby fellow, wore a top hat with a silk scarf tied round it? He that sat with her in the snug, while I lit the fire? I never saw him come to the house! How did he get in to see Mr Jacobus, if he ever did? He never came to the pub to ask for the key, not that day or any other.'

Now that, I thought to myself, is a very good point. And one I should have realised for myself the first time I met the relatives and their solicitor before the door, demanding to be let in. Had these previous visits been occasions when Perkins would call up and request that his father-in-law, Jacobus, throw down the key? Or did Perkins already possess a key to the house? When I first met him and his wife, they were standing in the street, angry that the police would not comply with their demands. But, possibly, they had gone to the house with their solicitor fully expecting to be able to open the door and walk in. After all, they knew Jacobus was dead. But they had still to be confident of gaining admission. They had not gone to the tavern and requested the key of the landlord. Finding the house secured, they had not only been angry, they had been shocked. Had it been then, when they found the house was officially guarded, that they decided not to reveal they held a key? Had Haynes, their legal adviser, recommended them to say nothing, lest they put themselves on any list of suspects? Tomorrow, I would need to talk to both Perkins and Mr Haynes.

'Daisy,' I told her, 'you have to go back to the Crossed Keys now. Tell Mullins he will need to find another potman, at least for the foreseeable future. Tomorrow morning, someone may come down to Limehouse and talk to you. But now, Mrs Ross and I would very much like to dine peacefully together in our own home.'

'All right, I'm going,' grumbled Daisy, standing up and shaking out her crumpled skirts. 'He's not going to like it, is Tom, when I tell him.'

'Oh, Daisy, one moment.' I put out a hand to detain her. 'You are well acquainted with Constable Biddle by sight, aren't you?'

'Of course I am!' she snapped. 'He's always sitting in your kitchen, stuffing his face!'

'I heard that!' Bessie appeared, outraged, brandishing a dishcloth.

'All right, Bessie, just keep calm,' Lizzie told her firmly. Bessie made an unwilling retreat into the kitchen and could be heard muttering.

'So you know him well enough. Now then, Daisy,' I continued. 'It's quite possible I may not be free to come to Limehouse tomorrow myself. If, either then or the day after, I should send Constable Biddle, or another officer if Biddle isn't available, to the Crossed Keys to fetch you to the Yard, you won't be alarmed, will you?'

'What?' squawked Daisy. 'You running me in, too, are you? There won't be no one left to run the pub at this rate, except Tom on his own – or are you planning on locking us all up?'

I smiled at her. 'There is no question of you being arrested, Daisy. At least, not on this occasion . . .'

My ill-advised attempt to defuse her ire with humour was not successful.

'Persecution, that's what it is!' Daisy struck a fine dramatic attitude, and her voice rang round the hallway. 'What am I supposed to have done, then? All I ever did was look after the old fellow. And that's more than his precious daughter and her husband ever did!'

If humour didn't work, I had to resort to low cunning, 'I have no plan to arrest you, Daisy. Calm down! It's just that I have a little ploy in mind and you'd play an important role in it.'

Daisy was not fully appeased, but she was intrigued. She put her head on one side, like the cockney sparrow she was, and surveyed me top to toe. 'Oh, I would, would I? Here! What are you up to?'

'All in good time.' I put a finger to my lips. 'Not a word to anyone at the Keys, mind, and particularly not to that lout, Mullins.'

When Daisy had left, and Bessie's ruffled feelings were soothed, my wife confronted me with a sparkle in her eye which meant she would not be fobbed off. 'What are you up to, Ben?'

'At the moment,' I told her, 'I hold one end of a very tangled piece of string. I believe it is starting to unravel; and if the guilty party or parties realise that, whoever is at the other end of the string may panic. If so, I am afraid the situation will get worse before it gets better.'

She frowned. 'Is someone else going to die? Is that what you fear?'

'I do fear it. But, at the moment, I don't know who it is. That's what makes it all so very difficult. I have to proceed with caution and not frighten the quarry. It only takes a moment to kill another human being.'

'And whoever killed poor old Jacobus was panicking?'

'Oh, yes, almost certainly.'

Lizzie considered the matter. 'So what are you going to tell Mr Dunn?'

'Dunn?' I had either forgotten or deliberately erased the superintendent from my mind. 'Oh, yes, Dunn!' I said now briskly. 'At the moment, I don't plan to tell him anything more at all. He'd only worry. Oh, he asked me to pass you his compliments, by the way.'

'I'm obliged to him!' retorted Lizzie, 'but I do wonder whether it is wise not to let him know what you plan to do.'

'Sometimes,' I told her, 'I think he secretly prefers not to know.'

Chapter Nine

'RIGHT, WOOD!' I said briskly to him the following morning. 'Here we have a set of people, all of whom have a declared interest in recent events that are currently being investigated by Scotland Yard. But none of whom own to any responsibility for anything that's happened. I, for one, am tired of all this shilly-shallying. It is time to put a cat among the pigeons!'

I was rather proud of this speech. But Wood eyed me stonily.

'We're to treat all this as one case, are we, sir? The Jacobus murder and the emeralds affair? Myself, if you don't mind my saying so, I wouldn't call the parties concerned to be one set of people. One lot live in style in Hampstead. That's the jewel theft parties. The others, a very different set, scrabble about for a living in Limehouse, sometimes on the right side of the law, and sometimes not. Where's the connection?'

'What connects them, Sergeant, is an old rogue, a receiver of stolen goods, by the name of Jacob Jacobus, lately deceased.'

'We've got to be able to prove it,' retorted Wood. He had

begun to look more than usually depressed. 'Not to say you aren't on the right track, Mr Ross, but suspicions aren't enough, not by a long chalk. We have to come up with some evidence. I don't see how we are going to do it.'

'Never thought of you as being faint of heart, Wood!' I rallied him.

'Got a plan, have you, then, Mr Ross? The superintendent knows about this?' Wood was searching in his coat pocket. I very much feared it was for the mint humbugs. A rustle of paper bag confirmed it.

'Please wait to pollute the atmosphere with those sweets until you are outside in the street, Sergeant.'

Wood took his hand out of his pocket and said, 'Yessir.'

I continued, 'As for your question, oddly enough, my wife asked me the same thing last night. I can only say to you more or less what I said to her. I see no need to trouble Mr Dunn unnecessarily. Now then, what I need you to do is convey a message to Mr Harry Roxby, requesting his presence here at the Yard at three this afternoon. Make sure only dashing young Harry gets the message, and his sorely tried parent does not find out. That could be tricky, as I also want you to find Sam Morgan again and bring him here. Sam, as we know, reports to Jeremy Roxby, who is paying him to follow young Harry about. It would be best if you could run Morgan to earth this morning, before he can report to his client. I'd also like to have had a chat with Sam before young Roxby comes at three. Oh, and if Sergeant Morris is about the place, ask him to come and see me.'

Wood departed and shortly afterwards Morris loomed into sight. 'You asked for me, Mr Ross?'

'I did. Have you completed a search of the premises in Limehouse?'

'Turned it upside down, sir. But we didn't find anything we have listed in our records as having been reported stolen. The old fellow was too canny to keep anything on his premises. However, we did find a quantity of gold sovereigns in the bedknobs.'

'*In the bedknobs?*'

'Yes, sir. I'm writing out a report on the whole search this morning, with an inventory. I'll have it done by the end of the day. The bedroom is above the room where the murder took place, the parlour. The bed has brass rails, top and bottom, and rather large bedknobs.'

I closed my eyes briefly, imagining the piece of furniture. 'Go on, Morris.'

'In my experience,' continued Morris, his tone encouraging, as if he realised I was struggling with the concept, 'it's not unknown for people to hide things in bedknobs. They usually unscrew and make very handy receptacles. And these, being larger than most, as I said, I suspected might have been specially commissioned to serve another purpose other than decorate the bed rails. So I unscrewed all four of the knobs on the old man's bed, and bless me! Out fell these gold sovereigns, thirty-two of them in total. His little secret stash, I reckon, in case of emergency. I knew, as soon as I unscrewed the first one, we were on the right track. It was so much heavier than it should have been, and there was a bit of tissue paper stuffed in it to prevent the coins falling out when he turned it, hole down, to screw it back on.'

A fairy-tale-like picture formed in my brain, truly something straight out of a story recorded by the brothers Grimm. Morris, a stern but just giant, standing in Jacobus's bedroom with gold coins showering around him.

'Where are the sovereigns now?' I asked, doing my best to sound as if this were an everyday sort of report.

'In the safe in Mr Dunn's office. Evidence, sir, of *something*, even motive on the killer's part.'

When was the superintendent planning to tell me he was now custodian of Jacobus's hoarded gold? Or had he been leaving that task to Morris?

'I wonder, Morris,' I mused, 'whether Mr and Mrs Perkins were aware of this little treasure trove, and that is why they were so anxious to enter the house on the morning after the murder. Well, as it happens, I am about to pay a call on their solicitor, Mr Haynes. I have a number of questions to put to that gentleman! Oh, and Sergeant, if you could order Biddle to go to Limehouse and locate the cleaner at the Crossed Keys, Daisy Smith. I'd like him to bring her here before three this afternoon, and seat her where she is not herself obvious, but where she can see who enters my office. She'll be expecting him and won't make a fuss about coming.'

Morris surveyed me with a touch of reproach in his manner. 'Mind telling me what's going on, sir?'

'Well, as you'll be aware, I am juggling two cases at the moment. But I suspect they are connected in some way not yet entirely clear to me. I believe, however, young Harry Roxby may have visited Jacobus in Limehouse, on matters of business.'

Morris looked shocked. 'Think the young gentleman is a thief, sir?'

'I hope he isn't,' I told him. 'But I need to eliminate him from any suspicion.'

Haynes had probably been expecting me to turn up in his office sooner or later, with uncomfortable accusations. But he kept his composure and invited me to sit down.

'You have news, Inspector Ross?' he asked courteously.

'I have questions, Mr Haynes.'

'Indeed, sir? I shall do my best to answer them.' He folded his pale, clerk's hands, with the clean, well-kept nails, on his desk top and raised his eyebrows.

Not only a cool customer, but a quick thinker.

'We have completed the search of the scene of the crime and the other rooms in the house belonging to Jacobus,' I began.

'Ah! Then my clients can now go in and begin an inventory of the contents. And the keys?'

'Oh, I suspect they've been able to get into the premises from the first. Either they, or you, hold a key, is that not the case?'

Haynes's face turned scarlet, then alabaster-pale. 'We hold a key here,' he admitted at last. His composure was gone. He looked furtive. 'What made you think . . . how did you . . .?'

I held up my hand to silence him. 'When your clients arrived in London, you took them at once to the building in Limehouse. You would not have done that unless you were confident of being able to walk straight in. To the dismay of all parties, you found you could not. The house was under police guard.'

'The fellow at the tavern held the key,' muttered Haynes.

'You did not know that, or you would have gone there first, and asked him for them. What is more, when we all did go into the tavern to escape the rain, you asked me on the way in if this was the public house that was part of the estate. You did not even know for certain it was the right establishment. Before that, you had made a great to-do about the key.'

Haynes rallied and made an attempt at defence. 'I had to protect the interests of my client, Mrs Perkins, and her husband. In the circumstances, immediately following the murder of Mrs Perkins's father, it was necessary. The Perkinses are themselves above suspicion. They are respectable people and were in Leeds at the time of the murder. I admit, we did not expect a police constable to be guarding the door, that black-bearded fellow, Higgins. But events had moved very fast. We were all of us, the Perkinses and myself, in a state of shock. I now see I was mistaken in advising them to say nothing of the key held in this office.'

'What was necessary, sir, was that you advise your client to make all relevant facts known to the senior investigating officer, that is to say, myself!' I told him sternly. 'And to do so immediately. You had ample opportunity to do that when we were in the snug of the Crossed Keys. You did not do so. When I arrived, you were all three genuinely angered at not being able to go inside and make an inventory. Was there perhaps something in particular that you either wanted to find or expected to find?'

'Inspector Ross! Neither Mr nor Mrs Perkins, nor I, had any wish or intention to interfere with police inquiries. But an inventory is essential and should be made immediately. Things do go missing after a death. It's a sad fact of life. Even the most trusted of servants may help themselves to some trinket or a set of silver spoons.'

I thought of my own mother's wedding ring and the willow-pattern meat dish. 'Yes, Mr Haynes, they do indeed. But anything in that house was safe because it was being guarded by the police. Besides which, there is the possibility that something in the house, something of value, might have been the cause of the savage attack upon Mr Jacobus. If that is the case, it is vital that we know it! Nor was there evidence of petty pilfering. You saw for yourself, when I took you inside, that the silver cutlery lay spilled and abandoned on the carpet in the parlour.'

'His watch and chain had been taken!' snapped Haynes.

'That theft was opportunistic. It occurred after the discovery of the body. The culprit is known and the items have been recovered.'

Haynes had momentarily been wrong footed, but he was regaining his composure and he was no fool.

'What did you, the police, find?' he asked sharply. 'I must insist you reveal the contents of any inventory made by the search team. In due course, naturally,' he added hastily, in case I took objection to being harangued.

'It will be,' I assured him. 'Mr and Mrs Perkins will be required to study the list of contents and tell us of any items they know to be missing. I suggest you bring your clients to the Yard tomorrow. You can then proceed to the house, with Sergeant Morris, and they can take a good look round.'

Haynes's gaze was fixed on me steadily now. '*Was* anything unexpected found by the searching officers?'

'A number of gold sovereigns, thirty-two, to be exact. They were hidden in the bedroom.'

'Good grief!' exclaimed Haynes, half rising from his chair in shock. 'That was extremely foolish of Jacobus! Had I had any suspicion that he was taking such a risk, I should have urged him forcefully to take the sovereigns to his bank.'

'His bank being . . .?' I asked.

'Coutts!' said the solicitor curtly.

I looked quickly towards the window and the view of a dusty plane tree outside. It was all I could do not to laugh aloud. I shall miss you, Jacob Jacobus! Villain that you were, you banked with the most distinguished names in the land, at the very best bank.

'There is one more thing I would like to ask about,' I said. 'I understand Mrs Perkins is the sole beneficiary, is that correct?'

'The will has to be proved,' Haynes returned cautiously. 'But when all the formalities are settled, including the investigation into the death being conducted by yourself, yes, Mrs Perkins is sole beneficiary.'

'But there is a codicil, I understand, drawn up two years ago?'

'Ah, yes.' Haynes hesitated. 'Mrs Perkins still inherits everything. However, there are provisions regarding one of the tenants of Mr Jacobus's properties. It concerns the adjoining house, at present used as a dwelling and a place of business, an ironmonger's shop.'

'Ah!' I exclaimed. 'Mr Overmann!'

'Indeed. Mr Overmann's tenancy of the property is protected for twenty years following the death of Mr Jacobus.' He paused and sighed. 'Mr Jacobus did not expect his demise to take place only two years later, of course. The clause is subject to Overmann remaining in a business, not necessarily the present one but a regular business of some sort, and paying the rent on time, subject to the going rate for properties in the area. He must remain of good character and not permit the use of the house for any illegal or immoral purposes.'

Considering that Jacobus himself had conducted some dubious deals of his own from his home, this seemed to me a case of 'don't do as I do; do as I say!' But it was a very generous clause, nevertheless.

'Why?' I asked simply. 'Why so generous to the Overmanns?'

'Mr Jacobus was not an unkind man,' replied Haynes reproachfully. 'Though undeniably an eccentric. Yes, I think it is fair to call him that. I have a suspicion of my own; purely my own, you understand. I am not speaking as his solicitor; but as someone who knew Mr Jacobus, and handled his property transactions over several years.'

He hesitated and seemed unwilling to go on. I decided to chance a question. 'This hasn't anything to do with the ancestor who came to England in the baggage train of William of Orange, by any chance?'

'Ah!' Haynes actually smiled. 'He told you about that, too?'

'I fancy he told everyone he met about it!'

'Just so. I believe he saw in Overmann someone in the mould of his ancestor: willing to leave all; and risk everything in a new country, confident that he would make a success of things here.' Haynes paused. 'Is there anything else I can help you with, Inspector Ross?'

'Not at the moment,' I told him. 'But I am sure we'll speak again soon.'

I left him looking rather unhappy at that prospect.

When I returned to the Yard I was greeted by Wood, who unexpectedly presented the opposite image. He was looking pleased with himself. I had never seen him so cheerful. Well, perhaps not cheerful exactly; we are talking of Sergeant Wood, after all. But definitely less morose than normal.

'I got him,' said Wood. 'Sam Morgan. I ran him to earth straight away. He's waiting for you upstairs.'

'Well done, Sergeant! How about Harry Roxby?'

'On my way to find him now, Mr Ross. Morgan has been very helpful. He says the young fellow is likely to be at a gymnasium in Bethnal Green where the boxers train. Roxby doesn't train there himself, you understand, being an observer, not a participant in the sport. But he meets others there who share his interests. If you ask me,' added Wood, 'that young fellow is heading for trouble. Mixes in rough company. Got no common-sense and too much money.'

'As I understand it, Sergeant, he *loses* too much money. That is generally a recipe for disaster. Time to have a word with him.'

Sam Morgan jumped to his feet as I appeared. He was, as usual, dressed much like a gamekeeper in his Sunday best, and clutched his bowler hat to his chest.

'Sergeant Wood says you want to speak to me again, Mr Ross.' He tipped his head to one side like an alert hound. 'Something new happened? If so, I don't know about it. If I'd heard anything at all, I'd have come in and told you about it, I swear it. Now that I know you're interested! I don't want Scotland Yard saying I've interfered with their investigations, of course I don't. I'm a respectable man myself. I just make my living following about those who aren't so fussy.'

'Don't be alarmed, Sam. Sit down. Now then, are you still being paid by Mr Jeremy Roxby to keep an eye on his son?'

Morgan looked unhappy. 'Yes, I am, Mr Ross, and it's beginning to be more trouble than it's worth. He pays me well, Mr Jeremy Roxby, for my reports. But I'm not easy in my mind, I don't mind telling you.' He contemplated the crown of his hat and gave it a rub with his sleeve. 'I've worn out that much shoe leather on this job, you wouldn't credit it!' he muttered, addressing the hat or perhaps just himself.

'What troubles you, Sam? Not a dangerous job, is it? Playing nursemaid to a foolish young man, who has never shown himself to be anything but harmless?'

173

Morgan leaned forward, fixed me with a bright nervous gaze, and said in a low voice, 'It's the sort of job that starts out all right; but can turn very tricky. I've had 'em before and I get the feel for them. I've got it now.'

'In any particular way, Sam?'

'I'm sitting here, talking to you, aren't I?' retorted Morgan. 'No offence, but once an inquiry starts to involve me with the police, I know it's time for me to think twice about the job. If the young fellow is as harmless as you say, then what's the interest of Scotland Yard in him? Why have I been called in here *twice*?'

I avoided a direct answer to this, instead asking, 'Tell me, Sam, while you have been tailing young Roxby around London, have you ever followed him to Limehouse?'

Sam squinted at me. 'May have done. He goes all over London to places he ought to keep away from.'

'Let me put it another way. Have you ever heard of a dealer in art and curiosities by the name of Jacob Jacobus?'

'He got himself murdered, just the other day!' Morgan said promptly. 'It was in all the London papers. I keep track of all the press reports. I read them at my local library. It helps me in my own investigations.'

'Just so, Sam, and very efficient. But had you heard of Jacobus before his death was reported in the press?'

'Heard of him,' admitted Sam. 'Never had any dealings with him.'

'In what context have you heard of him?'

Morgan was silent for a few moments, thinking out what he should say. It didn't worry him that I realised this, so I waited.

'It's like this, Mr Ross,' began Sam at last. 'Young Harry isn't the first young wastrel I've been asked to keep an eye on. Nor, I dare say, will he be the last. They run true to form, those young fellows. They gamble, they lose money, they order clothes from the top tailors and can't meet the bill. So they ask their fathers or guardians, or some doting old aunt, to pay their debts. But even the most tender-hearted of their friends and relations get to the point where they've had enough, and start to refuse. The young fellows get desperate, they start to pawn, or sell, or borrow money against some piece of jewellery or anything else of value in their possession. Say, a pair of gold cufflinks, or a stickpin. Or, maybe, some trinket bought earlier on the spur of the moment. But now he's lost interest and decides he'd rather he still had the money he paid for it. He could pawn it, but a pawnbroker has a sign over his door. It's the first port of call, if the family gets suspicious.'

That's true, I thought to myself. That's how I caught Obadiah Quigley. He went to a recognised pawnbroker like Carlotti.

'I follow where you're going, Sam,' I said.

'Thought you might!' retorted Morgan with a twinkle briefly in his eye. 'So, then, that's when the youngster in question asks his friends – who are much like himself – where he can go to raise the wind – the cash. But on the quiet, somewhere the family won't go and ask questions. The friends are happy to give him a name or two. Unofficial moneylenders, say, or someone who will buy a gold ring and not ask where it came from.'

'Someone like Jacob Jacobus?'

'You got it!' said Sam, with a nod of approval. 'There's always someone like that. The friends in question have done business with whoever it might be, and they are happy to recommend him. Jacobus will give you a decent price, they say. Any one of us can vouch for you. We'll introduce you.'

'Sam,' I leaned over my desk to emphasise how serious I was. 'You have taken Jeremy Roxby's money and you feel you are obliged to him. I understand that. But it is import-ant that you tell me everything. Did you ever follow young Roxby to Limehouse?'

'I did,' said Sam. The twinkle had gone from his eyes. He stared straight at me.

'To the house of Jacob Jacobus? It stands between an ironmonger's shop and a tavern called the Crossed Keys.'

'I know the place,' admitted Morgan. 'Yes, he went there twice when I was following him. Didn't stay long. I fancy he was expected. He didn't go directly to the house. He walked into the Crossed Keys first. But he didn't stay to drink. He was out again in minutes and he had a key to old man Jacobus's front door. That's what made me think he was expected. Jacobus must have told someone in the tav-ern to give him a key. Young Roxby did shout up to the window first, to let the old fellow know he was on his way up. Then in he went. He stayed only a short time, say thirty minutes, and came out looking very pleased with himself. He went back to the tavern, to return the key, I fancy, because he was only in there a moment. Then off he went as happy as a sandboy.'

'This happened twice?'

'While I was following him, yes. Same procedure, as

you might say. Call at the tavern, come out with a key, shout up to the window to warn Jacobus he was on his way, stay twenty minutes to half an hour at the most. Then out he comes looking like the cat that ate the canary, as I said.'

'And you put this in your report to Jeremy Roxby?'

'Well, I felt obliged to, Inspector. This was what he was paying me for. I played it down as much as I was able. I stressed how short a time young Roxby stayed in the house. I gave it as my opinion he was doing no more than selling some small object, on the quiet. His father was annoyed, I could see that. But it was no more than the sort of thing he already suspected, if you ask me. He didn't seem surprised, just irritated, as if all along he'd suspected the young man of doing something like that to raise a bit of cash. Anyway, Mr Roxby heaved a sigh and struck his fist on the table, muttering to himself about "the young fool".

'After that, he seemed to calm down, because he's a gentleman of means and something big in business. The likes of him don't let themselves down by shouting and carrying on generally in front of the likes of me. They got a reputation to think about and business rivals and so on. It doesn't do to let everyone know he's got troubles. I get about. Word gets about. So he calms down, and thanks me for my efforts. He wanted my assurance I would tell no one about this – about his son going to Jacobus for money – but I dare say he wasn't thinking that the police might request the pleasure of my company to ask about it.'

Sam paused. 'But the police have asked about it, and maybe others have too, because since then, someone has cut the old man's throat. I've had to tell *you*, Inspector! I can't believe it's the sort of thing Harry Roxby would do. I admit, I like the young fellow; and I don't reckon he is a killer. Can't see it. Why should he murder the old man, just because he might have reckoned he was being cheated over the worth of a souvenir of an Italian tour, a Pietro Douro paperweight or trifling *objet de vertu*, as they call it.'

How about an emerald necklace? I thought. Aloud, I told Sam, 'Let's hope you are right. But let me worry about that!'

Morgan frowned. 'So, I am now in a bit of a pickle, aren't I? Am I to report to Mr Jeremy Roxby that you've been making further inquiries of me about his son? Or keep it quiet? He won't like it, if he finds out that what I've told him I've also told you today. I mean, I'm in a corner, professionally speaking, aren't I?'

'Yes, I suppose you are, Sam. You were right to tell his father about Harry's visits to Jacobus. Now Roxby will want to know that you've told me about them. But give me time to question young Harry first. I intend to speak to him today.'

'I knew this job was going to turn bad on me,' said Sam glumly.

Just after half past two that afternoon, Biddle appeared with Daisy. She had dressed for the occasion. Even her hair was tidy. For her, this was clearly an outing. She wore a plaid skirt, a closely fitted black jacket and a little round pillbox hat atop her red curls. I could not have asked more of any witness. I had a short conversation with her and was more than pleased with what she told me. I then left her to

Biddle, who seated her in a shadowy corner nook where the corridor turned. She sat there quite happily with her hands folded, closely watching each passer-by.

At five minutes past three, Harry Roxby, escorted by a constable from the desk at the entrance downstairs, walked nonchalantly past her without taking any notice of her at all. He entered my office and declared: 'Here I am, Inspector! Just as you requested. I must ask you to excuse my slight tardiness, but the streets are very busy.'

'Thank you for coming, Mr Roxby,' I replied. 'Please sit down.'

So far, so friendly. I had a suspicion this pleasant atmosphere would soon change.

'I asked you to come this afternoon because I have reason to believe that you have paid at least two visits to a location in Limehouse, a house next door to the Crossed Keys tavern. It belonged to Jacob Jacobus at the time of your visits. It is now a murder scene. I am talking to everyone who had business there recently.'

'Who says I visited the old man?' snapped Harry.

'Do you deny it?'

He hesitated but decided to brazen it out. In the circumstances he could do little else. 'What reason do you have for saying I called at that place?'

'No, no, Mr Roxby,' I reproached him. 'I have my ways of finding these things out; and I am not obliged to reveal them to you at this stage.'

'Unless you tell me,' retorted Harry, 'you may ask me as many questions as you choose. I shall refuse to reply unless my family's solicitor is present.'

'That is probably very prudent of you, Mr Roxby. It is also curious. Such caution suggests to me you have good reason to conceal the nature of these visits, if not from me, then from your father. Mr Jacobus was a known receiver of stolen goods and sometime moneylender.'

'It is that quaint old fellow, Morgan, whom my father pays to snoop on me, isn't it?' demanded Harry. 'He has told you this!'

I ignored this question to say, 'You called at the tavern for the key to the front door. They would not have given it to you unless they had instructions from Jacobus to do so.'

Harry slumped back in his chair. 'Oh, so it is someone at the tavern who has told you about me. But they couldn't know my name!'

'You are easily described, Mr Roxby.'

He was recovering from his first shock. 'I'm not so different from a dozen other fellows. Put me face to face with your witness!'

'Very well, if you insist . . .' I rang the bell on my desk.

He hadn't expected me to comply with his demand so easily or so quickly.

'Sir?' inquired Biddle, appearing in the doorway.

'Bring in the witness, if you would, Sergeant.'

When Daisy marched in, smiling cheerfully, I almost felt sorry for young Roxby. His jaw dropped. I think perhaps, for a moment, he didn't recognise her in her best clothes. But she recognised him all right.

'Hullo, dearie,' she greeted him. 'Funny old place to meet again, ain't it? Scotland Yard, eh?'

'Why, she works at the tavern!' he exclaimed, half rising from his chair.

'Miss Smith does indeed work at the Crossed Keys tavern. But she also looked after Mr Jacobus. Perhaps, Miss Smith, you would be so good as to tell this gentleman what you told me.'

'Well, now,' began Daisy, settling to her tale. 'Amongst other things, I changed the bed linen for Mr Jacobus, and took anything requiring laundering to the washerwoman. Then I made up the bed with fresh linen. I'd done that on the day I heard you come into the house.' She nodded towards Harry, whose bravado had vanished. He had begun to look nervous. 'I was upstairs, in the bedroom, like I said. So I peeped round the newel post to see who the visitor was. You must have got the key from Tom at the pub. Up the stairs you came and went into the parlour to talk to the old man. I carried on with my work. I had just come out of the bedroom with my arms full of dirty linen when I heard the parlour door open on the floor below me, and voices. I stopped, just round the corner again. Out you came, still making your goodbyes to Mr Jacobus. I had a good view of you. But you never thought to look up, or you might have seen me. I dare say you were in a hurry to leave. I reckon you got what you came for, because you looked pretty pleased with yourself. Sell him something, did you? Anyway, off you went. I carried on downstairs. The parlour door was still open; and I could see Mr J, sat in his chair and looking at something in the palm of his hand, something small. What did you sell him? A ring? Bits of jewellery are very popular things for young gentlemen like yourself when they are hard up, and want to raise a bit of cash on the quiet. I called out to let Mr J know I was leaving and ask if he wanted anything else, before I went. He just called back, "No, Daisy, thank you!" and never bothered to look up.'

She stared thoughtfully at Harry Roxby and added, 'I'll miss the old feller, and so will you and your pals among the fancy, I reckon. You'll have to raise the cash somewhere else!'

Listening to all this, the wretched Harry looked quite deflated. He said nothing.

'Thank you, Daisy,' I told her. 'Please go with Constable Biddle and tell him what you have told me. He will write it down in a statement that you can sign, or make your mark to. Thank you for coming in.'

'Always happy to oblige!' chirped Daisy and followed Biddle out of my office.

Young Roxby made an effort to pull himself together. 'Very well, I admit I called on Jacobus two or three times. My father, as you must have realised, had been digging in his heels and refusing to pay my debts. In the past, I've managed to talk him round eventually. He's afraid of the scandal, you see. That kind of thing doesn't do in business. But it has been getting more and more difficult. Some of the fellows I know, they told me about Jacobus. Look here, Ross, I know the old man is dead. Worse, he's been murdered! But *I* certainly didn't kill him. I swear it. I wouldn't know how to go about such a – a grisly business, anyway.'

'His throat was cut. Anyone can do that,' I told him. 'And the opinion of the doctor, who came to certify the death, was that it was an amateurish attack. Very untidy, but effective.'

Harry shuddered. He was beginning to perspire and took out a handkerchief to wipe his brow. 'This is a nightmare! The whole thing is foul! I couldn't do it, not cut a throat; I don't care what you say. Why would I, anyway? Old Jacobus was pretty useful. I never stole any of the things I sold him. They belonged to me; and if I wanted to sell any of them, I was free to do so, and committed no crime. You have my word on it – if you are willing to take my word. Probably you're not, being a policeman. Crooks lie to you all the time, I dare say.'

'Yes, they do,' I agreed.

'Well, I'm not a crook! I repeat, nothing I sold the old fellow was stolen. They were all things belonging to me. Cravat pins, rings, that sort of knick-knack.'

What it is to be born into wealth! I thought. Expensive items of jewellery regarded as knick-knacks, to be disposed of casually to settle gaming debts. Again, my mind was drawn irresistibly to the missing necklace. That would settle many an outstanding debt of honour. But Harry would need to get his hands on it. And that, sadly, was where a seventeen-year-old girl who doted on him might hold the answer.

'For the sake of argument, Mr Roxby, let us imagine how much more money might be raised if a far more valuable piece of jewellery were sold. A necklace, for example, usually kept in a safe; but taken out to be worn that evening. However, the proposed wearer refuses to display it. When she is alone for a moment, she drops it from the window to the garden below. There waiting to pick it up is the young man she is so anxious to help.'

Harry had turned deathly pale and apparently lost the power of speech. He shook his head.

'Now then, Mr Roxby,' I told him, 'I realise you attended a very good school and must know your Latin. You will be familiar with the phase *cui bono*?'

'Who benefits . . .' whispered Harry. He made a determined attempt to get back his self-control, but with only partial success. 'I swear, I would never involve my cousin in such a sordid plot. Nor did I steal that blasted emerald necklace! It's not the sort of thing I could have taken to a canny old bird like Jacobus. He would be far too wary to touch it.'

'Yes, you are probably right,' I agreed. 'But, well, you must consider my point of view. Murder has been committed for quite trivial reasons. I know of several such cases.'

'I didn't – didn't do any of it,' stammered Harry. 'Are you really going to charge me with this murder? For pity's sake, I told you, I couldn't kill a man.'

I had frightened the young wretch sufficiently.

'I am making no charges at this time. I shall require you to sign a statement before you leave, Mr Roxby.'

'Yes, yes, whatever you want!' he replied impatiently, but he looked relieved. Then anxiety took hold of him again. 'Look here, are you going to tell my father about this visit?'

'I am not paid to report on you to your father, Mr Roxby. But I very strongly suggest you tell him yourself of your visit here, and include what you have told me this afternoon.

You might also consider changing your ways, now you see how your actions might be misconstrued.'

'Yes, yes, I suppose I must tell my father . . .' he muttered. 'Gosh, he's going to be jolly furious!'

Furious, certainly, I thought. Jolly? I don't think so.

Before the end of the day, I had more visitors. Mr and Mrs Perkins arrived, accompanied by their solicitor, Haynes. Mr Perkins looked apprehensive; Mrs Perkins was unusually subdued. Haynes, I fancied, looked a little sullen. I imagine he had had a difficult conversation with his clients.

'As I told you was my intention, Inspector Ross, I have brought Mr and Mrs Perkins to see you – and explain about the key,' he declared in a wooden tone.

'We are indeed very sorry if it has caused any inconvenience to your inquiries, Inspector Ross. We should not, with hindsight, have failed to give the key into your keeping,' said Wilfred Perkins. 'My wife and I were in such a state of shock that morning. The terrible news, the rush to catch the earliest possible train from Leeds to London . . . I assure you, there is nothing sinister in our overlooking the key, left with sundry documents in the charge of Mr Haynes. I could have kept it in Leeds. But it seemed safer and more sensible to leave it with Mr Haynes in London. Then, when we got to the house and found it guarded . . . Well, clearly you had a key already. We just saw no purpose in giving you our key.'

I wasn't putting up with this nonsense. I hadn't accepted it from Haynes earlier that morning; and I wasn't going to accept it from Perkins now.

'On the morning we met before the house,' I said sternly,

'you clearly gave me to understand you had no key. You were demanding the one the police held.'

'Well,' muttered Perkins, 'we were in something of a panic. We were bereaved. My wife had lost her father. Mr Haynes said there was no need to bother you.'

Haynes had been sitting silently after his opening words but now had to put up a defence. It was the same one he'd presented to me that morning. 'At the time, I felt it in my clients' best interests.'

'We didn't go into the house!' Mrs Perkins suddenly burst out. The long period of silence had clearly been unnatural to her and cost her much effort. 'We couldn't, could we? Not with that great black-bearded lummox . . .'

'My dear, my dear!' cried Perkins in distress, seizing her arm. 'You are speaking of a police officer.'

'He was still a big lummox!' declared Maggie Perkins. 'And he made no effort to explain the situation to us at all. Just stood there, with no more movement in him than Nelson's column, and said we couldn't go in. It was mortifying. And there was my poor father, lying dead in some morgue, all stabbed about with a knife.'

'His throat was cut, Maggie,' said Perkins pedantically, and unwisely. 'He wasn't stabbed, not all over.'

At least I had been successful in dismissing the image of a lion mauling its prey from his head.

'For heaven's sake, Wilfred! That doesn't make it any better, does it?' retorted his spouse. 'What's more, we've still not been able to make any inventory; and *now* we learn that gold sovereigns were found in the house and have been removed. Where are they, pray?'

'In safe keeping, Mrs Perkins, I assure you,' I told her. 'They are a possible motive for the mur— the attack on Mr Jacobus. Someone may have known he kept money about the house. He did occasionally act as an unofficial moneylender.'

'As if things weren't bad enough!' grumbled Mrs Perkins. '*Moneylending!* It's in the Bible as an ungodly occupation. Suppose they hear about that in Leeds? Our Lord chased the moneylenders out of the temple, didn't he? What other disgraceful business was Papa mixed up in, I wonder.'

I confess this met with silence on the part of all three of us. We could all have answered, I suppose, but discretion seemed the better part of valour.

'We understand,' said Wilfred Perkins timidly, 'that thirty-two gold sovereigns, in all, were found in the bedroom.'

'Exactly so, sir. They are safe. The officer in charge of the search of the premises drew up a complete inventory of pictures, ornaments and general knick-knacks. You will be asked to examine it carefully, and let us know if any item is missing that you know for a fact ought to be there.'

'Unlike the sovereigns that we didn't know *were* there, and have been removed!' snapped Mrs Perkins.

'Maggie, Maggie, my dear . . . Keep calm.'

Eventually they left. Haynes did linger to ask quietly, 'Were any of the items you mention, pictures, ornaments and so on, known to be unlawfully in Mr Jacobus's possession?' He could not bring himself to speak the words 'stolen property', it seemed.

'Not so far!' I told him briskly, in case he thought the matter closed.

'You see,' he said unhappily, 'Mrs Perkins doesn't know . . . doesn't know everything.'

'I don't know everything about this affair, either, Mr Haynes,' I replied. 'But I am working hard to find it all out.'

Elizabeth Martin Ross

I was busy with my household accounts that afternoon when I heard the clip-clop of hooves and rattle of wheels. The noise stopped outside my front door. I stood up hurriedly and went to the window. I was too late to catch sight of the passenger who had alighted from the hansom cab. But the rat-tat at the front door told me I had a caller. Shortly afterwards, Bessie came in, holding out the little tray that sat on a table in the hall for the reception of visitors' cards. Admittedly the tray's presence was conventional rather than practical, because I seldom receive formal calls. But today's caller was someone out of the ordinary, because there was a card lying on it. Picking it up, I read the name: *Ariadne Chalk*.

Now then, this was curious indeed. 'Please show Miss Chalk in, Bessie,' I said.

There could not be more than one Ariadne Chalk come to call on me. It must be the companion to Mrs Roxby. But why? Had she been sent, or had she come on an errand of her own? It could hardly be a social call of the usual sort.

Ben had described her to me as middle aged, slightly built, and plain. It was not a flattering description but I saw, when she entered, that it was accurate. I also felt a twinge of sympathy with her because there but for the grace of God, as they say, stood I, who had once depended on Aunt Parry for a roof over my head.

'Thank you for seeing me, Mrs Ross,' she said. 'I am sorry to disturb you.' She spoke rather abruptly, and I put that down to nervousness.

'Not at all! Please sit down,' I urged her. 'Bessie, bring us some tea. You will take tea, Miss Chalk?'

Bessie had been hovering in the doorway, eyes bright with curiosity, but instantly disappeared towards the kitchen. Distant sounds of the scrape of a chair leg across the tiled floor, and the rattle of porcelain teacups, indicated that she was standing on the chair to take out the best tea service from the highest cupboard shelf. I hoped she remembered to rinse the dust from them.

'I fear I am disturbing you, Mrs Ross. I believe you may know who I am.'

'Well, yes, I do,' I admitted, somewhat embarrassed.

The visitor had accepted the invitation to be seated but was still hesitant. I would have to find a way to put her at her ease. I admit, I was very curious to know why she had come all the way from Hampstead to call on me.

'You are companion to Mrs Roxby, are you not?' I replied and smiled. 'Have you come all the way from Hampstead by cab?'

'Oh, no!' she exclaimed. 'Only by cab from Broad Street Station. I took the train from Hampstead Heath Station into Broad Street. It was quite exciting.' Her whole manner and expression had brightened. 'The rail link is still very new and already very popular, I'm told. Many of those who live in the city now take advantage of it to make day trips to Hampstead. I suppose it appears like a visit to the country to them. Of course, Mrs Roxby would never travel by it. But she has gone to yet another whist party this afternoon. I took the opportunity . . .'

Her voice tailed away and she flushed. Perhaps she feared I thought her a chatterbox. From what Ben had told me of the lady I was sure she was not. To undertake the novel expedition by train, and unaccompanied, took courage. It could only mean she had a specific purpose in calling on me. She was also anxious that her employer should not know of it.

'I was once a lady's companion myself, to Mrs Julia Parry,' I said encouragingly. 'Do you know if Mrs Parry will be attending the same party as Mrs Roxby is attending today?'

'To the best of my knowledge, no, Mrs Ross. I don't think Mrs Parry will be there. The whist party is being held in Hampstead.'

That's a relief, I thought.

My visitor seemed to relax. 'I was told that you held the post of a lady's companion, Mrs Ross. The knowledge gave me the resolve to call on you. Otherwise I should not have been so bold, and I confess it freely. But Mrs Roxby being out this afternoon left me free. I thought I might not get another such opportunity.' She paused again and resumed, 'It is through a whist party that Mrs Roxby learned, from Mrs Parry, that you are married to Inspector Ross. The inspector is in charge of the search for the missing necklace known in the family as "the Roxby emeralds". You know all about that.'

'I do know of the theft,' I agreed. 'I understand there is still no clue as to the whereabouts of the necklace.' Was that why she was here? To find out what progress Ben had made in his inquiries?

Miss Chalk leaned forward and burst out passionately, 'Oh, Mrs Ross! You cannot imagine what trouble this necklace has given!'

Bessie arrived at that point with the tea, and the half of a sponge cake that was all that was left in the tin. But the best tea service gleamed.

'Sorry, there's no more cake, missis,' she said. 'I didn't know you were expecting company or I'd have made some jam tarts.'

This was an unfortunate speech at a moment when the visitor was just getting over her nerves. I saw poor Ariadne Chalk look distressed.

'It's all right, Bessie, just leave us,' I urged. When she'd gone, I said to my visitor, 'Please excuse the maid. She's a very good girl, but apt to speak her mind. I am sorry I cannot offer you better fare.'

'It's my fault,' whispered Miss Chalk, now looking quite dejected. 'I came unexpectedly . . . It has put you to trouble.'

'Oh, please don't blame yourself!' I begged her. 'I am delighted to receive a visitor. Otherwise I should have nothing but the grocery and butcher's bills to occupy me for the next hour. Now then, please try a piece of this sponge. It did turn out rather well, though I say it myself. And then let me know how I may help you.'

I was pleased to see my visitor appear to relax again. I realised it had taken courage on her part to knock at my front door. This was not an idle visit. Something worried her. As is often the way when someone has gathered up the courage for a difficult task, she plunged at once into the reason for her call, speaking a little jerkily, as if she feared she might lose her resolve.

'I do know that you've met Bella Gray. Oh, thank you.' Miss Chalk accepted the slice of sponge I held out. 'She is an impetuous child sometimes. Arranging to visit Mrs Parry, as she did, and asking Mrs Parry to invite you, so that she might pour out her worries . . . I was really cross with Bella, and I told her she must never do anything like that again. The fact is, she is very fond of that young wastrel, Harry Roxby. She is so afraid he will be blamed for the loss of the necklace. He isn't responsible for its disappearance, Mrs Ross, truly he isn't!'

'You seem very sure, Miss Chalk. I'm glad to hear he isn't involved. But may I ask why you are so certain?'

Her pale cheeks flushed. 'Please believe me, Mrs Ross, when I tell you that I have no kindly feelings towards Harry. He gambles, you know, and wagers money on horse races and prizefights. He is of no account whatever, and I do feel quite sorry for his father. He, Harry, is expected to take over the reins of the company eventually, you see, and he is totally unsuitable. But he is not – not a *thief*!'

She sighed and added, quite briskly: 'He hasn't the brains for it! Nor has he the resourcefulness or strength of character to plan the theft of something that holds great significance to his family. Besides, whatever would he do with it, if he did steal it? He wouldn't know how to dispose of it. He'd be too frightened to take it to a really important receiver of stolen goods. No one would ever give him more than a fraction of its worth and besides, they would not want Harry's business anyway. He's clearly such a muddle-head; and would be likely to confess to his father at any time.'

I reflected that this echoed what Ben had told me. Professional fences do not like to deal with amateur thieves.

Ariadne Chalk sipped her tea and then set down the cup. It rattled in the saucer. Her nerves were still not altogether under control.

'This may be difficult for you to believe, Mrs Ross. But the strongest argument against the young man being involved in the theft is, above all, that Harry is a *Roxby*. He has grown up knowing the significance of the necklace. It is the belief of the whole family that the fortune of the shipping business is tied to the emeralds. The necklace is the guarantor of its good fortune, of its prosperity. That may sound like romantic nonsense, but the necklace is the tangible witness to the history of the firm. It belonged to the founder's wife. It *is* quite a romantic history, in fact. The lady was Brazilian and very beautiful indeed. I have seen her portrait. Harry wouldn't be party to its loss! He is a fool, but not an insensitive fool. There!' She fell silent, folded her hands in her lap, and stared at me, flushed and defiant.

'Yes, I do see,' I told her. Of all the arguments she had put forward in Harry's defence, this last one made the greatest impression on me. 'What you have told me makes perfect sense to me. I do understand how concerned you are for Miss Gray. I must tell you I found her charming when I met her at Mrs Parry's home. But perhaps impetuous, as the young can be.'

My visitor had been nodding agreement with my last words. I was emboldened to ask, 'Have you any theory of your own about the disappearance of the jewels?'

'No, none!' she replied quickly. 'I think Inspector Ross suspects a ladder gang. There have been such robberies in the neighbourhood. Many of the houses are large and secluded. But, but I don't know. I really cannot suggest any answer.'

Her pale cheeks had flushed and she had begun to fidget with a little crocheted purse that hung by a cord from her wrist. There had been a distinct change in her demeanour. Perhaps she was regretting the impulse to come and see me. I realised that she was suddenly anxious to leave. But whether she had achieved her purpose in calling on me, I was not sure.

'I do thank you sincerely, Mrs Ross, for listening to me. Will you tell Inspector Ross what I have said?' She peered at me anxiously.

'I most certainly shall,' I assured her. At the same time, I couldn't help but wonder if she were short sighted. If so, why didn't she wear spectacles? Had this anything to do with her employer?

My visitor drew a deep breath. 'As you held that post in a household yourself, you will understand a companion's duty to be loyal to one's employer. Also, to be frank, comfortable situations are not easily come by.'

'I do understand, Miss Chalk,' I assured her.

She hesitated again. 'It can make life very difficult!' she added abruptly.

Yes! I thought, that is why she doesn't wear spectacles. She fears Mrs Roxby will begin to consider a replacement. She also fears that Mrs Roxby will return home from her whist party and, finding her companion absent, ask where she had been.

'If you are worried that my husband will tell Mrs Roxby you have called here today, I will ask him not to divulge it,' I promised. 'I am sure he will understand.'

'It is both a gift, and sometimes a burden, to understand others,' she said sadly.

At that moment, I confess a surge of respect for her, even admiration. But I still wondered what had really brought her; and what, now she was here, she had decided not to tell me. I couldn't help but sense she had not achieved what she had come to do.

'How will you return to Broad Street Station?' I asked. 'I assume you will take the train again, back to Hampstead.'

'Oh, yes, I bought a return ticket. I see you are near to Waterloo Station here. I will surely be able to take a cab to Broad Street Station from there.'

'I will send Bessie with you,' I told her. 'It isn't pleasant to walk alone in an unknown area of London, however busy it might be.'

'You are very kind,' she said gratefully.

And life, on the whole, had not been so very kind to her, I thought sadly.

Bessie was more than pleased to have a reason to leave

the house and her daily chores for a brief spell. I hoped Miss Chalk was able to make the return journey to Hampstead without any problems, and arrive home before Mrs Roxby, who must be something of a demon whist player, returned.

Later, when Ben returned home that evening, I told him all about Miss Chalk's visit.

'Good Lord!' he exclaimed. 'That is certainly an unexpected ingredient in the mix.' He frowned. 'She was far from anxious to confide in me when I called at the Hampstead house with Wood, to interview the staff. Perhaps I should have taken you along with me, instead of the sergeant.'

'I can't honestly say she confided in me, Ben. But I think she wanted to do so. Her courage failed her – or her fear of losing her place.'

'Yet she came,' murmured Ben. 'She did not have the courage to come to Scotland Yard and speak to me, or any other officer there. Yet she was desperate to speak to someone.'

'I believe she is very fond of Isabella Gray,' I said. 'Or "Bella", as she calls her. She appears to have been Mrs Roxby's companion for many years and must have watched the young child grow up in the Roxby household. Her chief wish, I am sure, is to protect Miss Gray, rather than any desire to shield Harry Roxby. She has the poorest opinion of him! But she does not believe he is party to the loss of the emeralds. Do you think he is?'

'I find it impossible to give you a straight answer to that, Lizzie,' he told me. 'But let me tell you what puzzles me most about this whole business. The Roxby emeralds themselves, the cause of so much dismay, appear to have disappeared completely. We, at the Yard, have put out word to all our sources. But we've received not a squeak in response. Have we missed some clue? Every time Reynolds runs into me, he makes some remark on my failure to track them down. It really annoys me. He knows that, and that's why he does it. I can't share his sense of humour; but he is absolutely correct. My inquiries so far have progressed not a jot. Not even any false information has been given to us! It is as though the emeralds have disappeared in a puff of smoke, as in a music-hall turn. A real magician's trick. I've never liked watching those fellows work, you know?'

'Which fellows, magicians?' I asked in surprise.

'Exactly. I know it is a trickery, or sleight of hand, when they make objects disappear, saw a woman in half, produce a rabbit from a hat. They have perfected the deception. They know they are ahead of me, and the rest of the audience, because we can't see how it is done.'

Ben smiled. 'Put it like this, Lizzie, I don't like being fooled, especially when I *know* I am being fooled. Somewhere, in all this, there is someone who is playing the role of the magician. He is mocking me, and I won't have it!'

'Ben,' I said, 'I do believe that Ariadne Chalk is very frightened.'

'Of what – or of whom?' he asked. 'Of the Roxby female? Or is it of the police that she is afraid?'

'I don't know, because she couldn't bring herself to tell me. But I feel sure she came here this afternoon with a specific purpose; and it was not merely to protect Harry Roxby.

Ann Granger

But, at the last moment, her courage failed her. I know that, as a police officer, you like evidence.' I smiled at him. 'I have none. I have only an instinct about it.'

'Lizzie, my dear,' he said, taking my hand. 'Believe me when I tell you that I have as much respect for your instinct as I would have for the best of evidence. But, alas, I cannot produce your instinct in court.'

198

Chapter Ten

Elizabeth Martin Ross

MISS CHALK, I learned the following day, was not the only person anxious to confide in me. A gangling boy in a page's uniform, a little too short in the jacket arms and trouser legs, brought a note mid-morning from the Railway Hotel. Mrs Perkins would be very grateful if I could find a little time to take tea with her that afternoon at three.

The parlour of the hotel was as dismal as it had appeared on my previous visit. As yet, no one had dusted the aspidistra leaves. There was a lingering odour of boiled vegetables that must be a memory of the previous evening's dinner fare. I wondered briefly why, since their stay in London was proving longer than they might have first expected, the Perkinses did not move to a more pleasant location. They could well afford it. The answer must be that they were not only lodging here. They were hiding here. At a better hotel, they might be more noticeable; and fellow guests more curious. They might even have been asked to leave when the lurid newspaper stories proliferated and their connection with a case of murder was realised. Here, on the other hand, fellow guests came and went rapidly, the majority staying only one night. They arrived tired late in the day; and left in the morning in a rush to catch their trains. Few, if any, cared about anyone else.

I thought that Mrs Perkins looked dejected. She had certainly lost her battle-ready demeanour.

'Very good of you to come, Mrs Ross,' she greeted me.

'This must all be a great strain on you and your husband,' I sympathised.

'You can't believe how much!' She heaved a deep sigh. 'It will take me months, *months*, to get over it. If ever I do get over it! I'll never be the same woman, there! You can believe it.'

'Courage, Mrs Perkins,' I urged her. 'You strike me as a lady with true strength of purpose. Don't be cast down!'

She brightened. 'Very good of you to say so, Mrs Ross.'

The same depressed maid appeared as on my previous visit. She brought tea and, as we were now in the afternoon, also a modestly sized fruit cake with scorched almonds stuck haphazardly round the surface.

'Look at that!' grumbled Maggie Perkins, pointing at the cake. 'You could mend a hole in the roof with that. I don't know who made it, but she didn't have a light hand, that's for sure. If you were taking tea with me at home in Leeds, Mrs Ross, I wouldn't dream of offering you such a wretched pretence of a Dundee cake. But beggars can't be choosers, I suppose.'

I did blink at that. I wouldn't have described Maggie or her husband as beggars. I understood them to be in comfortable circumstances in Leeds. Moreover, according to

Ben, and to what I had read in the newspapers, Mr Jacobus had left his only child a fortune.

'The cake will taste better than it looks, I'm sure,' I declared.

'Are you?' countered Maggie, unwilling to find solace in anything. 'I have no such hopes. I suppose, Mrs Ross, that Inspector Ross has told you about the key?'

I took my time before replying, not only because of the sudden change of subject; but because I did not want her to think Ben discussed every aspect of all his cases with me. He had told me about the key to the building in Limehouse, discovered to have been in the possession of Haynes, the solicitor. I replied diplomatically that I understood a front-door key to the Limehouse property had unexpectedly turned up.

'He had it all along, that lawyer fellow!' snapped Maggie. 'And my husband knew he had it. But *I* didn't know he had it. How should I? I never came down to London to visit my papa.'

It perhaps struck her that this did not cast her in the best light. She added, 'I considered doing so many times, but, for the sake of my dear late mother, I couldn't do it. But I never asked myself how Wilfred got into the house when he went to see Papa. He never told me. He would simply say he had called on my father, who appeared in good health. He certainly never told me he saw any suspicious persons lurking outside. However, to my mind, now that I have visited the district for myself, all the people in that part of London look suspicious. Some of those Wilfred assures me are seamen, from the foreign ships, look more like pirates! How do you pick out a potential murderer among so many ruffians? As far as I knew, we had no key to the house in any drawer in our house in Leeds. I must beg you to tell Inspector Ross that, if anyone has been less than frank in all this, it is that lawyer. Mr Perkins and I are not to blame.'

You are frightened, I thought to myself. That is what is behind this invitation to take tea with her this afternoon. I felt sorry for her, because she was genuinely unhappy. Perhaps she really had not known about the key held by the solicitor. But, as Ben had said, the fact that they had all gone to the house expecting to be able to enter it did suggest they had been confident of doing so. And it did seem that Haynes had not known that a key had been held at the tavern. That was odd. But the whole affair was very odd. I did wonder what manner of recriminations had been heaped on poor Wilfred Perkins's head.

'You have seen the newspapers?' demanded Maggie now. She pointed to a rack on the parlour wall where the day's newspapers were displayed. 'Everybody in London must have done so. They are full of the most lurid nonsense about my late father and his terrible death! You'd think nothing else was happening in the entire world. Isn't there a war somewhere they can write about? Isn't Parliament doing anything worthy of comment? I understand this to be an active social season in London, but there are hardly any reports on that. If there is any other news, no one would be the wiser. It is all about us, and my poor father's horrible demise, and vicious gossip.'

'The press, and the readers, like a crime story,' I told

her. 'Something else will happen soon; and their interest will change. It will prove a case of a nine-day wonder, you will see. Then you will be left in peace.'

Maggie looked undecided as to whether to be encouraged at the thought of being left in peace by reporters or insulted that any other affair might take precedence over her own troubles.

'I have never cared for London,' she announced. 'It's another reason why I never came down to visit Papa. It is full of immorality and vice!'

Mm, yes, I thought. The late Mr Jacobus might have known something about that.

Inspector Ben Ross

The gruesome murder of Jacob Jacobus had indeed seized the public imagination, especially that section of it which reads cheap paperback fiction, the 'penny dreadfuls' so loved by Walter Biddle. I could understand why. It did, as newspapermen like to say, have 'everything'. The victim himself had been a man of mystery in so many ways. Professional artists employed to illustrate such stories produced endless pictorial scenes of the crime – as they imagined it must have looked. The old, quaint house, its exotic (so the press described it) Limehouse location, the revelation of how wealthy the victim had been (that was the speculation of much excited theory), the discovery of a daughter (sadly, for the copywriters, neither very young nor beautiful), of whom no one had known anything; other than the wretched Haynes, of course. The solicitor must not be enjoying the notoriety his normally humdrum chambers had acquired. If it was worrying Haynes, serve him right! He must have known he was dealing with a ticking timebomb of a client in Jacobus. But perhaps we, at the Yard, should have been aware of it too.

'See here, Ross!' grumbled Superintendent Dunn, pointing at the front page of the latest edition of some scandal sheet, lying on his desk. 'These press fellows have been asking around. They have got hold of the information that you – and yes, you are named, Ross! – that you used to pay visits to the old devil. Look at this!' Dunn thumped the offending newsprint. ' "*How much did Scotland Yard know of the mysterious life of Jacob Jacobus?*" Well? How much did you know, Ross?'

'Not enough, apparently,' I admitted.

'The press certainly doesn't, because the reporters are making it up. Look! "*Was Jacobus a secret agent?*" A secret agent for whom? Reporting what? Find out who killed him, Ross. That is the only way to put a stop to this – this lurid rubbish!'

'Yes, sir, I am doing my best, sir.'

'Your best isn't good enough this time, Ross. This must be cleared up quickly.'

I retired 'in good order', as they say. As I walked back to my own office, I could hear Dunn still grumbling to himself aloud. 'Exotic? What is exotic about Limehouse, pray? Drinking and opium dens, dance halls, seamen's missions—'

I closed the door and cut off the rest.

For the next thirty-six hours, very little did happen. The day following Dunn's outburst about press reports on the case of Jacobus's murder was a Sunday. The weather was fine and perhaps everyone, including the wrongdoers of London, took a break from day-to-day activities. Perhaps some of them, like Miss Chalk, had taken advantage of the new rail link with Hampstead, and were disporting themselves innocently on the Heath.

A policeman, too, earns his day off. Lizzie and I went down to Putney, walked a little in the woodland there and ate an excellent luncheon at a pleasant riverside restaurant. It was the following Monday morning that a storm broke, though not a weather-related one. It was in the case; and the first event was both unexpected and tragic.

I arrived at the Yard to find Wood awaiting me with impatience. 'We've had an urgent message from Hampstead Division, sir!'

'What is it?' I asked sharply.

Before Wood could answer, Dunn strode from his office into the corridor to speak to me, a rare occurrence. I was usually summoned to his lair.

'Ross! Has the sergeant informed you?'

'He was just starting—' I was interrupted.

'You and he are to get over to Hampstead at once!'

'Yes, sir, but what—?'

'A woman's body has been found on the Heath. Well, don't linger here, Ross! Off you go!'

'I'll bring you up to date on the way, Mr Ross,' promised Wood. 'We are to be met at the new rail station they have there now, Hampstead Heath Station, it's called.'

'Well, what is all this about?' I demanded as the train rocked its way around London towards our destination. I would rather have hired a cab, as on our first trip. In a cab, one can have a private conversation. Not always so, in a railway carriage; although, at this time of the morning, we were fortunate enough to find one that was empty for most of the way.

'The body was discovered early this morning by a retired military gent, resident in the area,' Wood told me. 'He was walking his dog. Does so every morning apparently. To be precise, the dog found the body. Inspector Hawkins, of Hampstead Division, tells us the old gentleman recognised the dead woman, or claims he does.'

'Give a name?'

'Yes, sir. If the old soldier is correct, we also know her.' Wood gave me a sidelong, somewhat apprehensive, look. 'The witness identified her as a Miss Ariadne Chalk—'

'Dear Heaven!' I whispered. 'Of all people . . . What was she doing out on the Heath so early?'

'Body appears to have lain there overnight, sir.'

'Then, if she was missing last night, why on earth did Mrs Roxby not raise the alarm?'

'Don't know,' said Wood frankly. 'Mind you, Mr Ross, the military gent might be mistaken.'

'Yes, yes, that's certainly possible.' I had an unhappy premonition that the informant was not wrong. But such a tragic event following so soon on Miss Chalk's visit to my wife, and Lizzie's belief that her visitor had wanted to confide something, but that her courage had failed her . . . What was I to think?

Aloud, I said to Wood, 'If he is an old campaigner, he

will have seen his share of corpses. He will have been shocked, but he would have kept his wits about him.'

A uniformed constable was awaiting us at Hampstead and we soon found ourselves in a cab, being borne towards the scene of the crime.

The location was a patch of brambles and stunted trees, such as were dotted around the heathland, a short distance from one of the winding footpaths across the area. I made a quick mental estimation of the distance from Mrs Roxby's house. It could not be more than a ten-minute walk, even for a middle-aged lady at night, perhaps even less for a fit man.

'She must have had a lantern of some sort,' said Wood unexpectedly. 'Without one, she could have tripped and fallen, or her skirts might have got caught up on the bushes, if she left the marked path. I don't know why she would have done that at night, but she does appear to have left the path. Unless, of course, her body was dragged away from it by her killer, in order to conceal it.'

'The Roxby house is over there.' I nodded in the general direction. 'You'd better retrace her steps and time the walk.'

As always, following the discovery of a body, and the time it had taken us to reach the place, a crowd had assembled and was being kept away from the area by a pair of increasingly desperate young constables. At the murder site itself, there was also a good deal of activity. We couldn't see the body, because that was presumably still lying where it had been found. But a police photographer had arrived ahead of us and had been busy. He was now trudging towards us with his equipment balanced on his shoulder. An elderly gentleman of military mien stood a little way off, holding the leash of a spaniel dog and speaking to another constable who was writing down what he said. A uniformed inspector, whom I assumed to be Hawkins, had spied us, and came to meet us.

'Inspector Ross?'

I shook the hand he held out. 'Inspector Hawkins? We came as quickly as we could. This is Sergeant Wood.'

'It's a bad business,' Hawkins told us in a low voice. 'It's always worse when the victim is a woman. What makes it even worse is that this would appear to be a respectable lady, well known to many of the householders in the area. The gentleman over there . . .' Hawkins pointed to the military man, 'is Major Richards. He lives locally, retired, of course. His spaniel, which was running loose, came upon the body and would not return to heel when its master called to it. So the major went to investigate; and came upon the dreadful scene. It was made worse by his being able to recognise the victim.'

'How did he know her?'

'As I say, he lives locally. The victim, he says, is a Miss Chalk who is – was – companion to another local resident, Mrs Roxby. The major is a member of a group of keen whist players who meet regularly in one another's homes of an afternoon, to play. That is how he came to know Miss Chalk.'

'I also know Miss Chalk,' I told him. 'We have been investigating a theft of jewellery—'

Hawkins's demeanour changed. He stiffened and said brusquely, 'I am aware the Yard has been investigating the loss of the emerald necklace in question. I don't know why Mrs Roxby went all the way into central London to report the loss to the Yard. She could easily, indeed far more conveniently, have reported it here, to us, and we could have begun the investigation.'

'Have you met Mrs Roxby, Inspector?' I asked him.

'Not yet,' he admitted.

'When you do, you may find you have the answer to your question. She is – she is forceful in expressing herself; and inclined to have a strong sense of her own importance.'

'Oh,' said Hawkins. 'I see. Well, I shall have to meet her very soon. I am obliged to inform her of the situation. I would not, of course, delegate the task to a junior officer.'

'I'd be grateful if you would allow me to accompany you,' I told him. 'As the lady already knows me . . . and the sergeant here.'

'Yessir,' said Wood, who had been eyeing the major.

'Come with me, of course. It could help lessen the shock, since she knows you already; and you are trying to recover her jewels. Also, I'll have to ask her some questions and that could be difficult.'

'Trust me, Hawkins,' I assured him. 'The lady will be very difficult!'

'Well, then,' continued Hawkins, 'I believe the photographer has finished making his record of the scene, so, before the body is removed, perhaps you'd care to confirm the identity of the deceased, as you were also acquainted with her.'

'I should also tell you that she recently paid an afternoon call on my wife.'

That did startle Hawkins, who gaped at me. 'Did she, by gad!'

'My wife's impression was that something was troubling Miss Chalk; and she was anxious to confide whatever it was to someone. But her courage failed her and she left my house without telling my wife what was burdening her mind.'

'That's a great pity,' said Hawkins, after a moment of thought. 'Because it could suggest, to my way of thinking anyway, that this was not a random attack. I would have assumed the lady was walking on the Heath when set upon by some vagrant or other ruffian, although why she should choose to walk alone I have no idea. And after dark, leaving the main path. But now . . .'

'There is a possibility she came for the purpose of a rendezvous,' I finished for him. 'Well, we'll bear that in mind, certainly. I wonder if I might have a word with Major Richards. I see he has finished dictating his statement to your constable. But perhaps first of all I should look at the body. The photographer has packed up his equipment and the plates.'

For the second time, I found myself looking down at the body of someone with whom I had spoken so little a time previously. To gaze on any murder victim is an unpleasant experience. To see someone lying dead with whom one had had even a passing acquaintance in life brings home the twin realities of mortality and crime. Ariadne Chalk lay on her back in the middle of a circular patch of turf, surrounded by bramble bushes and shrubs that formed a natural amphitheatre in miniature. Somehow, in death, she looked younger. She was so slight in build. The tensions that had showed in her features had been smoothed away, making them softer. I noticed, for the first time, how fine her skin was. Her body was not blood spattered as had been that of Jacobus. No one had slashed her throat. Instead, a wound on her brow suggested she had been struck violently and with considerable force by some hand-held weapon.

Had she and the person she had met here argued? Or had this been a sudden assault without any preamble? Her clothing was not disarranged. There appeared to be no defensive scratches on her hands. Bludgeoned, I thought to myself. A sudden powerful blow had knocked her to the ground and extinguished her life, as a puff of air might extinguish a candle flame. I stooped and peered at the wound. It was recent enough to be still quite distinct and deep. It would become less obvious within hours. The skin had broken and bled but only a little. She had died instantly.

Even as I looked down at her, and speculated on the circumstances of her death, I could not help but think that this secluded location would suit the purposes of any ladder gang, seeking to conceal the ladder.

But I was now quite certain that the theft of the Roxby emeralds was not the work of a ladder gang, as I'd originally suspected. And this murder? Was that connected with the disappearance of the jewels? I could not, at this moment, see how. But my instinct is to mistrust coincidences. At least in policework. In life, as a whole, I dare say they happen all the time. Or how should it be that I had met Lizzie once again, at Mrs Parry's house, so many years after a brief encounter as children in Derbyshire?

'You can confirm the victim is Miss Chalk?' Hawkins asked me. His voice was quiet but it made me start.

'What?' I had been lost in my own thoughts. 'Yes, yes, that is Miss Chalk. Did you find a lantern?'

'Not as yet,' Hawkins admitted. 'But I am thinking that it might be hasty to decide she walked to that patch of bushes alone. She could have met whoever it was outside the house, or on the path, and her killer persuaded her to move to a more secluded spot, where they would not be disturbed.'

She knew him, I decided. *This was a meeting that she did not believe carried any real possibility of danger. She – and the person she met – were seeking privacy. On her part, that must be because she did not want her employer to know. But it is still all very odd.*

'How was the visibility here last night?' I asked aloud.

'Pretty good for most of the night. I looked out myself, around eleven, and I could see my garden quite clearly in the moonlight. Are you thinking that she finished up where she was found because she had become confused as to the direction?'

'I have been having a number of thoughts, Inspector. That was not one of them, but since you have suggested it, I won't dismiss it. But frankly, it seems to me too simple an explanation for her presence where her body was discovered. The whole business makes no sense at all. Here we have a respectable lady of a certain age. I imagine her to have been accustomed to keep to a daily routine. I think it unlikely it was a romantic tryst! Why, then, suddenly walk out of the house in the middle of the night and set off across the Heath?'

Hawkins offered no suggestion. Instead, he asked, 'Do you object to the body being removed to the mortuary now? The hearse is waiting and that crowds of ghouls over there is growing even bigger.' He scowled in the direction of the onlookers. 'Just look at them! It's an entertainment for them, I swear!'

'Indeed. Yes, let them remove the body. But I would still like to have a word with Major Richards, before we pay our call on Mrs Roxby.'

The major had been waiting patiently, almost at attention, as he might have been on parade. His spaniel had curled up on the grass and gone to sleep.

I introduced myself. 'I believe you knew Miss Chalk? I also had a passing acquaintance with her.'

'She was known to most of the respectable residents,' said the major crisply, in the manner of a man making a report. 'Dog found her. I walk here every morning, rain or shine. I let the dog off the leash and she runs around in circles. Looking to flush out game, you see. She's a spaniel. It's what she is bred to do. She ran into the undergrowth and didn't come back. I went to see what she'd found. I assumed, you see, she must have found something because I couldn't hear her crashing about in there. She was sitting by the body, waiting.' He paused. 'I saw it was Ariadne Chalk. Bad business. Decent sort of woman. Has someone told Mrs Roxby, her employer?'

'Inspector Hawkins and I will be going to the house now, sir, to carry out that sad task. I appreciate that you waited. I am sorry it was such a long wait. I am from Scotland Yard and it took time to get here.'

'Quite so. Any objection to my going off duty now? I have signed a statement.'

'We're very grateful, sir,' Hawkins assured him.

He didn't salute, though for a moment I thought he was going to do so. Instead, he simply called down to the dog, 'Come along, Bess!' The dog scrambled upright and the pair of them marched away.

'He served in the Crimea, I believe,' said Hawkins. 'And, as a youngster, was at Waterloo. We're lucky he found the body when he did. He didn't panic, having doubtless seen any number of bodies in his time, as you remarked earlier. At least this one wasn't blasted to smithereens by cannon fire. For a wonder, the rats hadn't found her either. He went to the nearest house and asked them to fetch us. Then he came back here, to stand guard in his words, and waited for us. He certainly kept any other walkers and sightseers at bay.' He glanced at me. 'Well, do we go now to see Mrs Roxby? I see the cab that brought you from our railway station is still waiting.'

We overtook Wood on our way to the Roxby home. The sergeant was walking at a steady pace towards the house, his gaze alternately on his watch, held in the palm of his hand, or sweeping the grass to either side, in search of a lantern or sign of a struggle. He did not glance in our direction as we rolled past.

'This is a fine property!' observed Hawkins as our cab turned into the drive of the Roxby residence.

'It is indeed. The Roxby business is in shipping. The firm is quite long established now.'

'Sort of family in which the ladies would be decked out in expensive jewels, then!' muttered Hawkins. 'Any luck tracking down the missing necklace?'

'So far, none whatsoever,' I admitted. 'It is a curious case.'

'It's probably been dismantled and disposed of bit by bit,' opined Hawkins.

'It may well have been. The family is hopeful of recovering it intact. It has connections with the history of the firm. I have explained to Mrs Roxby, and to other family members, that the chances of getting it back in one piece grow slimmer by the day. They refuse to believe me.'

'Difficult lot, then,' muttered Hawkins, as the cab rocked to a halt before the front door. 'Think the murder of this lady, Miss Chalk, is connected?'

'I am at a loss, to own the truth,' I told him. 'Ah, here is the butler. Ventham, he's named. My last visit, which was only an inquiry into the theft, scandalised him. I don't know how he'll cope with this one, concerning murder.'

Ventham was approaching the cab. He was a very different man to the disapproving figure he had cut on my previous visit. Then he had only reluctantly allowed us over the threshold. Now it was as if he had surrendered all his earlier authority over who entered and did not enter this house. His face was ashen. 'Gentlemen . . .' he greeted us, then fell silent, apparently unable to continue.

'He's heard the news!' muttered Hawkins.

'We are on a sad mission, Mr Ventham,' I told the butler. 'This is Inspector Hawkins of Hampstead Division. Is Mrs Roxby at home?'

'Yes, sir, she's waiting in the morning room. Is it true, then, the – report Joseph brought us of a – a woman's body? It is only that Miss Chalk cannot be found and no one has seen her since yesterday evening. So we are naturally concerned . . .'

A young footman had come from the house and joined us. I assumed this to be Joseph. He looked both frightened and excited.

'Mr Ventham sent me out earlier to find out if there was any news,' the footman burst out. 'People were saying a body had been found . . .'

Behind him, Ventham shuddered.

'That is correct,' I told them both.

'Is it—' began Joseph.

But Ventham had regained his sense of authority. 'That's enough, Joseph! If you will come in, gentlemen, I will tell Mrs Roxby that you are here. Am I also to tell her that . . .?' His voice tailed away again.

'No, Mr Ventham, I will give Mrs Roxby the news. That's my job. But before we go into the house, can you tell me when Miss Chalk was *first* discovered to be missing?'

'This morning, Inspector, at a quarter to eight, when the maid took up the early-morning tea. Her bed had not been slept in and there was no sign of her.'

'Who locks up the house at night?'

'That is my responsibility, Inspector,' said Ventham with dignity. When he was speaking of the household routine, he was in control of himself. 'I believe, Inspector Ross, I informed you of that fact on your previous visit.'

'So, to leave the house, Miss Chalk would have to ask for a key?'

'Well, no, sir, not in the sense that she needed to ask *me* for a key. She did possess a key to the French windows in the morning room. When I went to unlock those this morning, I found them to be on the latch. She must have left by that exit.'

She had her own key, I thought. Haynes had a key to Jacobus's house. A key suggests security. We lock our doors and believe ourselves safe. But Jacobus had not been safe; and Ariadne Chalk had not been safe. Was it only a coincidence that, in both cases, someone other than the householder held a key? A key had allowed the murderer to enter the quaint old dwelling in Limehouse. A key had allowed the victim to walk out of this fine residential property in Hampstead. That is the problem with keys, I thought. They are easily copied and may be held quite legitimately by several people. Ventham, the butler, would have a set of household keys to Mrs Roxby's home. Tom Mullins held a key to the dwelling in Limehouse; and it had hung in plain view behind the bar at the Crossed Keys. *Crossed Keys* . . . The very name of the tavern now seemed to hold a dreadful irony.

'They cause no end of trouble,' muttered Hawkins behind me.

'Keys?' I asked, startled. Had his thoughts been running parallel to mine?

'No, French windows, or French doors, whatever you call 'em. Always insecure. I don't know how many times

I've known burglars enter a house by breaking a pane of glass and putting a hand through.'

'None of the glass panes are broken,' interposed Ventham sharply. 'Miss Chalk held a key, as I said. She often went in and out of the garden by that route. She was an early riser. I – I first assumed that she had gone out for an early-morning walk in the garden. That was until Lily, the upstairs maid, told us her bed had not been slept in.'

What's more, I thought crossly, the fact that Miss Chalk had a key to the French windows is something I should have discovered on my previous visit. I had not asked her whether she had any keys, nor had she volunteered the fact. How significant was that? Had it been excess of caution that had motivated her, or . . . Oh, Miss Chalk, why did you not confide in Lizzie when you called on her? What was it you wanted to tell her, but had not the courage?

It was no use being annoyed with her now. But I did feel her possession of the key to the garden French windows was something she should have mentioned. If anything, I was annoyed with myself for not asking more specific questions about the keys, instead of accepting that the butler locked up at night and opened the house in the morning. *Call yourself a detective, Ross?* I told myself severely. *I should have sent Biddle, instead of coming myself. Biddle reads penny dreadfuls. I suspect he would like police work to be like the investigations in those tales. Perhaps he would have asked about keys?*

So then, Ariadne Chalk, to all intents and purposes, came and went at will. Had this anything to do with the disappearance of the emeralds? Had the first step in solving the mystery of their disappearance been readily available all along? *You have blundered!* I continued to berate myself. *The answers to the disappearance of the jewels and to the death of Ariadne Chalk – even, perhaps, to the death in Limehouse of Jacob Jacobus, all lie in this house!*

And where were the jewels now?

Hawkins and Ventham were both watching me. I assumed a professional calm I was far from feeling. 'Please go on, Mr Ventham,' I invited the butler.

'I was obliged to inform Mrs Roxby of Miss Chalk's disappearance,' said Ventham unhappily. 'And I sent out Joseph to make inquiries as to whether anyone had seen her on the Heath, in case she had decided to walk there.'

'And did she do that sometimes? Walk on the Heath in the early morning?'

'Very rarely,' said Ventham. 'But it seemed the only possibility . . .'

He stuttered to a halt and I realised he was close to a collapse. He was not a young man.

'Come, Mr Ventham,' I said encouragingly. 'Let us take over now. If you would be so kind as to announce us to Mrs Roxby.'

Given a specific order, he brightened. 'This way, gentlemen.'

It was into the morning room that he led us. Mrs Roxby sat on a low chair near to the very French windows through which, it now seemed likely, Miss Chalk had left the house on her last walk. Was it too speculative to wonder whether her employer had been sitting here this morning, with increasingly desperate patience, hoping to see the companion return, to walk back into the house via the exact same route by which she had left?

The lady wore an indigo-blue gown with cream lace trimming, and a dark-coloured widow's cap. It was as if she had already assumed a half-mourning, in preparation for the full mourning she would assume later, after we had confirmed the sad news. Her face was set rigidly, her eyes fixing me with a cold stare. She would not break down before Hawkins and myself.

'I am very sorry, ma'am,' I told her, 'to be the bringer of sad news.'

'A dead body has been discovered on the Heath, I've been told,' she said in a bleak, steady tone. 'You have come to tell me it is Ariadne Chalk's?'

'We have, ma'am.'

'Who has declared it to be hers?'

It was an obvious question, perhaps, but it was not the one I had been expecting.

'I have, Mrs Roxby, and before me, a neighbour of yours, Major Richards, had recognised her. It was Major Richards who came upon the deceased while walking his dog.'

She inclined slightly towards me. 'If anyone has the task of identifying the body, Inspector Ross, it is I. She lived for many years in this house as my companion. I do not think that either the major, or you, Inspector Ross, is better placed than I am to confirm her identity. She has – had – no family.'

And that is why she had taken a position as companion, I thought. Of course, Mrs Roxby was right in saying no one would be better placed than she was when it came to the sad task of confirming the identity of the deceased. Mrs Roxby would see it as her duty; and she would not want that duty to be usurped by myself or an elderly gentleman walking his dog.

But the lady is not only grieving, I thought, she is very angry. With whom is she so furious? With the killer, whoever that might be? With the hapless Major Richards? With the dead woman? With me? Or, perhaps, with Fate? I could have told her that the last would be a pointless object for her wrath. Fate does not care what we feel. Fate proceeds on its own inexorable path.

Without warning, we were interrupted. Someone else had arrived and was intent on joining us. Ventham could be heard protesting, in vain. The door flew open with a crash as it hit the wall and Isabella Gray burst into the room in some disarray.

'Is it true?' she demanded, without waiting to greet us, or be greeted by us. 'Has Ariadne had some dreadful accident? They are all saying it, all the maids, the footman, everyone! They are even saying she is dead. That can't be true, can it? Is she – is she dead?' She fixed her panicked stare on me. 'Inspector Ross? If you are here, then something must be terribly wrong!'

Hawkins was staring at Miss Gray in some wonder. He had not realised that another family member lived in the house. He had no idea who this wild-eyed young woman, with her hair tumbling loose about her shoulders, was.

I hastened to inform him. 'This is Miss Gray, Inspector, she is a member of the family—'

I was curtly interrupted by Mrs Roxby.

'Kindly allow me, Inspector Ross, to make the introductions in my own home! These gentlemen, Isabella, are both police officers. One of them you have met before, Inspector Ross from Scotland Yard. The other one is Inspector Hawkins of the local constabulary.'

Hawkins flushed angrily, probably feeling he had been demoted. But he had not met Mrs Roxby before. He had now learned, as had others before him, that the lady was not concerned with the feelings of others.

Mrs Roxby turned her attention to Miss Gray, saying curtly, 'You appear somewhat dishevelled, Bella. Go upstairs and have Peters attend to your hair.'

'Is Ariadne *dead*?' demanded Miss Gray, impervious to her aunt's icy tone.

'It would appear so,' conceded Mrs Roxby. 'Although I have yet to view the body and confirm identity.'

'Where is she?' demanded Miss Gray. 'How did she die? She was all right yesterday evening at dinner. We played cards afterwards. There was nothing wrong with her then!'

'Just one moment, if we may,' I interrupted. 'I am very sorry to tell you, Miss Gray, that your aunt's companion, Miss Chalk, was discovered lifeless on the Heath earlier by a neighbour of yours, Major Richards, who was walking his dog.'

'What was she doing on the Heath so early?' demanded Miss Gray. She had turned pale; but her reaction to the news was not to faint away or burst into tears. It was to go on the offensive. This young woman, I thought, has been raised from infancy by her aunt. She met disaster head-on and tackled it.

'Isabella!' snapped her aunt. 'Kindly ask Ventham to send a message to the stables to have the carriage brought round. Inspector Hawkins, you may accompany me to the mortuary. I assume that is where Miss Chalk's body has been taken? She has not been left lying on the Heath surrounded by the curious public?'

I was not to be bundled out of the house. I suspected that this resolve to go at once to the mortuary was partly to interrupt my inquiries and get rid of me.

'Miss Gray,' I addressed the young lady. 'May I ask, was that the last time you saw Miss Chalk, last night, after dinner?'

'Well, yes! We played cards for a while and then we all went up to bed. There was nothing different about the evening.'

'But Miss Chalk did not go to bed, Miss Gray. Her bed has not been slept in. She would appear to have left the house, probably shortly after the rest of the household retired.'

'Why would she do that?' Isabella Gray frowned. 'It makes no sense.'

'Not yet, perhaps, Miss Gray. Do you know whether Miss Chalk received any messages, or had any visitors during the day?'

'Not that I know of, Inspector. The usual post came.' Isabella hesitated. 'She may have had a letter.'

'Impossible!' snapped Mrs Roxby. 'Who would have written to her? She never had post. Don't imagine things, Isabella.'

Her niece's features set obstinately. 'She had a letter in the morning post. She slipped it into her pocket as if she didn't want anyone to see. But I saw it; and I am not imagining it!' Isabella turned to me. 'I can look in her room, if you like, to see if there's a letter up there.'

'I'm obliged, Miss Gray. But perhaps I could take a look around the deceased's room, before I leave?' I looked towards Mrs Roxby, who sat staring ahead of her and refusing to meet my eye.

'You have no objection, ma'am?' I asked.

Mrs Roxby hissed. There was no other description of the sound she made. I took it as meaning she would not try to stop me.

I smiled reassuringly at Miss Gray. 'We, as police officers, will get to the core of the mystery, never fear.'

She met my gaze frankly. 'Yes, Inspector Ross, I believe that you will. Ariadne Chalk was absolutely harmless. Whoever did this is wicked.'

No matter what anyone else in the family thought, I decided at that point, this young woman would make exactly the sort of wife Harry Roxby needed. At the same time, I felt some sympathy for him, if he had Isabella keeping a stern eye on him for the rest of his life.

Mrs Charlotte Roxby was by now white with rage. She rose to her feet. 'Come along, Isabella, we must make ready to go to the mortuary. Inspector Hawkins, you may wait here. As for you, Inspector Ross . . .' She glared at me. 'You may do as you please. It appears to be your habit!'

I was conducted to Miss Chalk's room by a disapproving Ventham, who watched as I examined the contents of drawers and a large oak wardrobe. Miss Chalk's possessions had been few. It might have been the room of a nun. She'd had a liking for the published journals of various travellers. Had she sought to escape in her mind from the cheerless routine of her daily life?

I found Wood waiting patiently for me at the gate, by the cab that had brought us, with Hawkins, from the murder scene.

'Find anything, Wood?'

The sergeant rolled a mint humbug round his teeth in the now-familiar way. 'No, sir. Sorry. I had a good look. It's a strange business. How did you get on in there?' He nodded towards the house.

'Deceased had her own key to the French windows leading into the garden from the morning room. She could have gone out at any time. Her bed had not been slept in. She appeared normal last night at dinner and afterwards, playing cards with the other ladies. It is possible she received a letter during the earlier part of the day. I searched for it in her room, but didn't find it – if it ever existed.'

We climbed back into our cab and, as Hawkins was to travel with the Roxby ladies in the carriage, told the cabman to take us back to the rail station.

'Been a murder, has there?' asked the cabbie, who had clearly not wasted his time and had made inquiries of his own.

'Unfortunately, yes,' I told him.

'That's what comes of having a railway station now!' opined the cabbie. 'Hampstead was a quiet place before this. Then they built that new station and every weekend the place is flooded with day-trippers and the like.'

I reflected that not everyone likes progress. I was about

to say something encouraging. But he had already whistled to his horse and we were in motion.

Wood, whose thought processes followed an inexorable path of their own, took up our conversation where it had been broken off.

'If it was a letter arranging a rendezvous in the middle of the night out on the Heath,' he said, 'your Miss Chalk will have put a match to it. It's not the sort of thing she'd leave lying around.' He cast me a sideways glance. 'Think it may have been a love letter, Inspector? Granted, she was no giddy young girl, but she might have formed an attachment. How about Major Richards?'

'The major, I think you'll find, is an old-fashioned sort of officer and gentleman. He wouldn't expect a respectable lady to meet him in the middle of the night in a remote spot. No, I am thinking of a much more devious sort of fellow.'

After a moment's thought, Wood said, 'It all comes back to that necklace, doesn't it?'

'Yes, Sergeant, I believe it does.'

'Do you think she was the thief? She saw it lying unattended in the young lady's dressing room, pocketed it, and later tried to sell it to old man Jacobus?'

'It's a plausible theory, Wood, but it has a major flaw.'

'What's that, then?' asked Wood, who clearly was attached to his explanation.

'Ariadne Chalk was not a thief. Quite the reverse. She was an honest woman. That is why she paid a visit to my wife. Her conscience was troubled. That is why she sought to put matters right in another way. And that, Wood, is why she is now dead.'

Chapter Eleven

OF ALL the distressing aspects to this latest murder, by far the worst for me was having to break the news to my wife. She whispered, 'Oh, no . . .' and turned so white that I hastened to fetch a glass of brandy.

'I am so sorry, Lizzie! I couldn't tell you any other way than bluntly; and I didn't want you to hear about it from anyone else or from the newspapers.'

She took a sip of the brandy and set the glass down. 'I do understand. Thank you, Ben, for telling me at once. It's truly appalling; such a dreadful crime and committed so – so senselessly. Poor Ariadne Chalk was the most harmless of creatures.'

'Someone thought differently . . .' I was obliged to say.

'Whoever it is, whoever committed this foul crime, he is either mad or wicked beyond belief!' Lizzie burst out.

I thought of the murderers I'd encountered in my career as an officer of the law: the insignificant-appearing, hitherto law-abiding, little clerks who had murdered their landladies, or shopkeepers who had murdered their wives. The devoted nephew who had battered to death a devoted, elderly – and wealthy – aunt. The women who had shown no remorse at all for a child battered to death when its life had barely begun; the poisoners who plotted so carefully, deliberately, cold bloodedly . . . For me, they were among the worst. But then I thought of Ariadne Chalk's pale corpse lying among the bushes on the Heath, her clothing damp from the morning dew. I thought of the missing letter that had lured her to a fatal rendezvous. And I drew the inevitable conclusion that whoever killed her was neither mad nor wicked in the conventional sense. This murder had been carefully planned. The murderer was someone who, unlike Obadiah Quigley, knew and understood every fine distinction between right and wrong; and who had chosen to do wrong. Possibly the killer was someone who had been driven to kill because of some extraordinary circumstance, but who, having now killed once, might, out of desperation, even kill again. Or had he only killed once?

But, worst of all, I could not help but think that, had I been successful in my inquiries to date, it would not have come to this. I remembered Miss Chalk sitting quietly in Dunn's office while her employer demanded the resources of Scotland Yard be deployed to recover a missing necklace, as if this theft were worthy to be ranked with the bloodiest of crimes. At the time it had not seemed to me to warrant such a drain on our resources at a very busy time. But now it did.

'I am at fault,' I muttered aloud.

'No, Ben! How can you be?' exclaimed Lizzie. She reached out and took my hand. 'You are not responsible for this.'

'I should have found that wretched necklace by now, or

at least discovered its fate. I was more concerned with who might have murdered old Jacobus!'

'You believe that poor Ariadne died because of the Roxby emeralds?'

'I can think of no other reason.' I kissed her hand and released it to stand up and begin to turn about the room. 'So much about all of this is that it may turn out to be down to sheer wrongheadedness. For example, it is a damnable thing, Lizzie, but everyone is so anxious to protect that wretched young man!'

'Harry Roxby?' she exclaimed, startled.

'Yes, young Harry! Has it not struck you how concerned they all are to protect him? They all know he is a wastrel. They know he likes to watch prizefights, men battering one another to a pulp in the name of sport. They know he wagers on the outcomes, on horse races, on cards, and he loses over and over again. Still, they all seek to protect the young lout! His young cousin, who manipulated your Aunt Parry into inviting you to tea, solely for the purpose of pleading Harry's case. His father, who has hired a private detective, Sam Morgan, to follow his son about London, so that the family may cover up any scandal. Ariadne Chalk, who told me herself that he was a wastrel; but who came here, at some risk to herself, to see you and enlist your support in his defence. Because that is why she came, Lizzie. If her employer had found out about her visit, she might have been turned out of the house which was her only home! But she still came.'

'She loved Bella Gray and wanted to protect *her*; I think,' protested Lizzie. 'It was not Harry she was worrying about, not for his own sake. But in case any scandal he got involved in might somehow reflect on his cousin Isabella. Mrs Roxby and Miss Chalk both hoped Isabella would make a good marriage. Harry could ruin her chances with scandalous reports of his behaviour.'

'And who knew Miss Chalk came here? Who knew she had called on the wife of the man charged with investigating the loss of the emeralds?'

'Oh, Ben . . .' whispered Lizzie, 'is that why she was killed? Because she came here, to see me?'

'I don't know . . . there is so much we don't know! I am sorry, my dear, to distress you more, I shouldn't have spoken that aloud.'

But my wife, given a puzzle, was concentrating on that. 'Nobody knew she came here. Her employer was out at a whist party.'

'And Isabella Gray, was she also out at some social gathering?' I asked.

'I don't know,' Lizzie admitted. 'I didn't ask. But surely, it is quite likely that she was. The impression I had was that Miss Chalk was very anxious that no one in the Roxby household should know of her visit here. Why, she even braved the train from the new Hampstead Heath Station, unaccompanied.'

'She had to plan her journey carefully, that much is obvious,' I agreed. 'She picked a moment when no one would require her presence or ask where she was. She slipped out of the house unaccompanied, and unseen. She then walked on her own two feet to the railway station. It took resolve and stamina.'

Lizzie sat silent for a few minutes, deep in thought. I continued to wander around the room, blaming myself for every aspect of this whole wretched business.

'What about the letter?' Lizzie asked suddenly. 'You told me that Isabella Gray claimed to have seen Miss Chalk hiding a letter that had arrived by the morning's post.'

'Only Miss Gray saw that. Mrs Roxby denied it. There was no letter in Miss Chalk's room and none was found on the body.'

Lizzie looked surprised and not a little shocked. 'Do you think Miss Gray imagined or invented the letter?'

'I don't know. She could simply have been mistaken. Perhaps it was a white handkerchief and not a white envelope that Miss Chalk was tucking away discreetly in her pocket.' It was all too much. It had been a long, tiring day, and it would linger in my memory. Perhaps that is why I added incautiously, 'But Miss Gray is another one anxious to protect Harry.'

'Isabella Gray wouldn't invent the letter, surely?' Lizzie protested. 'I agree, she could have been mistaken . . .'

'Ah, dear Lizzie,' I said, 'you have fallen under the spell of the young lady too!'

'Oh, don't talk nonsense!' retaliated my wife, rallying from her former despondency, as I was pleased to see, and becoming again her forthright self. 'I liked her, yes. She has a spontaneous charm and speaks from the heart. That is the impression I had.'

'And normally I would trust your judgement. But I should remind you that Mr Jeremy Roxby doesn't like her; and he has known her pretty well all her life. He is determined she shall never marry his son,' I reminded her.

Lizzie dismissed this. 'That is because he doesn't like Mrs Charlotte Roxby. One can hardly be surprised. From what you've told me, Mrs Roxby seems to be a most objectionable sort of woman.'

'She is, indeed. I agree, that could be one reason. It is the only one we know of at the moment. That doesn't mean there could not be other objections,' I suggested. 'For example, we do not know anything of the late Mr George Roxby. He was in business with his brother, Jeremy. But what was the relationship between the brothers outside the boardroom? They had inherited the family business. They did not establish it. They were not in business together from choice. They may have quarrelled or simply disliked one another. George was the elder. A younger brother sometimes resents the older sibling. Jeremy Roxby struck me as an urbane, sophisticated man. But one of strong opinions; and not easily persuaded to an opposite view in anything, be it in business or a purely family matter. I fancy there was a quarrel at some point, although I am the first to admit I lack any hard evidence for that.'

Lizzie looked thoughtful. 'Could it be when George married?' she suggested. 'Perhaps Jeremy disapproved of his choice of wife?'

'That could be the reason. At any rate, a quarrel, whatever it was about, could have festered, unresolved, for years, even after George's death.'

'It would still be unfair of him to visit his dislike on Isabella Gray. She is only seventeen years old—'

'Yes, yes, I know that!' I interrupted. 'But the girl is out of the schoolroom and has been launched on the social round. She is a worldly seventeen year old. That makes it even odder that she behaved so foolishly on the night of the dinner party. She did not prevent a valuable emerald necklace being taken from the safe, although she was determined not to wear it, and then left it lying unattended, in plain view, on her dressing table when she went down to dinner.'

'You don't forgive her for that, do you?' Lizzie challenged me, after a moment or two.

'It's not a question of blame. I leave that to her aunt, who may well blame her, I wouldn't be surprised. No, I am a detective; and I dislike loose ends and convenient mistakes.'

I received a message when I arrived at the Yard the following morning. It was from the solicitor, Haynes. Apparently, Mr and Mrs Perkins planned to return to Leeds later in the day, and would appreciate a word with me before they left regarding the state of inquiries into the death of Jacob Jacobus.

With the death of Ariadne Chalk now in the forefront of my attention, I could do without spending time with Haynes and his clients. But if they were returning home that day, it might be as well to make the effort. I wasn't surprised they were going home. Lizzie had told me what cheerless lodgings they had at the Railway Hotel. I told Wood I intended to be away only a short time and set off.

The clerk of the weather had decided to send us another

unseasonal downpour. It had been threatening since early morning and it chose to break as I set foot in the street. By the time I reached Haynes's office, I was drenched, irritable, and felt strongly that I was wasting my time. A police officer may qualify as a public servant. But that ought not to mean he was at everyone's beck and call for little reason. (Although in practice it often did mean that.)

'I am obliged to you, Inspector Ross, for making time to come,' Haynes greeted me, as I stood in the little lobby of his place of business; I divested myself of my wet coat and hat, handing them over to a sullen youth acting as porter. In an undertone, he added, *'They're going home!'*

Mr and Mrs Perkins, silent and unsmiling in their mourning black, sat side by side in the office; although Wilfred Perkins did rise to his feet as I entered.

'Good morning, Mr Perkins,' I said, 'and to you, ma'am.'

Mrs Perkins inclined her head graciously and her husband sat down again. I didn't know if it had been agreed between them that she should be spokesperson, but Wilfred made no effort to say anything, and she began without delay.

'We are obliged to return to Leeds, Inspector. My husband has a business to run!'

'I quite understand, ma'am.' I tried not to look too relieved.

'We had hoped,' continued the lady, 'that this whole sorry business would have been cleared up by now.'

'Maggie, my dear—' began Wilfred, but fell silent when she swept on, disregarding him.

Haynes made no attempt to speak. I thought he looked

a little less stressed today. The prospect of being distanced from these clients probably cheered him. But if he thought I had forgotten, or chosen to overlook, the matter of the front-door key to the Limehouse property, he was mistaken. I had other, more important matters on my mind at the moment, but should it prove necessary, I was well prepared to return to it. In the meantime, it did no harm to have him more than anxious to do anything he could to help. His clients, on the other hand, remained their discontented selves.

'You have still not identified the wretch who so foully murdered my dear father!' charged Mrs Perkins. She glared at me.

When did old Jacobus become her 'dear' father, I wondered? When she'd discovered how rich he'd left her? Time for me to speak up. I certainly wasn't going to sit here, in sodden footwear, while she berated me.

'These complicated investigations do take time, Mrs Perkins. It can't be helped. You will understand that we need a complete case to take to court. But rest assured; our inquiries are proceeding. Unfortunately, we now have a second murder to investigate.'

All three of them looked startled; and Haynes's relaxed manner evaporated. Unsurprisingly, Maggie rallied first.

'Has this anything to do with my father's murder?'

She clearly expected me to reply that it hadn't. I took unworthy satisfaction in saying, 'It may well have a connection, ma'am. But, as yet, the investigation is new.'

'When?' croaked Wilfred Perkins unexpectedly. 'When did this second frightful crime take place?'

'The body was discovered yesterday morning.'

'In Limehouse?' Haynes suddenly looked and sounded the keen professional.

'Not in Limehouse.'

'Then how can it be connected?' Perkins looked puzzled.

'Possibly it isn't. But until we have completed our inquiries, I am not yet in a position to say any more.'

'Oh, well, I suppose not,' grumbled Maggie Perkins. 'In any case, it can't be of any interest to us. I only want to know who is responsible for the death of my papa.'

She drew a deep breath and her manner changed from discontented to gracious, rather as a breeze causes a ripple across a pond. It was interesting to watch the transformation. She inclined in a sort of bow; and I swear I heard her stays utter a muted cry of protest.

'I'd be obliged, Inspector Ross, if you would tell your wife that I am most grateful for her support during this very difficult time. I've written her a note. Mr Haynes has it.'

Haynes picked up a white envelope from his desk, held it up briefly like a courtroom exhibit, and put it down again.

'I believe the Railway Hotel has not been a pleasant place to stay,' I said. 'My wife has described its shortcomings.'

'It's been dreadful!' snapped the lady.

I decided to address Mr Perkins. 'You have been able to complete an inventory of the contents of the house, I hope?'

'Yes,' said Perkins gloomily. 'Mr Haynes has that also.'

'A copy has been made for the police,' said Haynes, indicating a second white envelope.

Miss Chalk received a letter in a white envelope on her last day, I thought. It is probably no more than a coincidence.

'Then I'll take both envelopes with me now,' I said to Haynes. He handed them to me. 'We'll be in touch again, no doubt!' I told him.

He looked apprehensive. He had not forgotten the key either.

'Mr and Mrs Perkins!' I turned to them. 'I wish you a comfortable journey home.'

I decided to take the opportunity to call in at St Thomas's Hospital, where, as I understood, Dr Mackay had intended to carry out his postmortem investigation. In response to a message taken to him he came out from the mortuary in which he carried out his grisly work, and shook my hand briefly. I rather hoped he'd washed his own before he left his labours. He was in his shirtsleeves, signifying he had, at least, taken off his dissection coat.

'Death, in this instance,' he said, 'was certainly the result of a single heavy blow. The deceased's skull is rather thin. Not without interest from a medical point of view.'

'Any suggestion as to the type of weapon?'

'That's interesting, too. The point of contact with the skin suggests something rounded, small, possibly pat-terned. If so, the impression of any design has already faded. But I feel fairly certain that the surface was not a smooth one.'

'How about the head of a cane?' I asked. 'One topped with a pommel, perhaps?'

'Quite possibly. But you won't be able to match them

up. By tomorrow the dent will be quite gone. You can hardly see it now. Come and have a look, if you like.'

I thanked him and politely declined. 'I have already seen the poor woman, lying dead on the Heath.'

'Fair enough,' said Mackay. 'Otherwise, the lady was in good health. However, the really unexpected thing has not to do with the manner of her death. It has to do with her life.'

There was a gleam in Mackay's eyes that suggested he was going to spring a surprise and had been looking forward to the moment.

'Yes?' I asked.

'The lady had given birth at least once.'

'*What?*' I stared at him, stupefied. 'Are you sure? She was unmarried and utterly respectable. Also, I am sure that Mrs Roxby, her employer, would not have engaged her as her companion if there had been any scandal in her history.'

'There's many a scandal in respectable families!' declared Mackay cheerfully. 'And people are extraordinarily ingenious in hiding them. Haven't you found that out before now, Inspector? I think she was probably still young when she became a mother. I understand her age, at the time of death, to have been forty-three.'

My mind was abuzz with questions. 'What happened to the child? I mean, obviously we'll never know.' To myself, rather than to the doctor, I added, 'Did her family cast the mother out, and she was obliged to make her way in the world as best she could?'

'Can't assist you with any of the answers to those

questions,' Mackay told me. 'I can only say that it would appear to have been a full-term pregnancy. Her family may have conspired to hide her condition; and abandoned the infant to the care of the parish, in effect to a baby-farmer. The newborn child may not have survived for long. Such babies often don't; and some years ago, well . . . Things are supposed to be a little better now. But, in my view, not greatly so. There have been enough baby-farming scandals to attest to that; and, as a police officer, you will have known of such cases.'

'Yes,' I agreed. 'Yes, unfortunately, I have.'

'Anyway, it's all in my report.' Mackay clearly did not want to discuss the subject any further.

I had been given a lot to think about. I returned to the Yard and presented myself in Dunn's office. I told him all I had learned. He listened carefully and looked unhappy.

'The thing is this, Ross,' he said. 'Do we keep Miss Chalk's secret? Do we tell her employer, Mrs Roxby? Speaking for myself, I admit I had much rather not do so. To ruin the lady's reputation so late in the day can only harm the memory of her.' Dunn heaved a sigh. 'It's a not-unfamiliar tale, Ross. You and I are both well aware of that. As I see it, we have to ask, is it relevant to our inquiries into her death? I don't see how it can be. I know Mrs Roxby is a difficult woman, but you reported that she seemed genuinely distressed on learning of her employee's death.'

'It was the impression I got, sir. Mrs Roxby doesn't show much emotion, other than displeasure and impatience. But yes, I think her companion's death has caused much distress. Miss Chalk had lived in the household as Mrs Roxby's companion for a long time. It may have been a cheerless situation from the point of view of Ariadne Chalk. But at least it gave her a roof over her head, respectability and a comfortable existence. It may explain why, even when Miss Chalk was so anxious to confide something to my wife, she couldn't in the end bring herself to do so. She dared not risk her situation.'

'Mm,' murmured Dunn. 'When do you plan to call on Mrs Roxby again?'

'I thought I might call on her this afternoon. I can confirm the cause of death to her as a blow to the head. I can then encourage Mrs Roxby to tell me more about Miss Chalk, if, indeed, she knows very much about the companion's early life. In normal circumstances, the birth of an illegitimate baby would have been well hidden by Miss Chalk from everyone. But I can sound Mrs Roxby out about Miss Chalk generally.'

Dunn was nodding. 'Yes, yes, do so, Ross. In an investigation such as this, we need to know all we can about the deceased. But we don't want to shock Mrs Roxby into an even more uncooperative mood than she usually shows. Nor is Mrs Roxby a member of the deceased lady's family. She was only her employer. We are under no obligation to inform her of this – detail. Let us say we shall keep Miss Chalk's secret unless we are unable to do so for any reason. It would be quite improper to ruin the woman's reputation after death unnecessarily. Do you agree?'

It was not often that Dunn asked me if I agreed with him on anything. It was more in his nature to present me with his decisions. I realised that he had been moved by Miss Chalk's sad story. This made it all the more awkward to put forward a request I had. I began carefully.

'In principle, sir, I would of course agree. However, there is a line of investigation I would like to pursue. To do this, I need a request made of the Foreign Office, that is to say, it is a request involving consular records. I cannot ask myself. I need the request to go through you; possibly after consultation with the commissioner's office.'

'Good Lord, Ross!' exclaimed Dunn, who was almost goggling at me by now. 'What on earth is it?'

'Just bear with me, sir, while I explain. It concerns the young lady, Isabella Gray, who has grown up in Mrs Roxby's household and been treated as a daughter, although she is supposed to be Mrs Roxby's niece.'

'*Supposed?*' interrupted Dunn. 'Ross, are you about to suggest—'

I continued determinedly, ignoring his interruption. 'Her parents, we have been told, were Mrs Roxby's brother and his wife. Both of them were killed in a carriage accident while in Italy. Their baby daughter, Isabella, who had accompanied her parents with her nursemaid, survived.' I drew a deep breath. 'Or so we have been told.'

'Ross!' interrupted the superintendent. 'If I may complete the question I began to ask and which you so rudely interrupted! Are you about to suggest that Isabella Gray is, in reality, the child of Ariadne Chalk?'

'Bear with me, sir, for a moment longer, if you would . . .'

'You'd better be damn sure before we begin to go down that path! Good heavens, Ross! How do you propose to

241

find out?' Dunn was so exercised now that he almost levitated from his chair.

'It might not be so difficult, sir. In the case of a fatal accident involving British subjects abroad, the nearest British consular authorities would certainly be informed. They, in turn, would report the sad occurrence to the consular department of the Foreign Office here in London, so that the relatives here in Britain could be informed. The British departments of state are very good at keeping records, sir. If we might ask them to consult the relevant consular records for all fatal accidents in Italy, in particular one involving a British family with the surname Gray, fifteen years ago . . .'

Dunn had followed my reasoning. 'And if we find it on record that the infant daughter survived and was returned to England to relatives here, then Isabella Gray is truly the infant child of Mr and Mrs Gray, whom Mr George Roxby and his wife adopted into their own family.' Dunn drew a deep breath. 'But if the child died with her parents in Italy . . .'

'Then who is Isabella Gray?' I asked rhetorically.

'Damn it, Ross!' said Dunn heavily. 'We may start a hare with this inquiry that we may not wish to follow! Miss Gray undoubtedly believes herself to be Charlotte Roxby's niece. Whatever gives you the idea that a change of identity of the infant was enacted by George Roxby and his wife? We can't ask George Roxby. He's dead. We can ask Charlotte Roxby until we are blue in the face – she won't admit it! The question I have is for you. How sure are you that this exchange is on the cards?'

'Well, for one thing, sir, it has always puzzled me how determined Mr Jeremy Roxby is that his son, Harry, shall never marry Isabella Gray. Such a union, in addition to keeping the family business secure from outside interference, would solve the problem of the ownership of the Roxby emeralds. That, if nothing else. As the next Roxby bride, the necklace would be presented to Isabella on her marriage. The other puzzle is that Mrs Charlotte Roxby has never considered it a possibility that Harry and Isabella might make a match of it. Instead, she has been parading Isabella, at an unsuitably young age in my view, around London society for the purpose of catching a husband unconnected with the family. Miss Chalk, too, appeared to have no objection to that.'

'I will take it upstairs!' announced Dunn, after some thought with a furrowed brow, and accompanied by huffing and puffing sounds. 'You go and talk to Mrs Roxby with regard to Miss Chalk as a murder victim. But only as a murder victim. Ross, I beg you, be damn careful what you say!'

Mrs Roxby was in full mourning. She received me again in the small morning room, with the French windows opening on to the garden.

'Well?' she greeted me coldly. 'I hope you have come to report some progress. Your local colleague, Inspector Hawkins, has already called here. He is aware that, officially, this is not his case. But unrest in the local community is very much his concern. Ariadne Chalk was well known, as you will be aware. There is much alarm and consternation.

Hawkins has been trying to soothe people's fears. He seems to have had little success. If someone as inoffensive as Chalk . . .' Her voice tailed away. She turned her head to stare out of the window. 'People fear for their safety!'

'Inspector Hawkins and his men will do everything possible to make the area safe,' I said as reassuringly as I could.

'How could it happen?' she asked suddenly. She was still staring out of the window; and the question did not appear to be addressed to me so much as part of a mental conversation conducted with herself, possibly begun before I arrived.

I have learned over the years to interpret small gestures and the slightest of reactions to questions. Mrs Roxby was very distressed, as might be expected. She was also very unsettled. Well, perhaps that was not so surprising. But she's worried, I thought. Something is worrying her very much and it is not only the murder of her companion.

'I am well aware how much alarm the murder of Miss Chalk must be causing,' I continued. 'We certainly hope to apprehend the guilty party as soon as possible. To that end, all information is of help. I am aware that it must pain you. But if I might talk to you a little about the lady? Her origins, her background, how she came to be in your employ . . . all this might turn out to be of help.'

'I cannot see how!' Mrs Roxby snapped, turning back to face me. She drew a deep breath. 'However, if you insist . . . Chalk came to this house to live here as my companion thirteen years ago, following the death of my husband.'

'Prior to that, she had been a companion to someone else, perhaps?'

'To a lady of my acquaintance, who had recently died. So I knew Chalk a little. She was anxious to find a new place. I needed support in my early widowhood.'

'You had already taken into your household your orphaned niece, Isabella Gray,' I remarked as casually as I could.

'Yes.' That was the whole of her reply to that question.

'Was Miss Chalk in any way occupied with the care of the child?'

Mrs Roxby looked at me in surprise. 'Of course she wasn't! We had employed a very capable nursemaid.'

'Quite so,' I murmured. 'Is Miss Gray at home at the moment? I would like to talk to her.'

'Why?' demanded Mrs Roxby.

'I need to talk to anyone who knew the late Miss Chalk. The smallest thing might cast some light on this sad affair. It is the way of police investigations to follow up all possible leads, even if many don't help us.'

'It sounds a very inefficient way of working,' said Mrs Roxby. 'But you have your methods and feel obliged to follow them. I understand that. However, you cannot talk to Isabella. She isn't here.'

'I see. When, may I ask, will she return?'

'Isabella is very distressed. She was fond of Chalk and, naturally, she has never had any experience of an acquaintance being murdered. She has gone to stay with an old schoolfriend, who lives near Bath. The change of air and company will do her good, and she will not be badgered by police officers.'

I could have replied that the arm of the law was a very

long one. But I waited, sensing that Mrs Roxby was about to make some kind of declaration. She drew a deep breath and, still staring out into the garden, announced: 'Besides which, in the circumstances, she will no longer be able to accept any social engagements here in town.'

For the first time since I had met the lady, her voice trembled and she was briefly unable to control her emotion. She turned her face away from me again; but not before I had glimpsed the devastation in her expression.

Miss Chalk's death was hard enough to bear. But the sudden and definitive closing of the doors of fashionable households to her protégée, well, that was devastating. Mrs Roxby had invested so much in launching Miss Gray on to the social scene. Her hopes had been so high that Isabella would attract a wealthy and socially well-placed suitor. The cost must have been immense. Without warning, due to the murder of a member of the household, it had all come to a sudden and dramatic end. Not only was it impossible, as she had said, for Miss Gray to accept invitations to so many parties. Such invitations would now not be issued. Those already issued would be cancelled. Isabella's name had been struck from the guest lists of hostesses all over London. She might just as well be in the West Country. There was nothing, now, for her here in London.

I said, 'I understand.' In an attempt to distract from the loss of her hopes regarding her niece, I added, 'We are still working very hard to locate the missing emerald necklace.'

She turned her head slowly so that she again faced me; and fixed a penetrating stare on me. 'Do you think you will find it?'

'I begin to doubt . . . That is to say, I must repeat my warning that the necklace has probably been broken up.'

'I want to know where it is!' she said fiercely. 'Every last gem and fragment of the setting!'

At that moment we were interrupted by the arrival of the butler Ventham. 'I beg your pardon, madam . . .'

'Yes?' demanded Mrs Roxby. 'What is it?'

'The other police officer is here.'

'Inspector Hawkins?' I exclaimed.

'No, sir,' said Ventham apologetically, as if he might be at fault in not producing Hawkins. 'It is the sergeant. Sergeant Wood, sir. He is anxious to speak to you, Inspector.'

'Why not to me?' demanded Mrs Roxby. 'I am the lady of the house! If he has private business with Inspector Ross—'

I decided to take charge at this point. 'You will excuse me, ma'am? I don't know why Sergeant Wood has come, but it must be urgent. If you will allow me a few minutes?'

She nodded and waved her hand towards the door. She was probably glad to be free of my company even for a brief spell.

Wood was waiting in the hall. 'Sorry, Mr Ross. The superintendent sent me. He asks that you return with me at once. I have a hackney carriage waiting.'

I didn't know what all this was about, but clearly it was urgent. And private. Wood was not going to divulge the reason before any witness.

'Give me a moment!' I told him.

I went back to the morning room. Mrs Roxby stared at me in silence, waiting for my excuse.

'I am truly sorry, ma'am, but I have to return to the Yard. Thank you for seeing me this morning. I fully understand how difficult this is for you.'

'So you keep saying,' countered the lady. But she looked relieved at the prospect of my departure.

'Well, Wood?' I asked, as we rattled our way back to central London. 'What's happened?'

'The superintendent asked me not to tell you in front of that female dragon,' said Wood discourteously. 'But it appears the Roxby emeralds have turned up.'

'*What?*'

'Intact, too. The necklace is all of a piece.'

'Where? How? When? Who found it?' I realised I was beginning to lose my self-possession. I began again. 'Who has found it and where is it now?'

'It is at the Yard, sir. It was recovered from the Thames mud, earlier this morning.'

'Go on!' I croaked.

'The tide had gone out and, as you know, that's when scavengers descend on the mud to see what they can find. Mudlarks, they call 'em. One young lad found a bag, and when he opened it up, there was this magnificent piece of jewellery. It fair took his breath away. Couldn't believe his eyes, I reckon. Well, first he thought he had had a stroke of terrific luck! Normally, if he had found something like that, he'd have been off to sell it on. But then he realised it was too grand a piece for that. No one would handle it. So he decided to take it into the local police station, hoping for a reward, I dare say. And now we have it at the Yard.'

'It's been identified? By whom? We could have brought Mrs Roxby with us.'

Wood put his fist to his mouth and coughed discreetly, signifying there was more to be said. 'It looks like the one the young lady is wearing in that photograph, and answers the description. But Superintendent Dunn does not want to let Mrs Roxby know until we are quite certain. The fact of the matter is, he is beginning to be unsure of the lady's role in all this. And she has upset him with her high-handed ways.'

'That doesn't surprise me. But Jeremy Roxby could identify it. We could call him in.'

Wood shook his head in a sorrowful way. 'The superintendent doesn't want to trouble any of the Roxbys for the moment. He has sent a message to the offices of the insurers, requesting their help. When I left, they were awaiting the gentlemen from the insurance company to come to the Yard and give their opinion.'

'It's not even damaged?' I asked incredulously.

'Not as far as I could see,' Wood told me. 'Mind you, it stinks something awful, on account of the mud.'

Chapter Twelve

THE 'GENTLEMEN from the insurance company' had arrived a few minutes before me. They were both extremely well dressed in tailcoats and carried silk hats. They looked, in short, like men whose business was money, in one form or another. It was unfortunate that there was a lingering odour of Thames mud about the place.

Superintendent Dunn effected the introductions. 'Ah, gentlemen, allow me to present Inspector Ross, who has been conducting the inquiries into the whereabouts of the emerald necklace. Ross, these gentlemen are Mr Ferguson and Mr de Groot. Mr de Groot is an expert on gemstones of all kinds.'

I shook hands with each of the newcomers. Then we gathered round Dunn's desk on which lay a bundle that was the source of the smell of Father Thames. It appeared to be something wrapped in a hand towel.

'We have rinsed most of the mud off,' Dunn told us apologetically. 'But we did not presume to clean the necklace too – enthusiastically.'

'Quite right!' said Mr de Groot; and Dunn looked relieved.

'Perhaps you would like to be seated?' he asked.

Chairs had been brought and set round the desk so we sat down. We must have resembled some sort of séance. Mr Ferguson reached into an inside pocket of his coat and took out a folded document and a photograph. I guessed the document to be the insurance papers, which would have a description of the item in question. The photograph, I could see, was a close-up of the necklace lying on a dark background.

Dunn stooped over the desk and ceremoniously unwrapped the towel. There, before us, lay a mud-smeared but still resplendent piece of jewellery: an emerald necklace, with smaller diamonds, gold-set. Mr Ferguson consulted his photograph, comparing it minutely with the necklace on the table. Then he consulted the document he'd brought. His face remained expressionless throughout. At last, he appeared to have completed his inspection; he put away his documents and sat back in his chair.

'Mr de Groot . . .' invited Mr Ferguson courteously, indicating the necklace.

Mr de Groot, in turn, produced an item from an inner pocket. In his case, it was a jeweller's loupe. He put it to his eye and, picking up the necklace, began to examine it, inch by inch, stone by stone, in great detail. We all waited, with bated breath. It seemed an eternity before he replaced the necklace carefully on the towel and sat back.

'A very fine piece of workmanship,' he announced. 'I would guess it to have been made in France.'

'The lady to whom it originally belonged was Brazilian,' said Dunn.

De Groot inclined his head. 'You are speaking of the original necklace, I think. This one –' He reached out and indicated the jewellery on the desk. 'This one, of course, is paste.'

There was a stunned silence on the part of Dunn and myself. Ferguson merely looked disapproving.

'Are you saying?' Dunn asked in dismay. 'Are you declaring this necklace to be a fake?'

'It is a very fine piece of workmanship,' said de Groot. 'But not, alas, the real thing. Not if it is purporting to be the celebrated Roxby emeralds!'

'So it's worthless?' Dunn managed to croak.

'I wouldn't say that,' de Groot corrected him politely. 'Very fine pieces of paste jewellery, such as this, fetch high prices. But, naturally, still only a fraction of the value of the original and genuine stones in their setting.'

Dunn managed to rally. 'So, to be absolutely clear, this is not the missing Roxby necklace, as insured by your company?'

Ferguson took up the conversation. 'It is not. We certainly insured the original necklace. It remains insured with us. But this piece of jewellery is not that item. It merely replicates it.'

I spoke up to say, 'I understood no claim has as yet been made against the loss. In which case we don't know that the original necklace is missing at all!'

Ferguson turned to me and inclined his head. 'You are correct. In that sense, there has been no attempt at making a fraudulent claim – *as yet*. But the existence of this piece suggests that some kind of fraud has been contemplated.

What we wish to know, and urgently, is when and how this necklace was made; and the whereabouts of the original Roxby emerald necklace.'

Dunn put his hand briefly to his brow. 'So would we, the police! It would seem possible a false report was made to us. That is, if the original necklace was not stolen, but this copy was. On the other hand, who threw the copy into the Thames? And why?'

'And does the original necklace still exist? In which case, where is it? Hidden away somewhere? Or stolen in reality?' I put in.

But our visitors were making ready to leave.

'We must report this urgently,' said Ferguson. 'As it does seem that a switch has been made. But, in the absence of the original necklace, it becomes a matter of where, how and by whom.'

'And why,' I murmured to myself. '*Why* so much trouble has been taken to report the loss of a fake necklace, since no claim has been made on the insurance.'

'Yes!' snapped Ferguson.

'But until it is, the existence of this paste replica is not, in itself, a crime,' I pointed out. 'We have to find out who ordered this copy made and who, for reasons that are still unclear, decided to throw it into the Thames.'

It was unfortunate that, when it had been unwrapped from the towel and spread out on the desk for us to view, the necklace formed the shape of a smile. It was as if it mocked us.

'I have never enjoyed a magician's or a conjurer's act,' I added. 'I said so to my wife, just recently.'

Dunn looked at me, startled. But Ferguson regarded me with interest.

'Why not?' he asked.

'Because I don't like being tricked,' I told him. 'Particularly when I know I am being deceived, but can't see how.'

'Quite so,' agreed Ferguson. 'Then you will understand how the insurance company feels. Should you choose to retire from the police force at some later date, Inspector Ross, and take up work as a private inquiry agent, let me know.'

'Gentlemen, before you go!' Dunn spoke up suddenly. 'I understand you must report this to your employers. But, I beg you, do not approach any member of the Roxby family about it! Nor make the existence of this piece public. We have first to make a new, urgent investigation into the report of a burglary and theft of the necklace, as made to us by Mrs Charlotte Roxby. Starting from scratch and disregarding all she has told us hitherto.'

'Of course,' agreed Ferguson. 'It would be appreciated if you would keep us up to date with all your inquiries into this matter. We, naturally, shall let you know if any information comes our way.'

'Well, Ross, what do we do now?' asked Dunn, when our visitors had left.

'Do you wish me to return to Hampstead and inform Mrs Roxby of this find?' I indicated the muddy fake necklace. 'I can go straight away, if you think it wise to move fast. I feel we should, before the news of this discovery leaks out.' I paused and added, 'Ferguson and de Groot are models of discretion, I'm sure, but they must report it to their company. Once they have done that, other people, at first within the company but inevitably eventually outside of it, will learn of its existence. Besides them, there is the boy who found it and the officers at the police station to which he took it – to say nothing of several people in this very building who were here when it arrived.'

'Yes, yes,' Dunn interrupted irritably. 'There was no secrecy about it when it was brought in. I believe it is the talk of the Yard that the missing jewellery has been located.'

He sat with one hand pressed to his brow. 'Damn it, what are we to think? Ross, don't go back to Hampstead yourself. Send a message to the lady asking her to come here. I should like to show her this – article – and see her reaction for myself!'

The best-laid plans of mice and men are apt to go astray, or so the poet would have it. Mrs Roxby arrived at the Yard within the hour. However, she was not alone. She was accompanied by her brother-in-law, Jeremy Roxby. This was not only a surprise, because my understanding had been that they were barely on speaking terms, but it threat-ened to further complicate the situation. We could have done without that.

It was Jeremy Roxby who, as might be expected, appointed himself spokesman.

'I was paying a call on my sister-in-law when the mes-sage arrived that you have news, and wished her to come here at once. I – we – can only think that your news con-cerns the missing Roxby emeralds.'

'To which, Mr Roxby,' said Dunn, 'I can only reply both

yes and no! Perhaps you would both care to cast your eyes over this.' He removed the towel that had been thrown back over the necklace on his desk.

Charlotte Roxby was already seated. That was fortunate; because I believe that otherwise she would have fainted on the spot. She turned deathly pale and put both hands to her face at once, in shock, or else disguising her expression as best she could.

Jeremy Roxby also appeared thunderstruck. His voice, when he spoke, sounded compressed, as if squeezed through a tube.

'Where did you . . . How did you find that necklace?'

'You do well to call it "that necklace", Mr Roxby!' said Dunn. 'Because I can tell you immediately that, despite appearances, these are not the famed Roxby emeralds.'

Jeremy rallied at once. 'What do you mean? That is certainly the missing necklace! Do you think I don't recognise such a piece, so important in our family history?'

'It is a replica, sir, I am sorry to tell you,' said Dunn with every appearance of sympathy. (I had not known the superintendent to be such a good actor. He was, I knew, quite furious about this whole matter.) 'It has already been examined by a jewellery expert who has declared it to be so. As to where it was found: it was taken from the Thames mud early this morning by a scavenging mudlark, a young boy. He turned it in to the nearest police station.'

It was at this juncture that Mrs Roxby chose to faint away. The following scene can easily be imagined. General panic all round, calls for assistance, water, and a female in the building who might carry out the necessary task of unlacing the distressed lady's stays. It all took time and during it, Mr Jeremy Roxby regained his composure and attitude of being 'in charge'. He would learn he was not in charge, not while he was at Scotland Yard. However, the end result was that any interview was at an end for the time being. Mr Roxby announced he would accompany his sister-in-law back to her Hampstead home, and return at a later time.

'Of course,' said Dunn, still unbelievably sympathetic. 'Although there is no need at all for you both to go all the way back to Hampstead. Sergeant Wood will accompany Mrs Roxby, and remain in the house until she feels able to return.'

Jeremy didn't like that; and argued a little. But Dunn remained adamant, adding that he was sure Mr Roxby had business to attend to, and needed to get back to his office. In the end Roxby could do nothing about it but accept. The Roxbys departed, he on foot to his office, and the lady in a hackney cab to Hampstead, accompanied by Wood as nursemaid; although his manner was very much that of an arresting officer.

'Got 'em!' exclaimed Dunn, once they had left. He slapped the palms of his hands on his desk. 'They're going to have the devil of a task talking themselves out of this.'

'You think they knew, as soon as they saw the paste replica, that it was just that, a fake?' I asked.

'Of course they knew! Both of 'em. Didn't you see their faces? This, Ross, is no longer a robbery. It is now a case of an attempt to defraud the insurance company!'

It would be difficult to persuade him otherwise, but I had to try. 'I am not so sure, sir . . .'

'What do you mean? It's as clear as the mud on those glass jewels! And we need to keep the pair of them apart until we get statements from them. I don't want to give them any opportunity of hatching up another story.'

'I agree they both knew this necklace we have here must be paste,' I said. 'But I am not at all sure *when* they knew it. Or, at least, I suspect Mrs Roxby must have known it from the first because, well, the lady always did protest too much.'

'Shakespearean scholar now, are you, Ross?'

'But Jeremy Roxby did not know it when he came to my office the first time. I feel sure of that,' I continued. 'He was very angry with his sister-in-law for failing to keep safe a family heirloom. And let us not forget that the exact ownership of the necklace – the real one – is still in dispute. His anger was stoked by the fact that she had come to *us* to report it stolen! He believed she should have gone to him, and he would have gone about its recovery in quite a different way. That is, by putting the word about the criminal underworld that a substantial reward, with no questions asked, would be paid for its return.'

'Damn idiot!' growled Dunn.

'Very foolish, I agree. But I remain convinced that he did *not* know, at that time, about any possibility of it being a fake. Had he known, he would not have tried to get it back. He'd have been satisfied to know it had disappeared; and no one would ask why it was no longer being worn by any of the Roxby ladies. As to whether Mrs Roxby knew, that's another matter altogether.'

I added, 'And somehow, in some way that eludes me for

the moment, it is all connected with the murder of Ariadne Chalk. When I told Mrs Roxby the body found on the Heath was that of her companion, her shock and distress were genuine, although she tried to disguise both. Also . . .'

'Well, what else, Ross?' demanded the superintendent, still unwilling to give up his own theory.

'Jeremy and Charlotte can't abide one another,' I said simply. 'I just can't see them working together on any projected plan. Yet, this afternoon, he was paying a social call on her at home in Hampstead. Or so he would have us believe. He was there because they urgently needed to talk. The necessity was so pressing that he overcame his usual dislike of her, and went to her house. That's my guess.'

'Why so anxious to meet now?' challenged Dunn.

'Can't tell you that yet, sir. There is a good deal we just don't know. My instinct is to guess something of an emergency has arisen. Even natural foes have to work together sometimes.'

'So what do you plan to do now, Ross?' Dunn asked, squinting at me.

'I plan to question Obadiah Quigley again. He is holding out on us; I am sure of it.'

'What makes you so sure?' Dunn raised his bushy eyebrows.

'Because I begin to suspect that, again in some way I can't yet tell you, all this is connected with the murder of a receiver of stolen goods, known to us here: one Jacob Jacobus.'

There was a brief silence. Then Dunn spoke. 'Jacobus would have recognised a fake jewellery piece, were it offered to him.'

'Yes, he would have done so. But was he offered the necklace? And did he refuse to handle it on those grounds?'

Dunn was now scowling furiously. 'You are not over-looking the fact that the murder of Jacobus took place before that of Ariadne Chalk? That indicates a whole chain of events since the original report of the missing necklace.'

'I am well aware of it, sir, and that's why I need to talk to Quigley.'

Dunn's eyebrows now shot up to meet his hairline. 'Is he not awaiting trial?'

'Yes, sir, he's in Pentonville at the moment.'

'Oh well, go and see him there, then, if you must. Is there one specific detail he told you, when he was arrested over the matter of Jacobus's watch, which now makes you so keen to talk to the wretched fellow again?'

'Well, sir, it's something he didn't tell me that preys on my mind.'

'Then you will need to engage in a spot of mind-reading! If he still doesn't tell you whatever it is, perhaps you could consult a gypsy's crystal ball?'

With that, Dunn fell to chortling at his own wit, and I beat a hasty retreat.

I didn't escape without encountering a further minor obstacle. About to descend the staircase to the ground floor, I again encountered Inspector Reynolds. He stopped midway and looked up. A grin like the Cheshire Cat's spread across his face.

'I hear your emerald necklace has turned up?' he said cheerfully. 'Or rather, it hasn't! A paste replica, eh?'

'News travels fast around this building!' I couldn't prevent myself saying sourly.

'I knew there was something wrong about that burglary of yours,' Reynolds told me. 'There wasn't a hint of a rumour about it to be had anywhere. None of my regular informants had heard of it. I thought it was rum. Still, never mind, a paste necklace is better than nothing at all!'

'The real necklace is still missing!' I snapped.

'If you say so,' declared Reynolds. 'Well, well, it looks as though you will have to go back to the beginning and start again.'

He slapped my shoulder and proceeded on his way looking unbearably smug.

The really annoying thing was that he was probably right.

Chapter Thirteen

PENTONVILLE HAD been opened earlier in the century as a model prison. This aspect of it was never appreciated by its residents. At first, this was probably because, among other things, it had been a holding institution for convicts destined to be transported to Australia. A few years ago, such deportations ceased. But memories linger; and many present-day prisoners objected to being in Pentonville on principle. Obadiah Quigley was no exception.

'I'd rather be in Newgate,' he grumbled. 'You can always be sure of meeting up with a few fellows you know in Newgate; and if you keep your nose clean, no one bothers you. Here you're organised every minute of the day. Anyway, you can't be sure the government won't change its mind again, and bundle you on to a ship sailing off to the other side of the world!'

'That won't happen, Quigley. You have my word on it. Fear not, Australia will manage without you. It's no use grumbling. It's your own fault you are locked up at all,' I told him.

'The magistrate said I had committed a heinous crime!'

he squawked. 'It was too serious for his court and a matter for a judge. Heinous? I told him, I didn't even know what that was, so how could I have done it? He said it meant wicked. I told him that was nonsense. All I did was take a watch off a dead man, who didn't need it no more. But he said I was "of known bad character". Me! An honest working man! I don't say I was never pinched before for anything. But never anything *heinous*! Now I'm here, waiting to be sent up before the beak at the Old Bailey.'

I sighed. 'We've been through this before. Because Jacobus was dead, that did not mean you could help yourself to his property. You did, and that's why you're here. Listen, Quigley. Forget about the watch. I want you to cast your mind back to the day Jacobus died.'

'I didn't kill him!' squeaked Quig. 'Am I going to be accused of that too? Who am I? Sweeney Todd?'

'I am not suggesting you killed him, Quigley. I am here to ask about the day it happened. I believe there is something you have not told me. The reason you have kept it quiet is, I suspect, because you think the knowledge is something you hope to be able to profit from in the future. Your intention, in short, is blackmail.'

'Blame me for everything, why don't you?' demanded Quig gloomily.

'No, I am giving you the opportunity to help me and, in so doing, help yourself. But you have to tell me the truth, mind!'

Finally, something I had said seeped through the fog that filled his head. 'Do me a bit of good, you think?'

'If it's true. And I make no promises! But it might help

your defence, when you're in the dock at the Old Bailey, that you have cooperated to the best of your ability.'

'Go on, then,' muttered Quig sullenly.

'Cast your mind back to the day Jacobus was murdered.'

Quig's unlovely features set in a ferocious scowl. I took that to mean he was trying to remember. It was like attempting to have a conversation with a gargoyle.

'Who came to visit Jacobus that day?'

'You asked me before; and I told you, how should I know? I'm the potman at the pub. I'm not a ruddy butler, opening and closing doors all day!'

'If a stranger came to visit Jacobus, normal procedure was for the visitor to ask at the tavern first, because that was where a key to the house was kept. They were just hanging on a hook behind the public bar. Anyone in the pub could take it down and open up Jacobus's front door to a visitor. I believe that's what you did that day.'

'All right!' Quig surrendered. 'But listen, I wouldn't go letting into the house someone who looked like a murderer! Stands to reason. Anyway, it's not, generally speaking, my job. I got enough to do without running back and forth to old Jacobus's place. It was usually Daisy did that.' The gargoyle features grew even more grotesque. Quig was smiling. 'The old fellow liked Daisy around the place.'

'But on that day Daisy wasn't available? What time of day was it?'

'Middle of the afternoon,' admitted Quig. 'Daisy would've been out back, washing glasses. But the visitor, he didn't want to come into the pub. He was too grand, I reckon, or else he didn't want Tom or Daisy to see him. But I was outside. He called me over and give me a whole guinea . . .' Quig fell silent as he dwelt on this unheard-of piece of good fortune. 'So I reckoned he was all right. A gentleman, that's what he was. Very smartly turned out and carrying a cane. He wasn't the first swell to call on the old man. I'd seen others like him come and go. Usually young swells who've got themselves into a pickle over debts.'

'What did he say? Do you remember?'

'O' course I do! A gent who gives me a guinea! I've kept an eye open for him ever since.'

'And did you see him again, after that first time?'

'No,' said Quig sadly. 'Anyway, he hands over the guinea. *"Just let me into the house, my good fellow,"* he says. *"I need to speak with Mr Jacobus briefly. You can come back and lock up again later, in half an hour or so. I'll be gone by then."*'

Quig attempted to copy the visitor's way of speaking, when giving the actual words. The result was as if a ventriloquist's dummy spoke.

'It's what I did. I never saw the gent leave. But he'd gone when I went back, because I stuck my head through the front door and listened. I couldn't hear voices upstairs; not a sound. So I locked up and put the key back where it belonged, behind the bar.'

'You didn't go upstairs?'

'No! I was busy with my own work. You've been in that house. You know how it's built, just the one room on each floor, all of 'em opening on to the staircase. I'd have heard it, if someone was up there with the old feller.'

'When Daisy took Jacobus his supper tray, she found the street door open, Quigley! So I believe you did not go back to lock up the house. That last part of your story is untrue.'

He looked sulky and muttered, 'All right! I meant to go back; I swear it. But I was busy, like I said, and I forgot. I would've gone back to lock the door, but I was run off my feet, and that's the truth! I'm human, ain't I?'

'Yes, you are. All I ask is that you tell me the truth.'

'Well, I have done. Now you've heard it all and there ain't nuffin' else!'

'Now I believe you,' I told him.

Quig looked relieved. He tilted his head to one side and squinted at me. 'Reckon the smart gent killed old Jacobus, do you? Don't see it myself. He was a real dandy. He wouldn't want to get blood all over himself! Nor would he have given me a whole guinea. I'd remember a caller who gave me a guinea. Not likely to forget him!'

'Nor have you forgotten him, Quigley. You reckoned that anyone so free with his money has guineas to spare. He'd pay you to keep quiet about his visit. All you had to do was wait a while.'

'I reckoned without you, didn't I?' retaliated Quigley.

'Yes, Quigley, you did.'

I returned to the Yard and reported this interview to Superintendent Dunn.

'Bless my soul!' said Dunn, when I'd finished my account. 'Do you believe his story? Fashionable gentleman carrying a cane? It almost sounds like Jeremy Roxby! Is this some ploy by Quigley to get a reduced sentence?'

'Quigley isn't bright enough to invent such an incident, sir. At least, not entirely. In fact, Quigley often insists how stupid he is. He sees it as an excuse for his behaviour. No matter what he does, he does not accept any blame. He was dealt a poor hand of cards at the beginning of his life; and has only played them as best he could ever since.'

'He is not the first professional crook to plead that defence!' observed Dunn wryly.

'As for Jeremy Roxby, sir,' I continued, 'he carried a cane when he first came here to the Yard, to be sure. But so do plenty of other fashionable gents. Quigley also made a good point. A man who hands a guinea tip to a potman knows he will be remembered. Would Roxby be foolish enough to impress himself on Quigley's memory in that way?'

'He might, if he believed that a guinea buys silence,' countered Dunn.

I had to agree. 'I will see what Roxby has to say tomorrow morning. Perhaps a message could be sent to him that I'll call on him at his office. But first things first. Right now, I have to get myself over to Hampstead. Charlotte Roxby has had plenty of time to come to terms with the shock of seeing the fake necklace, and must have recovered sufficiently to be interviewed. Sergeant Wood will be wondering where I am.'

'Before you go,' Dunn opened a folder that lay on his desk, 'it may help you to read this. It is a copy of a report from the British consulate in Italy which dealt with the fatal accident involving Mrs Roxby's brother and his wife, both British subjects, fifteen years ago. It arrived from the

Foreign Office by special messenger while you were at Pentonville.'

I picked up the folder and glanced rapidly through it. 'Good grief!' I muttered. 'How will she talk herself out of this, I wonder?'

I was well on my way to Hampstead, by the train from Broad Street Station, before I remembered that I had not sent a message to Lizzie to let her know I would be late home for supper. It could not be helped. I walked from the Hampstead station to the Roxby house. It took me twenty minutes. It was not impossible that it had taken Miss Chalk's killer the same amount of time, if he'd been on foot and followed the same route.

The house was quiet and dark within, blinds drawn at most windows. This was a house in mourning. Ventham opened the door to me, but could hardly bring himself to speak. This was not because, as on my first visit, he disapproved of me. It was because an atmosphere of disaster hung about the whole place. Recent events had turned to tragedy and there was little hope they would improve in the short term. Mrs Roxby sat with Sergeant Wood in the little back parlour. There were tea things on the table between them. It would have looked a perfectly normal scene, had the lady not looked so tense.

Wood stood up as I entered.

'All right, Sergeant?' I asked.

'Yes, sir,' he replied dourly.

I bowed politely to Mrs Roxby. 'I hope you are recovered, ma'am?'

'I am well able to answer your questions, Inspector!' was the bleak reply. 'But I shall be unable to offer you any explanation for that – that mockery of the Roxby emeralds found in the Thames. I know nothing of it. I have told your sergeant here so.'

'In fact, madam,' I began, 'I would like to start by asking a few questions on another subject.'

She hadn't expected that; and looked at me in surprise. 'You don't mind if I sit down?'

'It appears to be your habit to make yourself at home.'

I sat down and nodded at Wood, who took out a notebook.

'So, as to my first question. Perhaps, Mrs Roxby, you could begin by telling me the true identity of the young lady, normally residing here, whom you have presented to the world as Isabella Gray.'

Shock rendered her speechless. All the colour drained from her face and then flooded back, suffusing her cheeks with an unattractive scarlet. 'Have you gone mad, Inspector Ross?'

Wood, also, was staring at me in considerable surprise. His hand, holding the pencil, had frozen in mid-air.

'No, ma'am,' I assured her, 'and I beg you will not waste my time, but answer my question.'

'How on earth am I to answer such a ridiculous question? Isabella Gray is the daughter of my late brother and his wife. They were both killed when Isabella was only eighteen months of age. It was in Italy that the tragedy occurred. The carriage in which my brother and his wife were travelling overturned on a mountain road. The infant and her nursemaid survived. My late husband and I had no children. We took in Isabella as a matter of course. But I think you probably know all this already, Inspector.'

'That is the story everyone has been told, I agree. But it is far from the truth, is it not? The child and her nursemaid did not survive. I must tell you that, just before I left the Yard to come here, I had the opportunity to read the official consular report on the accident. Tragically, none of the travellers survived; and I include the infant and her nursemaid. I must ask you again: what is the true identity of Isabella Gray?'

'Watch out, sir!' cried Wood, leaping up from his chair.

For the second time that day, Mrs Roxby turned ashen and fainted away. I was sorry for her at that moment, and sorry also that the interview was interrupted when it had barely begun. But it couldn't be helped. Ventham was summoned, and then Mrs Roxby's personal maid with the smelling salts. Wood and I retired discreetly to the study while the lady was restored.

'Blimey, sir!' whispered Wood in a hoarse undertone. 'That was a bit of a shock, for me, too! How long have you known that?' He fumbled in his coat pocket and produced a paper bag of boiled sweets. He was in need of some restorative support himself, so I didn't object when he put one in his mouth. He rolled it around his teeth and stared at me.

'Not very long, Sergeant. As I told Mrs Roxby just now, I only read the consular report just before I left the Yard to come here. I did suspect there was some mystery and it had to be brought out into the open.'

'Whatever put you on to it, sir?'

'Jeremy Roxby is so set against the girl marrying his son. And there had clearly been some serious falling-out at some stage involving him and his sister-in-law. He has been trying for some time to regain possession of the Roxby emeralds. They'd been given to his sister-in-law when she married his brother. That was the family tradition. The wife of the eldest son wears the emeralds until the next marriage of an eldest son. So why not encourage a match between Harry and Isabella, who were clearly very fond of one another? I became convinced there was some family secret; and they were determined to keep it hidden. I couldn't let that go on unchallenged, Wood. I admit to you privately, I am sorry to bring it out into the open. But this is a complicated case and unravelling it must mean starting at the beginning.'

'Does the young lady know?' Wood was now rattling the boiled sweet furiously against his teeth.

'No, I don't think she does. But she will have to be told she isn't the person she's been led to believe she is. It will come as a great shock to her. It will cause much distress. I am sure she really believes herself to be Isabella Gray.'

'Blimey,' murmured Wood again. 'So then, sir, have you got any theory as to who she might really be?'

'Yes, I do. But unless Mrs Roxby can be persuaded to speak out – or Jeremy Roxby does, it will be difficult . . .'

The door opened and Ventham reappeared. 'Madam will speak to you now, sir.'

'I hope you are recovered, ma'am,' I told Mrs Roxby. She looked far from well, very pale, and appeared to have developed a facial twitch. I had no wish to see her faint away again. However, the familiar stare of dislike was still fixed on me. I was confident I could question her. Predictably, she went on to the offensive from the start.

'You have no reason, nor any right, to inquire into *any* matter other than that of the stolen necklace.'

'Ah, but that's the problem, you see, ma'am. Once you report a crime to the police, inquiries begin. Who knows where they may end? It is something you should have considered before you went to the Yard and reported the robbery. Did you really think it would be so simple? That I would make some superficial inquiry and the matter would be shelved as an unsolved mystery? You should have had more confidence in us, Mrs Roxby, and known we would run down every clue. We are not amateurs, we are professionals.'

'I did not know you would be so shameless and impertinent!' she snapped.

'Sadly, it goes with the job,' I told her.

'So I have learned!'

'I can only repeat, ma'am, that you should have thought through your plans more carefully before you loosed the hounds on the trail of the fox. Now then, let us return to the identity of Miss Gray. Whose child is she?'

'This has nothing to do with the Roxby necklace.' Her voice was mechanical. It was a last attempt to put a stop to this line of questioning, but she knew it wouldn't work.

'That is for us to decide.'

We all three sat in silence for a few minutes. Wood looked like a man in desperate need of another mint humbug. He kept an anxious eye on me, wondering where on earth all this was going. I wasn't too sure myself. I had to win the battle of wills with the lady.

'Very well,' she said at last. Wood got ready to write in his notebook. 'Isabella is the daughter of my late husband, and a woman he had in keeping. It is a common enough arrangement for any gentleman of means. Our marriage had been founded on practical reasons. Money marries money, Inspector Ross.

'Sadly, my late husband and I had no children, despite consulting the very best doctors, here and in Switzerland. But his mistress had presented him with a baby girl. Then, I suppose, you might say Fate took a hand. My brother, his wife and young daughter were killed in a carriage accident in Italy, as you have been at such pains to investigate. My husband suggested to me that it was an excellent opportunity to bring Isabella, then only eighteen months of age, into our family, purporting to be my niece, who had survived the Italian accident. It took some time and a good deal of – arranging – but that is what we did.'

'And Isabella's mother?'

'She agreed willingly. An illegitimate child would have an uncertain future; but now Isabella would be living with her natural father. She would grow up in comfortable circumstances and her future would be secure, with every prospect of a good marriage.'

'And Mr Jeremy Roxby? He was not only your husband's brother but his business partner. How did he view this arrangement?'

She pressed her lips tightly together, as if to prevent a

frank reply. Eventually, she spoke in a flat, toneless voice, avoiding my gaze and fixing her own on some spot on the far wall. 'He was completely against it. There was a battle of wills such as can only happen when two Roxbys are at odds. It had occasionally happened before when there had been some business dispute. But this concerned the family; and at one point I began to believe it would threaten the stability of the firm. Eventually, George got his way. Jeremy finally agreed with very bad grace. But he made it clear from the beginning, and also as Isabella was growing up, that there could never be talk of a marriage between his son and Isabella. As brothers, they continued to run the company, as they were obliged to do. But there was no other contact.'

I ventured to interrupt and say, 'Yet the two young people have apparently always been friends.'

She dismissed that with a wave of her hand. 'The children, yes, one forgets that they have minds of their own. They were always good friends. But no more than that, Inspector Ross.'

Perhaps . . . I thought.

She was continuing. 'And then, sadly, my husband became ill with the influenza several winters after Isabella joined us, and he passed away. Jeremy made it clear that from then on, he would run the business. Even though I had inherited George's shares in it, I would have no say. The door of the boardroom was closed to me.'

She paused, then added briskly, 'I know you think me a difficult woman, Inspector. But my disposition is nothing like so implacable as Jeremy Roxby's. He is not a man to cross.'

I nodded. I believed her. 'So, tell me about the Roxby emeralds. Jeremy Roxby was demanding their return, was he not? Isabella Gray was wearing them around London's fashionable houses. He couldn't accept that.'

'No, he was furious. But I was equally determined that he should never have them. So, two years ago, I sent the necklace over to France without telling anyone, and had it copied. That copy was the necklace Isabella has been wearing to balls and other fashionable gatherings.'

'And the original?'

'The original was dismantled; and the stones and precious metal sold privately to a dealer in Russia. The same jeweller handled that sale. I heard, though I don't know if it's true, that some of the stones have been incorporated in a tiara and earrings that have been worn at the Imperial Court in St Petersburg.' She gave a smile that was truly chilling. 'At any rate, my brother-in-law can never have the Roxby emeralds, whatever he chooses to do.'

Wood, scribbling away, murmured something that sounded like 'Strewth!' I glanced at him warningly.

'How did the fake necklace come to be thrown into the river? Did you decide to get rid of it completely?'

She leaned forward, stiff as a board in her tight lacing, 'I cannot tell you how it came to be in the river, Inspector. You have my word of honour on that. I locked the fake away in the safe here in this house so that Isabella could wear it when she came out, as indeed, she has done. She still believes she was wearing the original necklace. Fortunately, she never liked it. Jeremy, as you can imagine, almost went out of his mind when it was reported to him that it had been seen at fashionable parties, worn by Isabella. He began again to insist I return it to him! He got to be such a nuisance that I decided to enlist Chalk's help in staging a robbery of the Roxby emeralds so that I could then report it to Scotland Yard as stolen.'

'But the ongoing presence of the necklace in this house had become something of a problem, I fancy,' I observed.

She pursed her lips. 'Yes, I had yet to decide what to do with it. Before your men examined the safe, I had removed the necklace again and hid it in a secret compartment in my late husband's desk. I was unaware that Chalk knew of the desk's secret. I can only suppose George foolishly told her of it. I was deeply shocked to learn it had been taken from the river, and I still don't understand how that could have happened. Jeremy, of course, still believed the real necklace stolen. He was already absolutely furious about my carelessness, as he chose to call it. When he was told that the necklace retrieved from the river was a fake, you saw how he reacted. Now he must be incandescent. But there is nothing he can do about it!' She gave a triumphant smile.

'When did you discover the paste replica was missing from the secret compartment?'

'Really, Inspector, have you not been listening? I repeat, I did not know it *was* missing! I thought it was still there. It was not until I received a telegram from my brother-in-law at breakfast-time this morning, alerting me that he was on his way to see me later in the day, that I opened up the compartment – and discovered it was missing. I was considerably shaken and was still distressed when I walked into Scotland Yard and was shown the replica, covered in mud, and apparently taken from the Thames this morning.'

'Did anyone else, other than Miss Ariadne Chalk, know that the necklace had never been stolen and was still locked up in this house?'

For the first time she showed a moment of weakness. She closed her eyes and swayed. I was afraid she might faint again and jumped to my feet. But she put out her hand to signal that I should stay seated. She opened her eyes. 'Only Chalk knew. She had to know in order for the robbery to be staged on the evening of the dinner party. I knew Isabella would refuse to wear the emeralds. But I put on a show of insisting she did; and took the necklace from the safe and up to her dressing room. Then we had a fine old argument, she and I. Isabella is half a Roxby, after all, though she might not know it! She got her way; and the necklace was left unattended in the dressing room. During the evening, Chalk slipped upstairs and dropped it out of the window into the garden below. After everyone had left, she retrieved it and locked it away again in the safe. I had to stay with my guests, of course, I couldn't do it.'

'You'd forgotten the matter of the insurance, I think,' I said.

'Yes, I had. I realised that to be really convincing, I should claim on the insurance, in due course. But I would not have done that. Whatever opinion you may have of me, Inspector, I am not a cheat.'

'That would have looked odd, as time passed and no necklace was ever found.'

'Yes, but I would not have put in a claim. I would have had to stage its rediscovery before it came to that.'

'Jeremy Roxby might have made a claim on your behalf.'

'I don't control what my brother-in-law does. That should be clear to you.'

'Now,' I said, 'tell me about Ariadne Chalk. Was she the lady your late husband kept under his protection, Isabella's mother?'

'Yes,' she said quietly. 'But if you are imagining some kind of *ménage à trois*, my husband, myself, and his mistress, under one roof, Inspector, put it right out of your head! While my husband was alive, Chalk never set foot in this house. But, not long after he died, she contacted me. She had fallen on hard times. She was no longer young and she was never pretty. I don't know what he ever saw in her. We came to an arrangement. She came here as my companion. She saw her child grow into a young lady. It worked well enough.'

Mrs Roxby might choose to believe there was never a *ménage à trois*; but in my view there was, if not the usual sort. Nor did I believe that charity alone had led her to invite Miss Chalk into her home. Miss Chalk knew the truth of Isabella's identity. She had to be kept under Mrs Roxby's eye.

'Now for another difficult matter, ma'am. The death of Ariadne Chalk.'

The satisfaction was wiped from her expression. 'I can tell you nothing of that, Inspector Ross, other than I suspect she took the necklace from the desk not knowing it was fake. She knew nothing of my having a copy made.

For that, I used another intermediary. At any rate, it seems she went out after dark, to the Heath, to make an arranged rendez-vous with someone she hoped would dispose of it. She had led a somewhat rackety life when young. Perhaps she had contacted someone from that period of her life, someone none too scrupulous? She misjudged how dangerous such a course of action might be. I speculate only, Inspector Ross, because, like you, I do not know.

'Possibly she was trying, in some wrong-headed way, to help. Don't ask me what she thought her accomplice would do. Did he agree to throw it into the river? Perhaps. I don't know what was on her mind at that moment. I do know that the continued presence of the necklace in the safe here had worried her a great deal from the start. When your men asked to examine the safe, she was terrified that you might search the rest of the house and find it. There would be a scandal and, by association, a shadow cast over Isabella's reputation. In my opinion, therefore, she decided to make arrangements herself to get rid of it. She was not an over-intelligent woman, Inspector.'

'Well, sir,' said Wood, as we travelled back into London. 'I've met some hard cases in my time, men and women, but that female takes some beating. You would have thought she would show some sorrow at the loss of her companion. They had been living there together for years.'

But I was remembering Mrs Roxby as I had seen her on the morning I went to break the news that the woman's body on the Heath was indeed that of Miss Chalk. I saw her in my mind's eye, sitting in the little morning room, staring out into the garden.

'For my own part, Wood, I believe she does mourn the loss of Ariadne Chalk. They were bound together by so much: her late husband, Isabella Gray, the years living under the same roof, as you say. But she will never admit it nor show it. It is not her way.'

Chapter Fourteen

Elizabeth Martin Ross

IT WAS very late and dusk had fallen before Ben arrived home. He looked exhausted and worried. Clearly, he had been dealing with some particularly difficult situation. He began to apologise for his tardiness, and for not sending a message that he'd be so late.

But I took his hand to interrupt him, and assured him he need not worry on that account, at least. Constable Biddle had taken care of it. As soon as he had been able to finish work for the day, our personal source of information had hurried over to our home, face shining with importance, to give both Bessie and me a full account of the day's developments.

He told it very well. Bessie and I had but to listen while Biddle – ever the dedicated reader of the penny dreadful – gave a full account of everything he knew to date, with thrilling detail and lurid description. Events included the retrieval of the necklace from the Thames; arrival of the gentlemen from the insurance company, quickly followed by their declaring the discovery was not the necklace at all, but was a paste replica. Then came the dramatic arrival at the Yard of Jeremy Roxby and Mrs Charlotte Roxby; the collapse of the lady and her being sent off home to recover under the supervision of Sergeant Wood. Finally came the inspector's own departure for Hampstead. Biddle deeply regretted he could not tell us what happened after that. We should have to wait until the inspector got back himself.

'Lawks!' said Bessie in awe, when Biddle at last fell silent and restored himself with a cup of tea. 'It's just like a book!'

'Thank you, Constable Biddle. You had better give Walter some supper,' I suggested to Bessie. 'Cover over the inspector's plate, and set it on the range to keep warm.'

'His dinner will dry out!' warned Bessie.

'Then perhaps you could go down to the public house on the corner and fetch back a couple of bottles of porter.'

'I'll walk down with you, Bessie,' said her devoted swain. 'But I can't go into the pub, on account I'm in uniform.'

I don't know if Ben noticed how dry his supper was, but he only picked at it before pushing it away. However, he drank the porter and began to tell me what had happened when he reached Hampstead. During his story, Bessie and Biddle somehow migrated from the kitchen to the parlour and sat in silence against the far wall, side by side, holding hands and listening, open mouthed.

'Poor Ariadne,' I said, when Ben at last fell silent. 'Now I realise what she wanted to tell me . . . and why when it came to it she could not speak. She wanted, above all, to protect her child from scandal. Only think what the newspapers would make of it all.'

'And will make, when they learn of it,' warned Ben. 'They surely will.'

I added, 'You know my father was a family doctor. I believe he knew of several cases in which an illegitimate birth was passed off as a legitimate one, by some subterfuge. Family members often arrange these matters between themselves. Do you believe Mrs Roxby has now told you the truth?'

'She has told me as much of the truth as she has been forced to do. There are almost certainly other details she has not told me. However, what I learned today may be enough.'

Silence fell on the parlour. We all sat lost in our thoughts.

'Biddle!' snapped Ben suddenly, turning to the constable. 'Not a word of this to anyone. I shall make my report in the morning to Superintendent Dunn. You won't utter a squeak to anyone! Nor you, Bessie. Understood?'

'Yessir!' they chorused in unison.

Inspector Ben Ross

I arrived at the Yard the following morning to find that Superintendent Dunn had arrived well before me and had been busy. Messages had been exchanged with Jeremy Roxby and I was expected at the offices of the shipping company at ten o'clock.

'And I,' announced Dunn, 'shall be coming with you.'

'You, sir?' I asked in surprise.

'You have some objection, Ross?'

'Well, no, sir, of course not. Do we take along Wood with us?'

'I see no need for that. To be frank, I am anxious not to have our arrival the cause of too much speculation. Wood is a good fellow, but he can be mistaken for nothing other than a policeman. You and I, Ross, might hope to pass as, well, something else. Some occupation less likely to raise gossip to fever pitch.'

'But everyone working there will know what we are!' I objected. 'We are expected, sir. You have just told me the appointment has been fixed.'

'So it has; and even now the staff will be awaiting us agog. I don't doubt it. But anyone else who might chance to be in the building when we arrive, a temporary caller, someone on business, might not. Don't be difficult, Ross. Allow me to know best.'

I was not altogether convinced by his argument but had to accept it. It seemed to me that whoever had insisted on Mrs Roxby being received by a senior officer like Dunn on her first visit was still intervening to protect the name of Roxby. I did not know who that was. Dunn might know but he would never tell me.

We were received at the offices of the shipping company at first by a page at the door. He was a pale, spotty youth, who gaped at us in awe before he quickly passed us on to a junior clerk. He conducted us briskly into the presence of the senior clerk, who in turn led us up to the boardroom. No mere office for us! I was beginning to feel we were being ushered into the presence of royalty. But that, after all, was the intention of the whole charade. Mr Jeremy Roxby was an important man. We were never to be allowed to forget it.

The boardroom into which we were shown was a

magnificent place, running across the width of the building, with windows on one side giving on to the street. The long wall facing the windows was hung with portraits. A highly polished teak table ran almost the length of the room, with chairs set to either side. Jeremy Roxby had been seated at the top of it, working on some papers. I wondered if this, too, was to remind us how important his time was. A desk set of silver-capped inkwell and pens in a silver tray, and an ivory-inlaid box for keeping sealing wax and other necessities, had been set out for his use. The prime minister probably did not work in better-equipped surroundings. As we entered, he laid down his pen, patted the papers into a neat oblong wad, rose to his feet and came to greet us.

'I am obliged to you, gentlemen, for your promptness,' he said.

Dunn had decided to play to his country squire image. 'Fine place you have here, sir!' he declared, indicating the room with a sweep of his arm. 'Those are, I take it, family portraits?'

'Yes.' Roxby responded by acting the host. He led us to the gallery of paintings. The central one hung above a fine carved marble fireplace. 'That is my great-grandfather and founder of the firm, Joshua Roxby.'

I thought Joshua had the look of a merchant adventurer about him. His hair was curled in the fashion of the seventeen-nineties, and teamed with magnificent sideburns. He had piercing dark eyes, and wore a silk brocade waistcoat under a blue topcoat with fitted waist. His beringed hand rested negligently on some document with a seal attached. The whole was pictured against a seascape on which featured a large sailing vessel. If anyone was setting out to found an empire of any sort, that man was Joshua Roxby.

'And this,' continued Roxby, moving to the next portrait, 'is my great-grandmother, painted shortly after their marriage.'

Here was the Brazilian lady for whom the emerald necklace had been created. She was, indeed, strikingly beautiful. She and Joshua together must have turned all heads. She was wearing the necklace and one could see at once that it had been created to complement her dramatic looks. This, then, was the cause of all the trouble.

Jeremy Roxby saw I was studying it. 'Yes,' he said, 'those are the Roxby emeralds. You will understand what an insult that shabby copy taken from Thames is to the original.' He sighed. 'I suppose we must accept that we shall never see the original again.'

'I fear not, sir,' I told him. 'Mrs Charlotte Roxby has told me that she ordered the jeweller in France who created the copy to disassemble the original and oversee the sale of the stones and precious metals. She claims she was told there was a buyer ready and waiting in Russia. It makes sense. Any attempt to sell the stones here would have aroused instant comment.'

'Wretched woman!' he muttered. 'George should never have married her!' He drew a deep breath and gestured towards the teak table. 'Let us sit down.'

He retook his seat at the top of the table, with the papers and writing materials before him. Dunn took a seat to his left and I the one to his right, along the length of the table. A casual observer who popped his head through the door would have taken it for a board meeting, not a police interview. But that was the intention of the whole theatre. Before either of us could speak, Roxby began again.

'You should know, gentlemen, that after Inspector Ross left my sister-in-law yesterday evening she wrote me a long letter, detailing all that had passed between you, Inspector. She sent it to me last night by the hand of Ventham, her butler. So you know that Isabella is the daughter of my late brother; and her mother was Ariadne Chalk, my brother's mistress. In short, you know almost everything.'

He sighed. 'When my brother George died, he left a wife without her husband: and a mistress without her protector. My sister-in-law needed to keep Chalk close. She dared not risk the truth of Isabella's birth becoming known. Besides, if Ariadne Chalk's circumstances became desperate, she might turn to blackmail. I warned George of all this when he told me he planned to adopt Isabella, while disguising the true circumstances of her birth. He wouldn't listen; but I was right, of course. After my brother's death, Charlotte took Ariadne into the house as a companion.' He gave a dry, mirthless, smile. 'Oddly enough, it worked after a fashion.'

I met Dunn's eyes across the table and he gave the merest nod.

'Mr Roxby,' I said. 'I am well aware that many of the questions I must ask you will be painful for you to answer. I do understand that, just as I understood how difficult it was for Mrs Charlotte Roxby to answer my questions about Isabella Gray.'

'You wish to talk about my son, Harry,' he said in a resigned voice.

'Yes, I do. I know you have hired a private detective by
the name of Morgan to keep track of the young man, to
report to you where he goes, his associates . . . I believe that
Morgan will have reported, at some stage, Harry's visits to
a dubious person by the name of Jacob Jacobus, who lived
in Limehouse.'

Roxby's features set tightly. I fancy he paled. When he
spoke, his voice was tense.

'I cannot deny it; since Morgan has already told you of
it. Harry has been foolish. He has been continually running into debt and eventually I lost patience. I told him I
would not pay his debts any longer. I spoke in anger. It was
an unwise thing for me to say because it meant that my son,
without changing his profligate ways, now looked elsewhere for money. I had learned, from Morgan, that he had
been visiting Jacobus. Jacobus was known, among other
interests, to handle stolen goods, especially jewellery, but
also small items of value, trinkets of one sort and another,
snuffboxes and the like.'

He fell silent and I prompted him. 'And then Mrs Charlotte Roxby reported the Roxby emeralds stolen, taken
from her house during the course of a dinner party. The
necklace had been left unattended in Isabella Gray's dressing room.'

'Yes,' he said. 'It was a ridiculous tale from the start.
That the necklace had gone, I did not doubt. But as to the
exact circumstances of its disappearance . . .' He fell silent.

I decided to prompt him. 'Forgive me, you thought it
possible the young people had plotted to steal them, sell
them, and solve all of Harry's money problems.'

'God forgive me,' Jeremy said very quietly. 'But I did. The circumstances of the theft seemed to me far too improbable. I thought Harry and Isabella, with the foolishness of youth, had thought up what they considered a splendid trick to get Harry out of his pickle.'

'It is understandable, sir. I thought it possible myself for a while. So, sir, you decided to pay a call on Jacobus, because that was the person to whom your son might well have taken the necklace to sell on. Jacobus had bought other, smaller, items from your son. Determined to know the truth and, if possible, recover the necklace, you visited Jacobus in Limehouse. That visit took place on the day the old man was murdered.'

Roxby was silent.

'You should know, sir, that the potman of the Crossed Keys tavern remembers you. You overtipped him when he procured the key of the house and let you in. That need not have mattered. But, unfortunately, the potman is light fingered. He was the second person to see the dead body, after it was discovered by a woman working at the tavern. Finding himself alone with it for a few minutes, he could not resist helping himself to the dead man's gold watch and chain. He did not want to risk being found in possession of the items, so he tried to sell them on at once. That led to his being discovered, and the watch and chain being recovered and identified by Jacobus's daughter.'

Roxby remained silent.

'What I believe happened, sir, is this. You called on Jacobus, having convinced yourself that Harry had offered the fellow the emeralds. But Harry had not stolen the emeralds. Thus, when you asked Jacobus about them, he denied any knowledge. You became angry.'

Roxby spoke at last, very quietly and with his gaze fixed on the writing materials on the table before him. 'The man had a collection of antique snuffboxes. They were set out as a display on a small table. I recognised one of them. It had belonged to my father. I knew Jacobus must have had it from my son. It convinced me that he must also have received the emeralds. I was furious about the snuffbox; but for the moment it was of secondary interest. Recovery of the necklace was my priority. I told Jacobus I would pay whatever money he had received for it, if he would only arrange for the necklace to be returned. But he kept insisting he did not have the necklace, he had not passed it on, he did not know where it was. There had been no talk of it among receivers like himself. If I had not been so enraged, I would have paid more attention to what he was saying, and realised that I was on the wrong track. Whoever was behind the disappearance of the necklace, it was not my son.

'But there was something about the rogue himself that irked me. He appeared to consider himself a legitimate businessman. He sat there, wedged into his chair, and – would you believe it? He offered me a glass of apricot brandy!'

'I do believe it,' I told him.

'I lost my head,' Roxby said simply. 'The whole taken together: his grotesque appearance, my father's snuffbox, the offer of some brew he had concocted – I took it into my head that the emerald necklace was there, in that room, hidden. I took advantage of his lack of mobility. I leaped up and began to search in the room, while the fellow sat there protesting. I pulled out drawers and opened cupboards . . . Of course I didn't find the necklace. A kind of madness had overtaken me. I thought he must have hidden it beneath the floorboards and began to try to lever them up with a large Oriental knife among the bric-a-brac I had uncovered. It is called, I believe, a kris. That was useless. Time was passing. Some other person might come to visit Jacobus; or the potman return to lock up again. So, I returned to where he sat, the kris in my hand. I stood behind him, so that he could not reach out and wrest the knife from me. I reached over and held it to his throat. I meant only to frighten the fellow into confessing the whereabouts of the necklace – if it was not in the room, what had he done with it? But he tried to lever himself up. I tried, with my free hand, to push him back down again. The knife . . . I had lost control of the knife and suddenly he let out a dreadful gurgle. I shall hear it, echoing in my head, until my dying day. There was blood spurting out everywhere. Fortunately, positioned as I was behind the chair, I was shielded from most of it. He stopped moving and no longer made any sound. His eyes were open and stared up at me. But he no longer saw me. I realised he was dead.'

It is an odd thing, but even when making full confessions I have often heard guilty men rewriting their actions in their heads as they speak. The unintentional slitting of Jacobus's throat, as described by Roxby, did not match the ragged tear I'd observed, or the wild sawing at the neck suggested by Dr Mackay. It is as if the murderer cannot face the true barbarity of his action; and wishes to believe that it was in some way the fault of the victim.

Roxby was continuing. 'I ran out of the room with the knife still in my hand and only remembered to put it into my coat pocket as I reached the door into the street. I knew I must take control of myself. I let myself out, closing the street door. I walked down to the river and, when I thought no one was looking, I dropped the knife into the water. The tide was high at that moment. I dare say some ragamuffin such as the one who found the fake necklace in the mud will find the knife eventually. He may already have done so. He would have been able to sell it easily enough to one of those ruffians who frequent that neighbourhood. He would not take it to the nearest police station, as happened when the necklace was found.'

'How did the paste replica come to be in the river?' I asked. I spoke quietly because he seemed to be in a mood to tell us all he knew. Some would suggest his conscience was troubled. For my part, I believe it troubled him more that he had mishandled the whole affair so badly.

There was a silence. I was afraid that Superintendent Dunn might break it and interrupt his confession. But Dunn was an old hand and stayed quiet.

'As I have explained, *at that time* I did not know the true circumstances of the theft; and I did not know that a paste replica had been made. Only when I read Charlotte's letter, detailing what she had told you, did I learn it all. But when I was in Limehouse, I knew nothing; and my actions grew from my ignorance of the fact.'

Roxby put his hand to his brow, took a moment to

control himself and began his narrative again in the earlier, even tone. 'It would have made so much difference if I had known of Charlotte's vicious plot to deprive the House of Roxby of its symbol. Of course, I would have been furious. I might even have tried to recover some of the gems from the Russian buyer Charlotte wrote of in her letter. But being entirely ignorant of the fact on the day I went to Limehouse, I left that strange old house still believing the real necklace had been taken. Charlotte let me believe it. It was her way of tormenting me. She is a vindictive woman without conscience. My desperate search for it in that cluttered room, while the old man squawked at me from his chair, the knife, the blood . . .' Roxby closed his eyes briefly. 'For nothing, nothing . . .'

'So, sir, when did you learn of the paste replica?' asked Dunn mildly. 'You knew, when you saw it on my desk, that it was a copy.'

'It did not make it easier when I saw it there, bedaubed with Thames mud! But when did I learn? When, out of the blue, I received a letter from Ariadne Chalk. In it, she requested a secret meeting. She could tell me what had happened to the stolen necklace. She did not want to come into town, for fear of being seen and recognised in my company. She suggested I meet her on the Heath, late at night, after the household had retired. I wrote back, agreeing.'

He fell silent again, so I said, 'She was seen with a letter, but we never found it.'

'I told her to be sure to burn it.' He drew a deep breath. 'I keep a carriage and pair of horses in town, in a mews not far from here. I also keep a single-seat phaeton, largely for

Harry's use. Earlier in the day, I went to the mews and told the head stableman, who also acts as watchman and sleeps on the premises, that I would have need of the phaeton that evening late. I would come at about half past ten and drive it out. I would return no later than two in the morning. He would be well compensated for the inconvenience to himself. The wretched fellow appeared amused. He seemed to think I would be setting out on some amorous adventure! Anyhow, I went as arranged and found the horse and phaeton ready and waiting for me. I drove myself out to Hampstead, to the spot agreed with Miss Chalk.'

He paused and, when he recommenced his tale, appeared overtaken by sadness. 'She was nervous, not because she feared me, but because of her own complicity in the deception. She explained there had been no robbery. It was an elaborate hoax. She was telling me this, despite the risk that she would be sent from the house and forbidden to return, because it had become a police matter. She believed the investigating officer – that is you, Ross! She thought you were suspicious. You had not accepted the story of the robbery as it had been told to you. She feared you would return and search the property again. Then she handed me a bag.

'"Why, what is this?" I asked her. I opened the bag and, in the moonlight, the necklace was revealed. I was unable to speak at first. I still thought, you see, that it was the real one.

'But as I held it in my hand and felt its weight I realised at once that it was a replica. When I told her this, she begged me to dispose of the fake. All I could think was that the Roxby emeralds were no more. I realised that Isabella Gray had been flaunting a mockery of the real thing around

London! I flew into a rage. "Do you not realise what a terrible thing has happened?" I cried out. "I have *killed* a man on account of this – this wretched impostor of a unique and beautiful object!"

'She gasped and put her hands to her face. She was muttering, "No, no!" I had brought my cane with me in the phaeton. The Heath is a deserted spot at night; and a gentleman alone, driving himself across it, might be attacked. I would have to defend myself. Now I struck out with my cane in my rage. The knob on the top of it hit her on the temple.' Roxby tapped his own head in the exact spot where the fatal injury to the lady had been. 'I did not mean to kill her. I did not even mean to injure her. I was only so angry . . .

'She fell to the ground, senseless. I knelt over her and tried to bring her round. But she was as dead as Jacobus in his chair. I seized the bag with the paste necklace in it, hurried back to where I had tethered the horse and drove back into London. I recalled how I had thrown the knife into the river, and decided to get rid of the necklace in the same way, although at a different location. So that is what I did. I believed I had disposed of the miserable impostor for ever! I didn't dream that it would rise up from the mud, as if possessed by some malignant demon, to be found by a ragged little mudlark. Last of all, I drove back to the stables where the fellow was waiting for me, still grinning, and saying he hoped I had spent a pleasant evening! I paid him well. I walked home. Dawn was breaking when I reached my house.'

'At such an early hour you might have been attacked in any London street,' I observed.

'No one accosted me,' Roxby replied. 'Perhaps I looked like a madman.' He patted the stack of papers before him on the table. 'I spent the time waiting for you this morning, writing out a detailed confession of all these events. I have signed it.' He picked up the pen and opened the inlaid box. 'I realise you would wish me to accompany you to Scotland Yard and make a statement there; and answer more of your questions. But I have said all I wish to say on the subject.'

He laid the pen in the box, and, when he took out his hand again, it held a pocket revolver.

'You understand that the head of the House of Roxby cannot finish twitching at the end of a hangman's rope. It would never do!'

He put the snub muzzle into his mouth, and, before the audience of his painted ancestors, and our horrified gaze, blew out his brains.

I constantly relive that moment and how the sound echoed around the room. It will never leave me. In my mind's eye I see him falling forward as we leaped to our feet, far too late to intervene. I see the blood and brains pooling on his confession, soaking into it; the revolver skidding across the polished teak. The door to the room flew open and the head clerk, who had heard the noise, ran in and then stopped, stock still, as if he had been turned to stone.

I still ask myself, vainly, whether, if I had brought Wood along with me that day instead of the superintendent, we might have moved fast enough to prevent it. Dunn expected Roxby to behave as a gentleman. He had told us he would come with us, and he would keep his word. He would not create a scene in his own boardroom and be dragged out, watched by all the staff.

That was Dunn's thinking. But Wood would never have expected any cornered lawbreaker to do anything other than act violently. He would have paid less heed to Roxby's final words, and kept a sharp eye on Roxby's actions. I should have done the same. But I took my lead from the superintendent. I should have known better. I should have remembered that other rule of the gentleman's code: death before dishonour.

Chapter Fifteen

Inspector Ben Ross

THE FOLLOWING days were also a nightmare. Our superiors at the Yard would hear no excuses; nor were any to be made. Dunn and I had failed to bring in our man alive. Sergeant Wood looked gloomier than ever, which I took to signify he was glad not to have been involved in the dreadful denouement.

'Well, Mr Ross,' he observed, 'I must say it proves the scripture right. As you sow, so shall you reap. All that fuss about a piece of jewellery, and all that deception about the identity of the young lady. It could only end badly.'

'I didn't know you were a chapel-goer, Wood,' I told him.

'Not me, it's the wife. She enjoys a good rousing sermon,' replied Wood. 'And the preacher, where she worships, is very hot on sin and retribution.'

The gentlemen of the press, as you would expect, had a great time with it all. We were besieged by a pack of them whenever Dunn, Wood or myself appeared in public. They even tracked me down to my house and lurked in the street.

I urged Lizzie to go and stay with Mrs Parry. But she pointed out that a choice between a horde of journalists at the door and Mrs Parry in the same room was to have no escape at all. She would stay at home, where she was needed. (I did need her and remain forever grateful for her steadfast support.)

Bessie, also, was pestered by the eager hacks whenever she ventured out to the shops, enraging the loyal Biddle, who spent almost all his free time guarding the kitchen door, once the newshounds had realised they could gain access to the backyard via an alley that ran along the rear of the terrace.

At the end of it all, what saved Dunn and myself, I fancy, was less our hitherto blameless reputations and good service records than the pressure from those unseen and unknown guardian angels of the firm of Roxby. They were not worried about a couple of police officers, even of senior rank such as Dunn. But they were worried about the falling value of the company's shares on the London Stock Exchange.

Also, Roxby's death meant there would be no trial at the end of it all, cheating the ever-avid press corps of even more copy. Eventually the crowd of newsmen dwindled and, one blessed morning, they were gone altogether.

There was, however, the coroner's inquest on the death of Jeremy Roxby to be got through. Dunn and I gave our evidence. The coroner ruled that Roxby had taken his own life while the balance of his mind was disturbed. This took much of the pressure off Dunn and myself. It also meant that the family could hold a funeral at which the presiding clergyman spoke of the deceased's successful career, and contribution to the economy. He regretted only that ill health, brought on possibly by his many responsibilities, had led to a temporary failure of judgement, loss of his senses and sudden decease. That he'd actually shot himself was not mentioned. (Nor that he had killed two people during this period of insanity.) That would have been indelicate. The ceremony was followed by interment and, in due course, the erection of a discreet headstone, giving only his name and dates of birth and death.

At the close of the inquest, when all there had begun to leave, there was an awkward moment for me. I found myself face to face with Harry Roxby. The young man, in his mourning clothes, presented a very different image to the ne'er-do-well young swell I'd met previously. He had lost weight, but gained in gravitas. He looked older. I expressed my regrets at having been unable to prevent his father's sudden demise.

'It is how my father wished it to end!' he said curtly. 'Do not blame yourself, Inspector Ross.'

I had noticed the absence of other family members, his Aunt Charlotte and Miss Gray. I ventured to inquire after their health.

'My aunt and cousin are both recovering from the many shocks they have recently endured by taking a brief sojourn at a health spa in Switzerland.' He fixed me with his defiant gaze. 'I understand, through our family solicitor, that the police will not be asking for charges to be brought against my aunt in the matter of making a false report of burglary. She was under great stress at the time, and remains in

Ann Granger

diminished spirits. Her doctors feel she should not undergo
further questioning. After all,' Harry fixed me with a steely
gaze, 'we cannot have two sudden and unforeseen deaths
in the family! Neither you nor I would wish that.'

Young puppy! I thought. But he knew he had the upper
hand – for the moment.

'Please convey her my compliments, when you next
write to her,' I said. 'I am sorry that it was necessary to
cause her so much upset. And Miss Gray? How is she?'

'My cousin has spirit and courage. I will take care of
her. As for myself, I am learning the shipping business. I
am not entirely ignorant of its complexities, despite what
many people may have thought. After all, I grew up among
people who spoke of nothing else. The firm of Roxby will
continue to prosper, rest assured.' He looked and sounded
very much like his father when he delivered the last words.

'I am sure it will,' I replied politely.

Suddenly, Harry burst out, 'Do you know, Ross? That
wretched little fellow, the private detective hired by my late
father to follow me all over London, has had the temerity
to present me with his final bill!'

'Oh? What do you mean to do about that?' I asked.

He stared at me coldly. 'I shall order it paid, of course.
The family and the firm of Roxby are both scrupulous in
meeting their obligations!'

Harry was indeed a Roxby.

Less illustrious beings also had their problems. Obadiah
Quigley found himself in a tight spot, as he had let the
murderer into the Limehouse property. But eventually it

304

was accepted he had no reason to suspect that such a respectable gentleman as the late Jeremy Roxby might cut the throat of the houseowner. In summing up to the jury, the judge stressed that it had been a recognised practice for visitors to be let into the house, after an employee of the Crossed Keys tavern had unlocked the door. Furthermore, Quigley had played an important role in identifying Roxby as a visitor on the day of the murder. Jacobus had hardly been of unblemished reputation; and had run the risk of being attacked as part of his trade. Quigley was undoubtedly a scoundrel, who had robbed a dead body, and had a previous record of petty thefts. However, he was of low intellect, declared the judge.

'What's my height got to do with it?' Quig was reported as having demanded indignantly.

He got three months. At the end of it, he went back to being a potman, though not at the Crossed Keys. Its new owner, Mrs Perkins, was content to allow Tom Mullins to remain as landlord, and Daisy Smith as bottle-washer and barmaid. But she refused point-blank to employ Obadiah Quigley, the man who had robbed her dead papa.

Wilfred Perkins had returned to London with his good lady, to settle the final details of her late father's estate. They had again taken up part-time residence at the Railway Hotel, dividing their attention between London and Leeds, until the Limehouse property had been completely refurbished. The plan then would be, as Wilfred explained when he called on me at the Yard, to rent it out to a respectable tenant. Chiefly, he had come to the Yard in order to thank me for my sterling efforts to bring the guilty to justice.

Maggie, unfortunately, still felt the justice system had failed her. She had therefore felt unable to accompany him to the Yard. But she wished me to be assured she bore me no personal ill will. She was sure I had done my best.

'My dear wife,' Wilfred Perkins confided to me, 'would be happy to see that fellow Quigley hanged. She believes him an accomplice. She can't understand why he hasn't gone to the gallows.'

'I appreciate her distress,' I told him. 'But Quigley is small fry. In the absence of your good lady, Mr Perkins, I am able to say to you that the way Jacobus conducted his business makes it remarkable he wasn't seriously attacked before.'

Perkins leaned forward, a man about to impart further confidences. 'I am able to tell you, Inspector, that, even in her grief, my wife has been able to take solace in the fact that her father was not done to death by some uncouth ruffian off the street. At least he met his end at the hands of a gentleman. Moreover, we understand that it was entirely as the result of a misunderstanding.'

There was no reply I could sensibly make to that! 'Quite . . .' I said feebly.

It was enough for Wilfred Perkins, who rose to his feet and clapped his bowler hat on his head. 'My wife would like you to know that, if Mrs Ross has no other engagements, she would be very pleased to renew their acquaintance, and take tea with her. Not at the Railway Hotel, as it has sad associations, but at some respectable and pleasant tearoom.'

I said I would pass the message on. Perkins shook my hand and departed.

Despite our best efforts at the Yard, we were never able to link Jacobus with any known stolen goods. I continue to harbour suspicions of that lawyer, Haynes, whom I believe always to have known more than he revealed to us. I don't forget how desperate he was to gain entry to the Limehouse property ahead of the police and before any official search or inventory could be made of the artwork and antiquities it contained. Nor do I forget how he failed to own up to holding a key until he had to. But suspicions are not enough. Evidence is required before any charge can be brought. Jacobus, that old fox in Limehouse, had made sure we should never find that.

Elizabeth Martin Ross

I did take tea again with Maggie Perkins, but this time at Fortnum and Mason. It was in startling contrast to the parlour of the Railway Hotel. I think this was partly because Maggie was adjusting to having come into a small fortune (however dubiously acquired by the testator), and partly because she was embarrassed by the memory of former meetings in such dingy surroundings. This time she was, as popular parlance has it, 'splashing out'. She was still in mourning, of course, but had acquired an obviously new and startling hat bedecked with the plumage of some unidentified bird. Even so, I thought she looked a little nervous when we were seated and she looked around her.

'My dear Mrs Ross,' she whispered, leaning across the lavishly laden tea table. 'I had no idea, before we came here, that it was such a – fine place. So many fashionably dressed ladies!' With a return to her normal assertive manner, she quickly added, 'I would not have you think that we have no respectable tearooms in Leeds. Indeed, we have several establishments of excellent reputation and beautifully equipped. And when it comes to dress, well, I can assure you we know about quality garments in Leeds!'

'So I have always heard,' I replied.

She relaxed somewhat. 'Of course, London style is somewhat – different.'

She was momentarily distracted by the cake stand and, after some study, selected a millefeuille.

'When your period of mourning for Mr Jacobus is over,' I suggested, 'you will be able to take some comfort in a new wardrobe.'

'I dare say,' she returned a little less confidently. 'But I would not wish to appear to be "showing off", you understand. The ladies of the Temperance League would not approve.'

'Naturally,' I replied. 'And I am sure you could never be accused of any such conduct. But your late father would have wished you to enjoy your inheritance.'

(I didn't add 'and not give it all to the Temperance League'; although I might have done, because I was fairly sure Jacob would not have approved of that.)

'My poor dear papa,' said Maggie with a sigh. 'He worked so hard in order to leave me a respectable sum. Not forgetting the properties, of course. Although I shall not tell the ladies of the League that one of them is a public house! They wouldn't understand.'

'There is no need for you to tell them anything of your private business,' I said firmly.

'That is exactly what Wilfred says!' she told me. 'Will you not try one of those little strawberry tarts, dear Mrs Ross?'

I returned home able to inform Ben that Jacobus's reputation appeared to have been completely restored in the eyes of his daughter. He had gone from a deceiving and neglectful husband to Maggie's mama to respectable businessman, and Maggie's dear papa.

'I have the impression,' I concluded, 'that very soon she will want to put a plaque in his memory on the wall of that funny old house.'

Accompany Inspector Ben Ross on more adventures in . . .

THE TRUTH-SEEKER'S WIFE

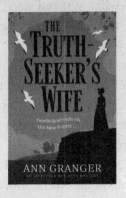

**Death descends on the New Forest in Ann Granger's
gripping eighth Victorian mystery featuring Scotland Yard's
Inspector Ben Ross and his wife Lizzie.**

It is Spring 1871 when Lizzie Ross accompanies her formidable Aunt
Parry on a restorative trip to the south coast. Lizzie's husband, Ben,
is kept busy at Scotland Yard and urges his wife to stay out of harm's
way. But when Lizzie and her aunt are invited to dine with other
guests at the home of wealthy landowner Sir Henry Meager, and he is
found shot dead in his bed the next morning, no one feels safe.

On Lizzie's last visit to the New Forest, another gruesome murder
took place, and the superstitious locals now see her as a bad omen. But
Lizzie suspects that Sir Henry had a number of bitter enemies, many
of whom might have wanted him dead. And once Ben arrives to help
with the investigation, he and Lizzie must work together to expose Sir
Henry's darkest secrets and a ruthless killer intent on revenge . . .

Available now from

HEADLINE

**Discover Ann Granger's Cotswold village
mysteries featuring Mitchell & Markby . . .**

DEADLY COMPANY

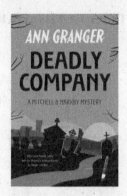

No one feels safe when there's a murderer in their midst . . .

Superintendent Alan Markby and his wife Meredith have retired for
the night when they are disturbed by a visitor. It's not the first time
someone has called at the Old Vicarage in search of a priest, but in
this case, having just found a dead body in the churchyard, Callum
Henderson needs the police. Accompanying Callum to the graveyard,
Alan declares that this has all the hallmarks of a murder scene.

News of the incident travels fast in the market town of Bamford,
but no one seems willing to admit to knowing the dead man or how
he ended up in the cemetery. As Alan and his team search for clues,
Meredith becomes convinced that something must have been
overlooked. Meanwhile, despite Alan's warnings, Callum appears to
be in cahoots with the team's latest recruit, DS Beth Santos. While
every lead points to yet more foul play, nothing can prepare Meredith
and Markby for the shocking truth behind this mystery . . .

Available now from

HEADLINE

**Don't miss Ann Granger's short story collection
of murder, mystery and mayhem . . .**

MYSTERY IN THE MAKING

Throughout her distinguished career, Ann Granger has penned
an array of hugely entertaining and gripping short stories. This
collection features eighteen of these compelling mysteries to
delight and enthral crime fans everywhere.

From a nosy neighbour who trusts no one to a jealous nephew
protecting his inheritance, and from a ghostly apparition on a cruise
ship to an Oxford undergraduate who cannot escape his past, Ann's
short stories transport readers from the Highlands of Scotland to the
rugged coast of Cornwall and from the Victorian era to the present
day. In each story there is an intriguing mystery to captivate the
most avid crime fan, making this a collection to treasure.

Available now from

HEADLINE